A LION'S HEART
A Shadow Shifters Rebellion Novel

A.C. ARTHUR

AN ARTISTRY PUBLISHING BOOK

A LION'S HEART, Copyright © 2017 by A.C. Arthur
First Edition: 2017

Excerpt from A COUGAR'S KISS, Copyright © 2017 by A.C.
Arthur
First Edition: 2017

www.acarthur.net

Cover Design by Croco Designs

THE SHADOW SHIFTERS SERIES
READING ORDER

The Awakening
Temptation Rising
Seduction's Shift
Passion's Prey

DAMAGED HEARTS TRILOGY
Mine To Claim
Part Of Me
Hunger For You

THE UNVEILING
Shifter's Claim
Hunger's Mate
Primal Heat

THE WOLF MATES TRILOGY
READING ORDER

The Alpha's Woman
*Story appears in Claimed by the Mate Vol. 1
& the Growl anthology*

Her Perfect Mates
*Story appears in Claimed by the Mate Vol. 2
& the Wild anthology*

Bound to the Wolf
*Story appears in Claimed by the Mate Vol. 3
& the Hunger anthology*

GLOSSARY OF TERMS
Shadow Shifter Tribes

Topètenia-The jaguars
Croesteriia-The cheetahs
Lormenia-The white Bengal tigers
Bosinia-The cougars
Serfins-The white lions

Acordado-The awakening, the Shadow Shifter's first shift
Alma-The name of the spa at Perryville Resorts Sedona.
Means "soul" in Portuguese
Amizade-Annex to the Elder's Grounds used as a fellow-
ship hall

Companheiro Mate/Companheiro calor-The scent
shared between mates

Companheiro/connection-A telepathic link between
mates

Curandero- The medicinal and spiritual healer of the
tribes

Elders-Senior members of the tribe
Ètica-The Shadow Shifter Code of Ethics

Joining -The official union of mated Shifters

La Selva-The name of the restaurant at Perryville Resorts.

Means "the jungle" in Portuguese

Oasis-The underground world created for the Shadow Shifters after The Unveiling

Pessoal-Secondary building of the Elder's Grounds which houses the personal rooms of each Elder

Rogue-A shadow shifter who has turned from the tribes, refusing to follow the Ètica, in an effort to become their own distinct species

Santa Casa-Main building of the Elder's Grounds that is the holy house of the Elders

Stateside Assembly-Body of shifters selected to help govern the Shadow Shifters living in the United States

The Assembly-Three elders from each tribe that make up the governing council of shifters in the Gungi

The Stateside Assembly Leader-The shifter who has been selected to lead their people, guided by social equality and dedicated to upholding the laws of the Ètica

STATESIDE SHIFTER HIERARCHY

Stateside Assembly Leader- Roman "Rome" Reynolds

Mountain Zone Faction Leader- Sebastian "Bas" Perry

Pacific Zone Faction Leader- Jace Maybon

Central Zone Faction Leader- Cole Linden

Eastern Zone Lead Enforcer- Dominick "Nick" Delgado

Eastern Zone Lead Enforcer- Xavier "X" Santos Markland

Mountain Zone Lead Enforce- Jacques Germain

Lead Guards- Ezra & Elijah Preston

A LION'S HEART Name Pronunciations

Decan (dee-k-an)
Jalil (jah-leel)
Kyss (kiss)
Lial   (like Dial)
Nisa (nee-s-ah)
Keller (kel-er)
Zyon (z-i-ahn)

PROLOUGE

———◆———

The Unveiling

SITTING IN A RECLINER WITH a cup of hot tea cooling in her hands, Kalina watched the television screen as if she expected something to jump through it at any moment. She was still a bit stiff as the stiches in her side healed. Beside her in another chair Ary sat close, rubbing her hand over Kalina's back in an effort to keep her and the baby she was carrying calm.

"He's alright," Ary said slowly, her gaze also intent on the television screen. "They're all coming back to us, Kalina. You cannot think otherwise."

"They're everywhere," Kalina said softly. "Just everywhere and they're killing whatever is in their way. Humans and shifters."

In the corner, as was his favorite spot in any room that he occupied, Baxter held Shya in his arms, rubbing his chin along the little girl's soft ebony curls. She'd flourished so much in the weeks since the blood transfusion from Ezra. Her chubby cheeks were the highlight of her cherub-like face, she had a smooth heavily-creamed coffee complexion and hazel brown eyes. She'd even grown two teeth at the bottom front of her mouth and now held tight to the spirit filled stick that had been converted into a rattle Baxter had given her the day she was born. Magdalena had given him the stick when he'd first left the Gungi to travel to the states with the Reynolds family. It was for protection, strength and solace, so Baxter had given it to Shya as the first born of the newest shifter generation. The Seer had already sent another spirited object for the first child of the Assembly Leader upon its birth.

Watching Kalina as she worked her fingers together, released and started the process again, Baxter wondered if that would come to fruition. The First Female looked tired after the injuries and subsequent surgery she'd endured because of the car accident. She'd lost a little weight but Ary assured them all that the baby inside her still thrived.

"There's so much death," Kalina whispered. "So much hate."

Ary sighed. "I know. I know. But Rome is a good leader. He'll get them all out of there. I know he will."

But even to Baxter's ears she did not sound confident.

In the next few minutes the mood in the tunnels shifted quickly. The first SUVs came barreling into the parking area. Calls came in rushed screams over the intercom system that had been installed into each room and the hallways of the tunnel. "Medical assistance needed! Medical assistance ASAP!"

Ary immediately rose from where she was seated. "You stay right here," she told Kalina. "Do not move. I'll come get you if it's Rome."

Kalina had already come to the edge of her seat, about to get up.

"Baxter, make her stay," Ary called to him.

Baxter moved slowly from the corner, going to kneel

in front of the First Female. "I need you to hold Shya, while I make sure all is well. Sit back and hold the baby," he told her.

She looked up at him in a way that said she knew exactly what he was doing and wasn't fooled one bit, but she did take Shya into her arms, cuddling the little girl close to her chest. Standing, Baxter nodded to Ary and watched the *curandero* rush from the room to take care of the wounded.

Within the next hour more trucks came in with more wounded Shadow Shifters, some already dead.

When Kalina thought she would go out of her mind, and Shya had fallen asleep in her lap, she stood. With a resigned sigh and no knowledge of exactly how much time had passed, she lay Shya in the cradle that had been brought down for her. As she stood, still fighting back the tears of dread, a hand touched her shoulder. Tears fell as she exhaled slowly, her entire body filling with warmth at his touch.

"*Meu companheiro*," he said in his deep voice and Kalina's shoulders began to shake. "Don't. Please don't cry," Rome said, turning Kalina to face him.

She fell into his embrace, holding onto him so tightly she thought she might actually break him, or her arms, in the process. "I was so afraid," she whispered into his shirt. "So afraid for you and for everyone."

He rubbed his hands down the back of her head, then cupped her face and tilted her head until she stared up at him. "I am safe and I am here. I love you," he told her, letting one hand slip down to rub over her protruding belly.

Kalina nodded. "You are safe and I love you."

"ROME'S CALLED A MEETING IN half an hour," Eli said after he and Nivea had walked from their truck to the room one of the guard's had directed them too. It was sparsely decorated with just a bed, one table and one chair, but the bathroom had a shower and they were told their clothes had been brought down here. "We have just enough time to grab a quick shower, stop by the infirmary to check on Ezra and then get to the meeting on time."

He continued to talk, not sure why it was so imperative to keep moving. Especially when he knew Nivea had come in and sat on the edge of the bed, remaining very quiet.

"Jax called me on the eband to say that Ezra's already in surgery. Ary's working on him," he said while pulling clothes from one of the bins that had been labeled with his name. "I want to get down there as soon as possible."

Nivea still didn't speak.

"He also said your sisters were doing well," Eli continued. "I asked about your parents, too."

"Stop," she said softly. "Just stop."

Eli did. He turned to face her and wanted to hit something, curse, or simply collapse at how sullen and helpless she looked at that very moment. Instead, he summoned the strength to go to her, sitting on the bed and wrapping one arm around her.

"It's done," he said. "We can't go back and change it. We tried to stop it, but it's done."

Tears streamed from her eyes. Eli didn't look at her but he could smell them, salty and sad and something clenched inside his chest tightly.

"They're dying," she told him. "I saw Pete die. That white lion took him down." Her breath hitched and more tears fell. "We couldn't stop it."

"No," Eli told her. "We couldn't."

"What will happen now?" she asked.

"I don't know," he replied honestly. "I really don't know the answer to that question, Nivea."

Then Eli moved and he lifted Nivea onto his lap, wrapping one strong arm around her waist, using his other to lift her face and cup her cheek. "All I know right here and right now is that I love you more than life itself. And I don't ever want to lose you, not in battle, not because of some disagreement or lack of communication. I just want you, always."

She looked at him through eyes blurred by tears, human eyes that had seen and experienced far too much in her young life. And he wanted to give her the world. Of course he didn't know which world that would be, but Eli didn't care. All he knew was that he was looking at his future, his life, the reason why he'd survived all that he had.

"I love you," he told her again, touching his lips softly to hers. "I love you."

She sighed into his kiss, whispering over his lips in response, "I love you, too."

"WE HAVE NOT BEEN ABLE to contact Cole," Rome said solemnly as he stood in front of what was left of his leadership team. "It is too soon to send a team out to search for him, but we will first thing in the morning. Ezra is in critical condition. Zach and a number of others are dead."

At the table, Eli reached for Nivea's hand. He'd seen his brother with tubes running all over him, eyes closed as he lay in the medically induced coma that Ary assured Eli would help him heal even faster than shifters normally did. It had taken a part of him to see his other half lying so still as if he were already dead, but he'd flattened his hand on his twin's chest and felt his heart still beating. Nivea had stood right by his side, as Dawn had covered Eli's hand with her own. For as much as Eli had been against his brother mating a human, he was at that moment happy that Ezra had found someone to love him the way he deserved to be loved. So he did not move when her hand rested on top of his and when Nivea leaned in, adding her hand on top of Dawn's, his heart had swelled.

"We have been exposed," Rome continued. "The humans now know without a doubt that there are Shadow Shifters living in this world with them. There will be repercussions for that revelation and there will most likely be more death."

It was a solemn declaration, but one that was true nonetheless.

Nick and Ary stood stoically just behind Rome. Kalina sat in a chair to his right. Jax was ever present next to the First Female. X and Caprise who had sustained a pretty violent looking gash at her neck, stood to Rome's other side, forming what, to Eli, would always be an impenetrable alliance. Baxter and Elder Alamar were all the way to the back, looking as grief stricken as the others felt.

"I'll organize the recovery teams to go out at first light to search for the others that are missing," Eli volunteered, wanting to take some of the stress off the Assembly Leader's shoulders.

"I'll help with that," Bas said, speaking for the first time since returning to the tunnels and learning that Cole was missing.

"I'm going out to look for him myself," Jace told the room in a tone that dared anyone to speak against him.

Nobody argued.

They would all go out to look for the Faction Leader.

"Right now it's best if we try to get some rest," Rome told them. "Teams will be assigned and briefed at five a.m. Then we'll go out to search for survivors."

"That's not a good idea," a new voice sounded throughout the room.

All eyes went to the man now standing in the doorway,

the human that was familiar to some. He was surrounded by two shifters that had what looked like a death grip on his arms.

Nivea immediately stood. "What are you doing here?"

X and Nick both moved to the doorway to confront Agent Dorian Wilson.

"That's a damned good question," Nick said, staring into the man's face.

"I was given directions," Dorian told them. "By Rayna."

"That bitch!" Nivea whispered and Caprise nodded her agreement.

"Hear what I have to say first," Dorian insisted, his gaze seeking and resting on Rome. "You want to hear this before you decide how to proceed."

A T ELEVEN A.M. ON A Saturday morning, Eli walked behind his Assembly Leader as Roman Reynolds, Nick Delgado, Xavier Santos Markland, Sebastian Perry, Priya Drake and Agent Dorian Wilson were escorted into the Oval Office.

They crossed the room with solemn footsteps, their feet moving softly over the United States of America Presidential seal painted on the floor. Coming to a stop, Eli made sure to count each member of the Secret Service in the room. Their job was to guard President Wilson Reed, just as Eli's was to guard Rome.

The President looked grim as he stared at Rome.

"You lied to me," was the first thing the older man said, his glasses pushed up high on his face.

"I never lied," Rome countered. "I did not tell you what you did not need to know."

Wilson slammed his palms down on his desk. "I didn't need to know that there were damned animals roaming around my country? Are you kidding me?"

"First," Rome began. "The animals you refer to are

housed in a zoo. What have been walking and mingling amongst the humans for hundreds of years are called Shadow Shifters. And up until last night you had no idea we existed."

"That's exactly what my problem with you is Reynolds! I allied myself with you. I supported you and your firm and the charities you reached out to."

Rome interrupted. "Because those were the right things to do. I have always been an upstanding citizen, a successful lawyer and a contributor to this community as well as others. There was no need for you not to offer your support just because you had no knowledge of my DNA."

"Don't give me that smooth-ass lawyer crap! You should have told me!" Wilson was clearly outraged and he was afraid.

Sweat pricked his forehead and his hands shook after he'd slammed them on the desk, so he pulled them down to his lap instead. He was afraid of the shifters that had seemingly invaded his office.

When in truth, it was Priya and Dorian who had arranged for the private meeting as a form of damage control for the United States Government—to whom many countries were now looking at with thoughts of terrorism against their citizens, as last night's attack involved several of their highest dignitaries. And for the shifters whose true nature had finally been unveiled... The President's staff had jumped at this opportunity, but Rome had insisted it be a private meeting instead of a nationally-televised press conference.

"Now I want you to tell me where the rest of your kind are hiding and what you all plan to do now that you're here," Wilson told Rome.

The Assembly Leader shook his head. None of them had been overly optimistic about the human government being able to come to amicable terms with the shifters.

That had been one of their greatest fears with exposure. But they'd agreed to the meeting, agreed with Dorian that it looked better for them, and it put forth the peaceful approach the agent now believed the shifters needed to take.

Dorian's appearance had also been a huge question. But the agent had explained how he met Rayna and how the Lormenian shifter had wanted to help the Shadows by exposing and killing Boden. She'd wanted her sister's safety, but she'd also wanted them to be able to live cohesively with the humans in this world. She'd left him a letter with the directions to the tunnels—which she knew because she'd been there to help them work on the construction—and she'd told him that if she did not return to the hotel by a certain time that night that he should assume that she was dead and get to Rome as quickly as possible. The agent had done just that.

"We are a peaceful species," Rome told the President. "What happened last night was not our fault."

"Big ass cats jumping over cars, biting and killing people, that's not your fault?" Wilson inquired "When I've been told that you are yourself one of the big cats."

Rome paused a moment, the room going completely silent as everyone waited for his response.

"Yes. I am one of the big cats. I am the Stateside Assembly Leader of the Shadow Shifters," Rome said with confidence and pride.

Wilson stood then, squaring his shoulders so that his stance mimicked Rome's.

"Then I command you to release the names and locations of every member of this species. I demand to know where every one of you are hiding so that we can deal with you appropriately," Wilson said without hesitation, his angry gaze locked with Rome's.

"I will not do that," Rome told him calmly. "There's no reason for any of us not responsible for last night's fiasco to be, as you put it "dealt with". And furthermore, I will not stand for the persecution and execution of my kind."

Wilson nodded as if in resignation, before saying, "Then you have made the United States and possibly the entire world your enemy."

Rome's reply was immediate and was said just seconds before the Assembly Leader turned and left the room, his team following dutifully behind him.

"No, Mr. President. It is my goal to work with the humans, with your government, so that there will be no need for any of us to be enemies," Rome said seriously. "You knew my parents. You know what type of man I am. You know what I stand for and what I believe. There is no reason for us to work against each other here. The Shadow Shifters simply want peace."

Wilson Reed looked from one of his advisors to the next, then back to Rome and the others who stood with him. He sighed heavily, smoothing down his tie as he lowered himself slowly into his seat.

"I only want peace for my country," the President said to Roman. "Can you promise that from your people?"

"We only want peace as well," Rome told him. "So yes, I can promise you that. And if we all work together peace and harmony shall be what we have."

CHAPTER 1

———◆———

20 Years Later
Oasis

"SHE'S YOUNG," FIRST FEMALE KALINA Reynolds told her husband, Assembly Leader Roman Reynolds.

"She's smart," he replied.

Kalina nodded. "She's tenacious."

Rome agreed before adding, "And stubborn."

"Intelligent," Kalina said as she moved across the room.

"Beautiful." Rome followed her. "She is the best of both of us and the best Topétenia guard of this generation."

Then the composure that she was known for possessing, the cool and always in control leader that the Assembly had come to expect whenever their First Female was around, slipped.

"I don't care about that, Rome. She's our baby and we're letting her go into unchartered territory with a lion. We're campaigning for first place in the bad parenting department."

Rome knew it was coming and had been waiting patiently while she took her time admitting what was obvious. He resisted the urge to smile and stepped closer to his *companheiro's* side, wrapping an arm around her shoulders. After all this time with her he still couldn't believe she was standing by his side. So much had happened in the years since he first met Kalina in his office at the law firm. Some good things and some bad, but everything—from that very first day—impacted them together. One unit. One joining. With one daughter. The love of their lives.

"We're doing what is necessary," he said. "You were the one who came to me advising that she was restless."

"Well, we should have found her a hobby. Not send her off to another part of the world, to do who knows what. The very unstable world that we now live in, I might add."

Her hands had been clasped in front of her. Now they moved as she folded her arms across her chest and then dropped them again only seconds later. Before he could speak her hands were moving once more, this time to link at the back of her neck as she inhaled deeply and exhaled slowly.

"I do not regret coming to you after seeing how unhappy she was," Kalina said finally, rotating her head and then letting her arms fall heavily to her sides. "But I did not expect this. You very wisely waited until the last minute to tell me about a new assignment."

Rome leaned in to kiss her at the temple. He inhaled the sweet floral scent that was distinctly Kalina's and shook his head.

"None of us expected things to turn out like this," he said quietly.

"Magdalena's prediction came too late," she replied, turning slightly to look up to him.

"Yes, Baxter delivering the news from the Seer was ill-timed. Her prediction of death and destruction. The complete end of the race or a catastrophic change in who and what we were. All of that should have been known to us sooner. However, I don't know what we might have done differently," he said.

"I might not have wanted a child as much as I did," she commented quietly.

They both looked through the soundproof glass shield that served as a window stretching the length of the main hall of Assembly Headquarters, where their daughter stood. Oasis was where they had been living for the last twenty years since the shifters had been unveiled to the world. The underground haven had begun as a series of tunnels to carry the shifters quickly from one place to another secretly. The night that all hell—or rather all the shadow tribes—had broken loose, those plans changed and for the last twenty years Commanding Officer Nick Delgado, as head of security for the Assembly, had worked alongside the other Faction Leaders to turn the tunnels into the shifters' underground world.

Nobody knew they were here, no humans and no shifter that wasn't in agreement with them and their desire to keep a low profile during the continued unrest above ground in the human world.

"We both wanted her and we're both proud of her," Rome stated solemnly.

Their daughter was a beautiful twenty year-old with her whole life ahead of her. She was packing the back of a black Tracer which was one of the Shadows' vehicles that were specially re-designed for them and their new way of life underground. Among the many shifters in Oasis, a Bosinian couple who at one time had worked for a large automotive company above ground, had technologically enhanced the SUVs the Shadow guards and enforcers drove. They created the Tracer, Wrangler and Attacker vehicles for them to use on the mostly matted clay roads throughout the tunnels. Guard teams mostly drove the Tracer. Enforcers and upper level command used the Attacker, while the Wrangler was designed solely for personal use.

Nisa Reynolds was scheduled to drive her Tracer from Assembly Headquarters in the eastern zone to Central Headquarters located just beneath the state of Texas where Jace, the Pacific Zone Faction Leader and acting Central Zone Faction Leader, was waiting to meet her. Jace and Rome had worked together for going on thirty-five years now. He was a friend and Rome trusted him with his life. Now, Rome thought heavily, he was trusting him with his daughter's life.

"She can do this," Rome said. "I trust that she can get the job done."

"I don't doubt that," Kalina replied. "You've taught her everything there is to know about being a good leader. What I'm more concerned about is how well she's going to adapt to taking instructions from someone other than you and Eli. And what's going to happen to the person who has to teach her that lesson."

That person was Decan Canter.

A Serfin, white lion shifter.

He was standing next to the vehicle behind the one Nisa was loading another duffel bag into. Tall, around six-feet five-inches, muscular build, keen and intelligent eyes, United States military and Shifter Tactical Team trained, Decan had been Rome's first and only choice for this assignment. Rome needed someone he could trust and someone he knew could protect Nisa during the trip to Central Headquarters. Decan's father, Jalil, had been of great assistance to Jace as he'd worked to get all of the Shadows in the Central Zone entered into the Shadow Shifter database and scanned into the intricate security systems developed as the primary source of entry into Oasis. The Canter family was from Houston where Jalil had, at one time, held a job in telecommunications. Decan, had been one of the few Shadows able to secretly continue throughout the human school system after the Unveiling. He'd graduated with honors and immediately enlisted in the United States Marines.

"He looks hard and rigid," Kalina continued, tearing Rome's thoughts away from the dossier on Decan Canter which he'd reviewed for the hundredth time this morning.

"He's a trained soldier with excellent tracking skills. He comes from a tribe reputed for its integrity and strength. He's exactly what we need right now," Rome told her.

"I fear this outing you're sending them on is no longer about what we need as a species, but instead, how well these two will get along."

Rome watched as Decan approached the back of the Tracer where Nisa stood. Even from this distance he could scent the tension rising between those two—the lion shifter and the jaguar one. Kalina was right, this was a test of sorts. One which he hoped with all his being his daughter would pass. Because if she didn't, Rome had no idea what he would do with his spirited child. He had no idea how he could continue to protect her.

"I'LL TAKE US SOUTH," NISA said when she smelled the lion coming up behind her.

Each feline in the Shadow family had a different scent. The Serfins possessed a very dominant fragrance, like burning cigars. This one had something else, a more potent aroma that doubled the intensity of his presence. Nisa refused to turn to face him, just as she decided not to explore his scent and how or why it was so different from any other shadow she'd met before.

"We'll make it to Florida tonight and in the morning

we'll begin our journey west. There's a high population of Croesteriia once we get into swamp territory. So far they haven't been too much trouble in the eastern region, but Jace has reported needing to police them a little more in central and pacific. My thought is they're restless. The tunnels do not provide enough space for satisfying the need to run and stretch. They want to go above ground more frequently," she continued.

When her bags were as neat as she could get them in the tight space left after she'd ensured she had all the supplies needed for this trip, Nisa gave herself a little nod for a job well done. She took a step back and had to come up on her toes to reach for the door to close it. Just before her fingers could touch the cool metal, she watched as he came closer, one rope-veined arm extended as he pushed the door so that it came down slowly but still closed with a thud. He leaned against it then, crossing his arms over his chest as if he now wanted applause for his assistance. Nisa wasn't about to give it to him. Nor was she going to acknowledge the quick leap in her heart rate at the sight of him up close, dressed in full guard uniform looking like he should be on a door length poster for hot hunks.

"I'll drive," he said while she thought about what else she wanted to say to him.

"We'll be in Florida before nightfall. There's a secure location near the Everglades where you can go above ground and run. Tomorrow we'll move out early and make it to Central Headquarters by nightfall. You can have another run then."

His voice was deep, not so much as her father's, but still a low timbre with a raspy edge that rubbed something inside her in an unexplainable way. Nisa kept her gaze trained on his icy blue eyes. The strong line of his jaw masked by a light coating of a beard and the black and white spray of tightly curled hair was of no interest of her. None at all.

"This is my truck. My mission. My call," she asserted and just to make sure he knew she was serious, Nisa took a step forward, folding her arms over her chest as well.

His gaze immediately dropped to what she realized when she finally followed it, was the generous swell of cleavage displayed with her actions. Her uniform jacket was in the front seat where she'd tossed it earlier. For now, she wore only a blue tank top with a sports bra that didn't offer her as much support as her size D cup breasts required.

Instantly annoyed, and much warmer under his perusal than she thought was acceptable, Nisa snapped her fingers and waited while he slowly dragged his gaze back up to her face.

"It might also be a good idea to stay focused on this mission. We might be underground but there are still dangers lurking," she told him in what she hoped was a supervisory tone.

Even as a senior guard in the Assembly, Nisa had learned a long time ago that male shifters did not like dealing with the Assembly Leader's daughter, unless it was to flirt with her. She hadn't wanted the latter with any of the ones that had ever crossed her path, so she'd decided the light frost in her tone and steady eye contact usually hammered that fact down pretty quickly.

To his credit, this Shadow didn't look like the type to argue. Nisa supposed that was a good thing. While she could easily out-argue someone—according to her best friend and daughter of one of her father's best friends, Shya Delgado—she was relieved that he didn't seem interested.

Relief dissipated almost instantly, leaving Nisa a bit deflated as he came closer to her and lifted a hand to smooth over his beard. No, that's not what he was really doing. The arrogant lion was showing her the band of white stripes around the wrist portion of his jacket.

"I'm a Senior Enforcer," he told her, in case she couldn't count the stripes that marked his superiority. "This mission is mine to lead. We're leaving in five minutes."

Before Nisa could even consider a reply, he'd moved past her and was heading toward the driver's side of the vehicle.

Names she could call him, ways she could insult him for being obnoxious and everything short of stomping her foot in anger, crossed her mind. But the tingling at the base of her neck held her still a few seconds. Then, she turned slowly, tilting her head back until she could see them.

Roman and Kalina Reynolds, the best parents a Shadow could have. As for a young woman, well, Nisa was certain that she was not the only person to go through the phase of wishing her parents would let her go without doubt. From the looks on their faces—even though her mother was waving and her father was giving her his best political smile—they were filled with doubt about letting her go on this mission.

She remained still while anger bubbled inside. This wasn't how this was supposed to go. Nisa wanted to scream, and then she wanted to yank the Senior Enforcer's smug self out of the driver's seat of *her* vehicle.

That thought only fueled her anger.

Hadn't she aced her tactical training, moving quickly up the ranks to become a Senior Guard at just twenty years old? Didn't she know the Shadow Shifter history as far back as the very first jaguar shifter in the Gungi rainforest? Hadn't she been instrumental in designing the new holodeck in the main control room? Didn't she know all there was to know about each tribe, Magdalena the Seer, Baxter the Overseer and even the enemy Rogues? What more could she do to prove to them that she was ready?

Finding Cole Linden, the Central Zone Faction Leader, would be a start.

Cole had been missing since the night of the Unveiling twenty years ago. However, Nisa wasn't as certain as her father and his friends that he was still alive. Even with that in mind, Nisa's plan for this mission was, to lead this team from east to central without incident and then to help Jace Maybon and the Lead Enforcer in that region to train their guards on how to use the new boards that she'd designed to assist them in logistics and strategic mission planning. Eventually, that would lead to Jace recommending to her father that he turn the region over to her. Then, finally, Nisa would be in a position to not only lead, but to help her father in the battle he refused to fight against the humans that would see their entire species terminated. How was she going to do that now, with Mr. "This mission is mine to lead" on her back?

Nisa's parents were her life. They meant everything to her. In turn, she was determined to make them as proud of her as she was of them and all that they'd done for the Shadows. That was her focus, her one goal in this life, and she would not let anyone or any situation deter her.

Not even the sexy lion who had already aroused pricked the cat inside of her.

S HE WAS SITTING TOO CLOSE to him. Even with the console and their ready box between them as he drove, she was too close. Her scent was too strong. Her breasts too alluring. The sound of her heartbeat too loud. The slight parting of her lips as she read over the maps on the board—and hand-held replica of the holodeck she'd created for the control room at Assembly Headquarters—she'd pulled out of her pack was too sexy.

He should have declined this position.

But the message that had come from the Assembly Leader a week ago was simple and really left no room for negotiation.

"I want you to escort my daughter to the Central Zone. Jace has a project there that Nisa can help implement."

That's how this particular situation had begun.

Decan's fingers gripped the steering wheel as he recalled that two days after receiving the transmission via his comlink, he'd stood in Roman Reynolds' office. There had been no nervousness, no anxiety, and no fear. He did feel immense respect for the shifter who had built a democracy for his species outside of the rainforest in Brazil where their kind had originated. It was an honor to be in his presence and Decan had no intention of ever forgetting that fact. Still, whatever he may have thought or felt before stepping into that room, Decan had tucked it securely away. It was a trick he'd learned after his first shift and one that had saved his life for a long time after. He pressed it all back, with the strength of the fierce cat that lived inside of him. Everything was moved out of his mind and his being so that there was just the basic human body. He'd done that so easily for so long that when the time had come he'd been almost useless against the attack executed on him. But that was long before the meeting with the Assembly Leader. And even longer before he'd first seen her.

"I can do that," Decan remembered his response to the Assembly Leader.

"While you're there Jace has some new information he's uncovered through the help of some lycan friends above ground, to run past you."

"There are other shifters above ground?" he'd asked, astonished by that knowledge as there had never been any mention of another species besides the humans and the shifters.

"There is a lot up there that you, nor I, know about," had been Rome's reply.

Decan hadn't been given a chance to think about that as Rome had continued to talk about Jace and the lead he had on Cole Linden's whereabouts. He was the FL who had disappeared amidst the chaos of the Unveiling. Decan didn't know if the shadow was still alive or not, but he wasn't going to argue the use of resources and manpower for this continued search. His time in the human military had taught him to never leave a man behind.

"Why me?" he had, however, asked because he'd needed to know.

His father had been sure it was because Rome recognized what a good leader Decan would make, but then Jalil tended to think the world of his only son. Decan was to be everything that Jalil would not allow his girls to achieve. That's why, when Decan was just ten years old, his two sisters had gone underground with the rest of the family while Decan stayed with his mother's adoptive parents above ground and continued with his human education.

"You are the one for this job," Rome had assured him. "I trust you to take care of my daughter and to deliver her safely. Jace will keep me apprised of how things work out with you and his lead."

In other words, Jace would report back to Rome on how good or bad a job Decan managed to do. So this was a test. Decan had never failed a test before and he wasn't about to start now.

Clenching his jaw and staring straight ahead through the dark cavernous tunnel as he drove, Decan silently declared Jace's report to the Assembly Leader would be phenomenal. So much so that Rome would have no choice but to name him the new Central Zone Faction Leader.

"There's another set of tunnels just past the Virginia marker that might get us down there quicker."

The feminine voice echoed throughout the otherwise quiet interior of the vehicle and Decan resisted the urge to turn to her. He knew how she looked. He'd seen that face on and off in his mind for the last six months, since the first time he had a glimpse of her at the quarterly meeting. He'd only been in Oasis for five months at that time, but his father had made sure he knew everything there was to know about the new haven for the Shadow Shifters the moment Decan had returned. Jalil had been excited to introduce Decan to all of the FLs at the meeting and finally, to the Assembly Leader.

"We don't need to rush. We're not expected at Central Headquarters until tomorrow night," he replied and continued down the bumpy path.

After the initial tunnels were constructed, more emphasis had to be put on building the bunkers that would house all of the Shadows, as they'd been migrated underground fairly quickly. So most of the tunnel roads still remained unpaved. As evidenced by the multiple craters he drove over in the next few seconds. The vehicle took the shock like a champion and he was only slightly jostled as he continued to drive. She, on the other hand, dropped the board and cursed as she leaned forward to retrieve it.

"The roads on the alternate route have smoother passageways," she snapped.

Decan did look over at her this time. He wanted to make sure she wasn't hurt. He did not want to take in anymore details of her attire. She'd put on her jacket which had been a blessing, so her delectable cleavage was no longer on display. But her mission pants were tight, and as she'd bent over, her jacket and tank top rode up her back, giving him a glimpse of smooth chocolate toned skin that his fingers ached to caress.

"The priority was to build the bunkers for the families to occupy and the leadership to meet. Oasis needed to function as our new world. Going back to re-do the roads is taking time, but they will all be finished soon," he said, still staring at her body as she sat back slowly in her seat.

"What are you a brochure for Nick Delgado's construction team?" she asked.

His lips clamped shut tightly as he dragged his gaze up to her face. Such a pretty face, even if she frowned frequently and spent a lot of her time arguing with others. She had a pert little nose and sexy lips. Her hair was a short cap of springy dark curls that suited her compact, no fuss appearance. She didn't need any fuss, every natural part of her was enough. It somehow felt like too much, for him at least

"It's better if we stay on the main roads. Security cameras are embedded in the tunnel walls and there are always enforcers watching. This is the safer route, but I'll do my best to hit the upcoming bumps as softly as possible."

As if in response to his words and probably because he was paying more attention to her than the road ahead, the vehicle traveled over another crater section in the road and they were both rocked by the sudden motion. Decan was positive, though, that his chest didn't look half as alluring as hers did during the incident.

"Wow," she said then. "If that's your best—"

Her words and the curse he was silently reciting to himself for letting his physical urges override his professional training, were both interrupted by another thump and more shaking of the vehicle.

Decan cursed as his fingers tightened on the steering wheel. Nisa echoed his sentiment as she now saw what he did.

Cheetahs, two of them, standing on the hood of the Tracer, teeth bared and ready to attack.

CHAPTER 2

———◆———

DECAN SLAMMED ON THE BRAKES. Exactly what she would have done, Nisa thought as she quickly undid her seat belt and popped open the ready box to retrieve her weapon. She was certain she could take the two cheetahs that had just slid off the hood of the Tracer and were now growling and hissing from the ground. But tactical teams were now trained to avoid hand-to-hand contact whenever possible. Lead Enforcer and trainer Eli Preston, lectured the trainees relentlessly on the Assembly Leader's new directives. They were not to shift during an altercation. Nothing was to be done to confirm the human's belief that the Shadows were nothing more than animals.

These opponents, however, were Shadows and they were underground, aggressive and in their cat forms. Nobody would blame her if she shifted and let her jaguar beat the crap out of them. Nobody but the Senior Officer who she'd been forced to travel with.

Nisa jumped out of the vehicle, gun set on stun.

"Stand down!" she yelled.

The first cheetah came for her, stopped just about two

feet away and then bobbed its small head and hissed.

"We're on official business and you're out of order," Nisa repeated. "Now stand down, or be shipped back to headquarters to face the Assembly Leader."

The second cheetah once again jumped on the hood of the Tracer, just as cheetah number one lunged at her. Without a second thought, Nisa fired, distributing a million volts through cheetah number one, and sending his wiry ass down to the ground instantly. At the same time, Decan grabbed cheetah number two by the neck, yanking him down and throwing him to the ground.

"Get back in the vehicle!" Decan yelled at her. "Now!"

Nisa ignored him, taking a step toward the cheetah she'd downed watching as he attempted to fight the stun but ended up shifting back into his human form.

"I gave you an order!"

That's what Nisa heard next before her arm was yanked and she turned to see that Decan had moved very quickly to appear right beside her in just seconds.

"I don't take orders from you," she told him and then noticed the other guards that were traveling in the vehicle behind them had stepped out with their weapons drawn as well.

Nisa snapped her lips shut tightly. She would not make a scene. Nothing could happen on this trip that she did not want reported to her father. Standing here arguing with the mean 'ole lion was definitely not going to show her father that she could lead an entire zone of shifters.

"And anyway, they're down now, so we can get back into the vehicle and keep driving," she told him before snatching her arm away from him.

The cat inside was quick and vicious as it hissed and pressed against her bones in rebellion. She wanted out, now, which confused the hell out of Nisa. She held her cat on a loose leash, letting her out as much as she could, but usually only when they were alone. This new press to break free was unexpected and just a little disconcerting.

"Not so fast," another female voice spoke.

As far as Nisa knew, she was the only female in this travel party. In the vehicle behind them were four guards, all dressed in the navy blue mission jacket, pants and a lighter blue button-down shirt, which completed the guard uniform. Senior enforcers, such as Decan, wore all navy blue—mission pants, shirt and a jacket with their tribe insignia on the front left side and white stripes around the wrist cuffs which signified their rank.

This female, Nisa noted when she turned quickly away from Decan, wore a skintight black bodysuit with a bright yellow jacket and steel-toe boots. Her black hair was pulled away from her face in a tight ponytail that hung long down her back.

"We were only bringing you information," the newcomer stated before tilting her head.

She walked slowly, stepping around the cheetah that Decan had dispatched and the one who had shifted back to his human form, still writhing from the shock of Nisa's gun. There was a twenty-foot ceiling in the tunnels, with a double lane capacity of seventy-five feet. Their vehicles were in the center of the tunnel and the female took her time coming around the vehicle until she was only a short distance away from Nisa. Decan, who had been still standing behind Nisa, moved forward until he stood between her and the newcomer.

"Oh," she said. "There you are. I knew the Assembly Leader wouldn't send his only offspring out alone. Quite a yummy bodyguard you've got here, Miss Nisa."

"What's the information and who sent you?" Decan asked before Nisa could reply.

Again, the female's head tilted, this time causing her ponytail to shift and dangle over her shoulder. Her cheekbones were high, eyes a simmering amber hue. She looked exotic, even to another shifter. But Nisa wasn't impressed.

She moved around to stand beside Decan.

"Yes, tell us who sent you?" Nisa asked.

"Nobody sends me anywhere," she said. "I come and go as I please. Which is how I came to be in the possession of knowledge about the recent murders above ground."

Nisa paused. "Why should we care about that?"

To her knowledge, in the years since the shifters had been underground—which equated to all her life—their dealings with the human world had been slim. Her father and his team had only been concerned with building and maintaining a safe environment for the shifters.

"So naïve," the woman quipped.

Her lips spread into a smile that Nisa could only describe as breathtaking.

"And cute too," she continued. "Assembly Leader Reynolds and First Female Kalina sure did produce one lovely little jaguar."

She'd taken another step closer as she spoke and from behind Nisa could hear one of the guards growl in response.

"You should get to the point," Decan stated evenly. "Now."

There was definitely a tension here, one that filled the tunnels like an invisible smoke. Nisa kept her finger on the trigger of her gun, wondering if she should have switched it from stun to kill.

The female nodded and clamped her hands on her hips.

"The Ruling Cabinet family members are being killed. It's a message to Ewen Mackey and his suit and tie band of murderers."

"Again, that has nothing to do with us," Nisa said, but suddenly felt like her words sounded false and, as much as she hated to admit, naïve.

The female chuckled this time and then looked to Decan. "I know you know better than that," she said to him.

"Continue," was all Decan said in response.

His entire body was tense. This was the first time Nisa actually let herself acknowledge that. He didn't have his weapon drawn, but his hands were fisted at his sides, his legs spread slightly a part.

"I picked up Lial's scent at the scene of the most recent murder. He was there."

Decan frowned. His brow furrowed and his strong jaw, even covered by the light black and white beard, clenched. He knew what she was speaking about.

"So he's killing? For who?" Decan asked.

"That's what I figured you'd want to find out," she stated.

"Who are you?" Nisa asked.

Her confusion was growing. She did not like that. Her father and Commanding Officer Xavier Santos Markland—another of her father's best friends and the shifter who had taught her everything she knew about technology—hadn't mentioned anything about murders above ground when this mission was first discussed.

"I'm Kyss," she said, purposely hissing the latter part of her name, Nisa was sure. "Croesteriia, like those two over there."

Her eyes shifted then, turning cat in seconds while she gave a very human and alluring smile. Nisa could only stare. Decan, on the other hand, had moved again, this time taking Nisa's hand and pulling her toward the passenger door of the Tracer. She'd never had her hand held before, not by someone who wasn't her parents anyway. It felt oddly comfortable, but she knew that wasn't right. It wasn't supposed to be right. But before she could think about pulling away, Decan was opening the door and edging her inside.

"We continue as planned," he told Nisa.

Then he pushed the door to close as he turned back to Kyss.

Nisa had quickly stuck her foot out so that the door didn't close all the way and she could hear him speaking.

"Do not repeat what you've just told me to anyone else," he said and handed Kyss a card he'd taken from his jacket pocket.

The cheetah woman moved closer, until her pert breasts rubbed against Decan's arm. She leaned into him before whispering, "Yes, sir."

Decan moved around her in the same swift and efficient fashion he'd been doing everything in these last few moments. He came around the Tracer and Nisa hurriedly pulled her foot inside and closed the door just as he was opening his. When he was secure in the driver's seat, Decan pressed the ignition start button and pulled off without further warning to the remaining cheetahs that were still in the road. They scuttled out of the way quickly.

"What just happened?" she asked when curiosity threatened to strangle her and her cat.

"Nothing," he replied nonchalantly.

"Liar!" she snapped. "I know about The Ruling Cabinet. If a shifter is killing these humans that means the war against our kind will be intensified. They'll find out where we are and attempt to exterminate us."

Nisa knew she was overreacting. The scent of her rattled nerves was ripe and she chastised herself for not being in better control of her emotions. But this was her first real mission, the first time she'd heard firsthand of the violence going on above ground and realized how deeply their species was still involved in the human world. Besides all that, her hand was still tingling from where his had once been pressed.

"Our mission is to get you to Central Headquarters. You are to assist the FL and then I will return you to your father. That is all that is happening here."

"You suck at lying," she told him as she picked up her

board once more. The stench of untruth wasn't potent, but it was definitely there. He didn't want to tell her. That was fine. But she would know. She would simply find the information on her own.

"Even your cat is rebelling against your lies. Or he's aroused by that sexy cheetah with all the pertinent information," she continued and then snapped her lips shut.

Why had she just said that? How had she known what a lion was thinking or feeling for that matter?

Decan was staring at her with his icy cool eyes silently asking her those same questions.

H OURS PASSED BEFORE EITHER OF them spoke again.

A huge stretch of time traveling through the long tunnels with the other vehicle close behind. All the while thoughts flew with lightning speed through Decan's mind.

Yes, he'd heard about the killings above ground. After the first murder three months ago, he and his childhood friend, Gold, had gone above to investigate. Lial's scent had been strong at the scene then too. This was why Kyss' words did not shock him, but her appearance had.

Decan had no idea who she was. He did not know why she'd come to him with this information or how she'd known that he would be traveling on this particular road with Nisa. Her knowledge was eerie and in Decan's experience, eerie usually led to trouble. Which was why he'd communicated with Gold through their comlink to take Kyss with them. He'd done this the moment she appeared on the scene and came too close to Nisa because he'd first thought she was a threat to the Assembly Leader's daughter. Now, he was thinking the cheetah might be a threat to something even bigger.

Gold was riding in the second Tracer. As the leader of

this mission Decan had personally selected who would travel with him on this expedition. He was also well aware of Nisa's preferences, something he had no idea why he bothered to consider. Still, he'd been sure to add two Topétenia guards who had trained with her. Roman Reynolds and his beautiful mate had produced a spirited and stubborn daughter. One that Decan had spent a good amount of his time watching, when he should have been paying more attention to other matters. Namely, Lial, the rogue cougar shifter.

Humans were being killed. In all likelihood by shifters. That was not a part of the plan.

Decan felt his facial features easing into a scowl as he made a quick left turn that took them off the main road.

Nisa had spent most of this ride reading on her board. No doubt trying to find any information on the Ruling Cabinet and its dead family members that she could. She was not going to let Kyss' appearance or her words go. Decan knew that as surely as he knew that the well-trained hellcat sitting across from him was not going to react kindly to the place where Decan had planned for them to spend the night.

"Why are we turning here?" she asked as her head came up and she stared out the window and then over to him. "Where are we going?"

"We're going to rest for the night," Decan told her without any plans to elaborate.

"These are the unmarked tunnels," she said. "This territory hasn't been excavated yet."

He knew she would know. Decan had no doubt that Nisa Reynolds had studied everything that had ever been written about Oasis and the Shadow Shifters' life down here. It made sense, especially since she had never been anywhere else. This was her world and she was the Assembly Leader's daughter. It was her duty to know everything about this place.

Just as it was Decan's duty to keep her inquisitive and attractive ass alive.

"This location is secure," Decan said as he killed the lights on the Tracer and slowed the vehicle down to a crawl.

The wide passageway had quickly turned narrow, just enough so that the vehicle could get through, but not without some concerted effort.

"Does my father know about this place?" she asked then. "Does he know where you're taking me?"

"Do you tell your father everything you do?" he asked and avoided looking at her.

Their eyes could shift to night vision with one blink. Either the cat's eyes, or the human ones, they could see through the pitch darkness of this tunnel as easily as if they were above ground in broad daylight.

His question had silenced her but only for a few seconds.

"Would you like me to tell my father you're not following his command?" she snapped back.

Decan silenced the vehicle's engine and released the locks on both front doors. He turned slightly in his seat and looked at her, but for a moment was startled from his original purpose. Her cat's eyes blinked back at him. The smallest black dot surrounded by a green so murky it almost looked translucent, and a yellow outer ring. Her long lashes folded down over them as she blinked and Decan swallowed hard.

"You can tell your father whatever you like," he said when he'd finally gotten his thoughts…and his seemingly raging libido together. "But I'll still be the one in charge at this moment."

Before she could reply and while he had at least a semblance of control, Decan climbed out of the vehicle and circled around to her door just as she was about to jump down. He held the door and took her arm. She wanted to pull away, but her pride wouldn't let her. He was amused and impressed by that fact. She would recognize both their positions in this situation, but she didn't like it. He figured that was fair. He didn't like it either.

CHAPTER 3

———◆———

THERE HAD BEEN CHANGES SINCE the last time Decan had been here. Both to the physical structure of this bunker, and to the reasons why he was here.

"Where are we?" Nisa asked the moment they passed through the oval walkway.

She had already moved by him and was surveying her surroundings no doubt, while she waited for his response.

"We're in the Florida territory. The Everglades as you mentioned earlier."

Decan watched as she moved.

At five-feet-five inches she was neither tall nor short. Just right was the way he would put it, as the top of her head came to his chin, causing her to have to look up to him. He didn't know why that filled him with a gust of dominance as potent as a physical blow. Her booted feet were soundless over the carpeted floor.

"This location is not on any of the tunnel maps," she continued. "That means it's unsanctioned. Why do you know about unsanctioned locations and the Assembly does not?"

"How do you know they don't know?" he asked as she moved past two rows of round tables and chairs.

The eight tables lined one half of the space, while an elaborate white column shot to the ceiling. The top of the column fanned out like the top of a cone and around that cone a metal sphere held egg-shaped LED lights equal distances apart.

"If they knew, then so would I," she replied as she stepped over to the other half of the room.

There were sectional couches on that side, three in an off white color and four in a dark orange hue. The colors matched the striped carpet and worked well with the darker beige paneled walls. They'd come in on the ground level, so the ceiling was lowest in this room, no more than ten feet high at most.

"You do not have upper level clearance," he replied and then held up his hand because even from across the room, he knew she would respond quickly to that statement.

"You're a Senior Guard," he told her. "That's level 3 clearance. As I'm sure you are aware only Lead Enforcers and FLs have level 6 clearance."

Her lips were clamped tightly, eyes boring into him like tiny chisels. He almost grinned at how easily he could anger her. He knew all her buttons to push and continued to push them, even when it wasn't his intent.

"Then I should not be here at all," she snapped and folded her arms over her chest.

The stance might have seemed childish or temperamental to anyone else, but Decan knew it for what it really was. Her shield.

Nisa Reynolds loved a good puzzle. She'd excelled in tactical training because she could quickly figure out the logistics of the battle and then was able to, just as fast, configure her best odds for survival. It worked for her every time. It was that same need to unravel the mystery and come up with a solution that had led her to the installation of the holodeck—which was a control center much like the humans' Internet, for the shifter universe. She had been able to migrate all of the databases that had been created for the shifters and generate an entire system that included maps of the tunnels, blueprints of all of the bunkers, plans for the vehicles they used, the weapons that had also been specially enhanced for them, the genetic breakdown of each tribe and so much more. The system was intricate and far more advanced than most of the shifters in Oasis. Along with that accolade, Decan had been especially impressed with the network Nisa had helped Nick Delgado design, called ViceSecure. This was the system that scanned the genetics of each shifter from the moment of their birth so that there was no way an undocumented shifter could enter Oasis because the locks on the doorways were all DNA scan protected.

"This is where you belong for the moment, Nisa," Decan replied to her intense gaze.

He'd lost seconds just staring at her wondering how all of that intellect and ability could be so neatly and attractively stored in one shifter.

"Before you ask any more questions just remember that your father assigned me to this mission. That means I'm responsible for you. I know you don't know me that well, but rest assured, I have no intention of letting the Assembly Leader down. So just relax, you're safe here. Trust me."

"I don't trust anyone who won't answer simple questions," she said, but her arms fell to her side as she turned and continued to move about the room.

"Well, I see you arrived safely."

Decan looked away from Nisa long enough to see that their host had arrived.

"We did," Decan said with a nod and then extended his hand for a shake.

Keller Cross was six-feet two-inches tall and at least

two hundred and thirty pounds. He wore dark gray pants and a shirt that barely stretched over his broad chest and large arms. His skin was a deep golden color, his eyebrows thick over imperial green cougar's eyes. He was probably the only shifter that wore his cat's eyes all the time.

Decan noted Keller's glance going over his shoulder and turned to see that Nisa had come to stand right behind him.

"Keller Cross, this is Nisa Reynolds. Nisa, this is Keller Cross."

"You're not a rogue," she said, her eyes keen as she watched Keller lift her hand and bring it to his lips. "We know there are some hiding down here, but your scent is clean."

Keller smiled just as Decan reached over and removed Nisa's hand from his. The cougar's smile faltered only slightly as he glanced quickly at Decan and then back to Nisa.

"It's a pleasure to meet you, Nisa. It's also good to know that my scent pleases you," Keller said.

"She didn't say that," Decan snapped. "She said you didn't smell like a rogue. There's a difference."

Keller shrugged. "I guess you're right."

"Where are we?" Nisa asked. "What is this place and why is it not on the maps?"

Keller was quick and replied without Decan's assistance. "Ah, yes, you are the lovely brain behind the holodeck and its wealth of information."

"I seem to have missed something pretty prominent," she replied and then looked around the room. "I'm guessing this bunker has eight levels, this one being the lowest. It's built up instead of out like most of the others down here. The tunnel floor is almost thirty-one thousand feet down. That leaves a lot of space to build up, but it would have taken some time. And approval."

"Well," Keller said with a chuckle. "Now that we've

gotten the logistics out of the way, can I get you a drink, Nisa? Or something to eat? I'm sure you're starving after your long ride."

She looked at him skeptically and Decan expected her to decline and demand he tell her where they were or take her out of here one more time for good measure. He wasn't going to do either, but he wouldn't deny that he liked her tenacity. It almost matched his.

"Fine," she said and then accepted the hand that Keller immediately offered her. "I can eat."

The moment Nisa's fingers touched Keller's, Decan felt it. The immediate and almost painful push of his cat against the wall that he always kept erected. He had to take a step to keep from falling with the force. Nisa looked back over her shoulder at him and when their eyes connected he could have sworn she was smiling. Her cat, that is.

It was a strange thought, one Decan had never had before. A Shadow Shifter's sex drive could be insatiable. A full grown white lion could be skating along the human lines of being addicted to any and every sexual act. Decan declared himself somewhere in between. He also, once again, prided himself on his restraint. He chose who, when and how. Every time.

Nothing a female did could arouse him if he was not in the market for sex. And when he was in the mood, there was usually no female willing to turn him down. Tonight, Decan wasn't in the mood. Or rather, he knew in his mind that he wasn't. So why was his cat, and hers, doing some odd type of mating call?

NISA WAS CORRECT, THIS FACILITY was built up. They took the elevator to the third level where the dining room was located. This circular room had only two tables, fifteen-feet each of dark glossed wood with high-back red cushioned chairs lined along each side like soldiers. These walls were smooth and painted a cool green color that wasn't too bright or too dark. The carpet here was a tree bark brown and Decan immediately got the vibe that he figured whoever designed this space was going for. He'd never been to the Gungi rainforest where the Shadow Shifters originated and he'd never wanted to go. Tonight, was no exception.

"Have a seat," Keller told Nisa.

She looked up to him and had even smiled before sitting in the chair Keller had pulled out for her. Decan grit his teeth in an effort to hold back the growl that wanted desperately to break free.

He pulled out the chair across from her and sat down heavily because he felt like he was being pushed.

"Our chef can make anything. He used to work for some fancy restaurant above ground and he had a television show. Tonight, in honor of where you are traveling to, I had him prepare barbeque."

Keller was talking as he sat at the head seat. It was his favored spot, Decan recalled.

"I've had barbeque before," Nisa told him.

"I'll bet you have," Keller continued. "I'm sure the chefs at Assembly Headquarters are top notch."

"I've never seen you at any of the quarterly meetings," she stated.

Keller glanced at Decan who was still trying to figure out what the hell his cat was up to tonight.

"I don't attend them," Keller answered.

"Because you're not a Lead Enforcer? You're not part of the Shifter Tactical Team at all, are you?" she asked.

Decan lay his hands flat on the table and drummed his fingers. Nisa immediately stopped talking, her head snapping toward his movement. He stopped. She looked up at him. He inhaled deeply and was just letting out a whispered curse when trays of food were brought out and placed on the table between them.

He immediately reached for the glass of water that had been placed in front of him. He watched her, watching him, as he drank.

"Well," Keller spoke a little louder than he had been before. "I am not part of the STT, but I assure you that it's perfectly safe for you to be here for the night. Isn't it, Decan?"

Hell no! Decan almost roared.

He had a dreaded feeling that it wasn't going to be safe for her to be anywhere around Keller. Not for long anyway.

"So you're a renegade with enough money and manpower to get this place built. I'm guessing that you probably also have someone in the Assembly helping you keep all of this a secret," Nisa said to Keller, with her gaze still locked on Decan's.

"He's no renegade," Decan answered. "He's a friend, doing me a favor."

"Yes, I am," Keller replied with a deep chuckle.

Three loud chimes sounded at that moment and their host, who seemed to be enjoying this moment way more than they were, went silent.

"I have to go," he said seconds later. "You two enjoy your meal. One of the staff will be along when you're done to take you to your rooms."

"Our rooms?" Nisa said. "So this is like a shifter hotel?"

Keller was now standing and he looked down at her, giving only a half grin this time. The look had Decan fisting his fingers and Nisa raising a brow in what...was that flirtation? Decan stood then, clapping a hand on Keller's shoulder.

"I'll find our rooms," he told the host who was definitely doing the most with Nisa right now. "You go and take care of your business."

Keller nodded, his grin disappearing as he stared back

at Decan. "Yeah, and you should be careful with yours."

Their gazes locked for a moment, until Decan turned away and listened to the cougar as he exited the room.

"Tense," Nisa stated and lifted a finger to her lips to lick away some sauce.

The growl was like an earthquake moving through Decan's body in a trek from the pit of his stomach until his lips peeled back from his teeth, letting the sound break free. Her head jerked up instantly, her eyes shifting from human to cat.

"Very," he replied and stepped closer.

She pulled her finger slowly from her mouth as if her ultimate goal in life was to tease him to the point of distraction. Well, Decan admitted, even if momentarily, she'd done a damn good job of that. Her hand continued to move slowly down until now it rested in her lap. Decan gripped the back of her chair and pulled it out from the table far enough so that he could move to stand in front of her.

Beneath the zipper of his pants Decan's cock twitched as her mouth was only a couple of feet away. In his mind, he could already feel her there, licking his length, sucking him deep, drawing everything from him in the blink of an eye.

"Look at me," he demanded.

The man was surprised to see her immediately do as he'd requested. The lion inside was not.

"What are you doing?" he asked in a last ditch effort to figure out what the hell was happening at this moment.

She shook her head, her tongue skirting out to touch her lips before replying, "I'm not doing anything."

His palms tingled with the thought of feeling her soft hair as he grasped the back of her head and pulled her closer. It would take only seconds to free his now raging erection and put her mouth to its tip. Just a taste. He'd give her only a little and then he'd pull back. He'd forget this ridiculous urging. Even as he thought it, the lion dismissed the notion. Just a taste would not be enough, not for either of them.

"Liar," he whispered through clenched teeth. "Sexy, sneaking, liar."

"No," she snapped quickly, her eyes shifting back to human as she abruptly stood to face him. "I'm not the one lying here, Decan. You are. I can smell it. And I don't like it."

N ISA WAS STUCK.
In this gorgeous suite, closed in her private bathroom, standing beneath the hot spray of water from the massaging showerhead. Her cat was stuck in her human body, because of a world that rejected it. Her desire to be more, to do more, with her life was stuck in the hands of a lion shifter with secrets that carried a distinct stench which should not have permeated her senses the way it had. Yet, it did.

From the moment he'd approached her, Nisa had scented it. Now, she tried her best to rid her mind, her senses and her cat of its effects. That, however, wasn't going to be easy. More pertinent and shocking to recently admit was her desire to be sexually satisfied. It was stronger now, had been in the last few months at Assembly Headquarters. She hadn't understood the overwhelming urge then and she definitely didn't now.

Sitting on the bench which lined one of the shower walls, she lifted a leg, propping her foot on its end and let her hand fall to the bare skin of her juncture. It was smooth and warm as she separated her thick folds, moaning at the slickness that awaited her.

Her awakening had come when she was fourteen years old, much earlier than her mother's, and a year earlier than was normal for female shifters. As she'd already known what she was, Nisa had been waiting anxiously to meet the cat that would share her body for the rest of her life. She'd had no idea that the cat would bring with it an urging that would threaten every sane part of her being. That's how it felt, the arousal of a shifter. It quickly took over any and all thoughts. Nisa had been lucky that there had been very few shifters living in her part of Oasis that turned her on. But the few that had, the feeling that had warmed her to the point of her entire body trembling whenever she'd been around them was intense and pushed her to a point where she'd known something had to give.

But her father was Roman Reynolds.

In addition to being the Assembly Leader, he was a black jaguar with as much predatory power as any king of a jungle. Oasis was Rome's jungle and Nisa was the second untouchable under his reign. Every shifter across the world knew this. They were not to speak a disrespectful word to Kalina, or give Nisa a second look. It was that simple and that serious at the same time.

The warning hadn't bothered Nisa since all she'd ever wanted to do was work toward building a better future for the shifters. Yet, she'd still had to figure out a way to deal with the urgings without risking another shifter's life by asking him to be with her. The answer had been fairly simple. She would slake her own need. It worked, she enjoyed the independence and that was it. She moved on to the next thing. At least that was how she normally handled the situation.

Tonight was different. She was not only trembling, but her cat was pacing and making a rumbling sound that echoed in Nisa's mind. The cat needed and Nisa wanted, unlike either had before.

She shouldn't. That was a given. Decan Canter was a lion and mixed joinings were frowned upon by some in the shifter community. Most commonly opposed was the shifter and human mating, but when her father met her mother while working at the law firm he used to own, neither of them had known that Kalina was a shifter. Ezra, Lead Enforcer, had joined with Dana, a human. Sebastian "Bas" Perry, the Mountain Zone Faction Leader, had joined with Priya, also a human. And there were countless others, she'd seen their names as she'd helped enter them all into ViceSecure. So the shifters as a whole had been moving toward accepting that union. As for the interspecies joinings, well, they were still a bit away from totally accepting that. Part of the reason was that Shadow Shifters themselves were a sort of anomaly. Half man and half cat, they had a complex DNA to start with. Mixing the half man, half cat, with a different variety of cat, was another level of the unknown. In the event of an offspring, what would it be? Which cat would dominate and how would the human half respond to such a mixture? It was something, that, to date, had not been answered because the different tribes had remained separate when it came to pairings.

Tonight, however, a jaguar was so turned on by a lion, she thought she might actually jump out of her human and cat skin if she did not receive some relief from these urgings.

She wanted to believe they'd come on quickly, but that wasn't totally true. She'd been feeling restless and needing release more frequently in the past few months. Tonight, the need had morphed into an all-out hunger. One that seemed to be battering her senses. Why else would she allow herself to stay here without calling her father to intervene? Why hadn't she blasted Decan with questions and more forcefully demanded the answers required when he decided to bring that cheetah along with them? Why...? The cat hissed and Nisa bit her bottom lip as she, finally pressed a finger into her center. The warmth immediately sucked the first digit in deeper and she let her head fall back against the gray marble walls of the shower. Her legs were already shaking slightly in anticipation as she pressed another finger alongside the first one.

Yes, her mind screamed.

As she began to pump her fingers into herself slowly, her chest heaved with each breath and she lifted another hand to grip her breast. It felt heavy in her palm, her nipple already tightened. She squeezed that nipple until her creamy walls clenched her fingers. With her eyes closed, Nisa's breaths quickened and she continued working her hands and fingers in an effort to reach her pinnacle soon.

Her cat growled then because it was not enough. Nisa knew it too.

She thought about him, let his image form in her mind as she moaned.

He was so tall, even taller than X's six-foot four-inch stature. And he was broad, his shoulders wide, arms thick and muscled. No, she hadn't seen him naked, but she hadn't needed to, his enforcer's jacket did nothing to hide his build or the strength she suspected he and his cat carried. There was power in his hands, strength in the fingers with the blunt-tipped nails. Even his face was sort of rugged. The beard that was neatly trimmed, the thick curls atop his head and those eyes. Like glass dyed the lightest hue of blue. Cool and slick like a glacier. He was older than her, there was no doubt, and not just because of the mixture of black and white hair, because shifters rarely showed physical signs of aging. No, she guessed it was because he could not be a Lead Enforcer at her age.

Nisa pulled her fingers out and circled them over her clit as she thought of his hands moving over her now wet body. He would know how to touch her in just the right way, there was no doubt. He was worldlier, she guessed because she'd never heard his name mentioned in Oasis. She hadn't seen it on the ViceSecure and there were no whispers about him. There was no doubt that a shifter that was this hot and this decorated on the STT would be sought after by men in leadership and females in need. She didn't know where he'd been in all her years or why he was suddenly here now. And while she wondered, the question of how good it would feel to have him over her, sinking deep inside of her, was one she was most curious about at the moment.

With that thought her fingers slipped into her warm, wet pussy once more, pumping fiercely in and out until she was gasping, her cat growling. It was getting hungrier and she was only whetting its appetite with her futile attempts at release. Her body felt tight, as if she were just on the precipice of relief, but couldn't quite get there. She wasn't going to get there. Not like this. Not this time.

With her curse she let her leg fall from the bench and pulled her hands away from her body. It wasn't going to work. She needed more.

It only took another few minutes for her to wash and slip on sweat pants, a t-shirt and tennis shoes. Then Nisa was slipping out of the room that Decan had escorted her to a half hour ago. This was the third floor, from the elevator control board she saw there were nine floors to this bunker. What she sought was up there. Pressing the appropriate button she eased further back into a corner of the car, keeping her head down while it took her to her destination.

Security would be tighter on the highest floor and hopefully—if this bunker was designed like the majority of them in Oasis—the security systems would give her some idea of who lived here and why this place was off the Oasis grid.

She stepped out of the elevator after the door quietly opened on the ninth floor. These halls were dimly lit and painted a muted gray. That was the first difference. Within all the Oasis bunker plans, the only floors kept without much light were for storage only. They could afford to conserve energy on those floors. Storage was never kept on the top floor of a bunker because that's where the shifters housed their weapons. In this one, if a human or rogue happened upon the doorway above ground that lead to Oasis, they would enter on this floor. She wondered why.

Nisa kept moving, going to the right and keeping close to the wall. She looked up in search of the square of green dots which traveled across the ceiling from one end of the wall to the other. This was the signal for an operational security line, one that could be monitored by guards at the holodeck. There was none. There were also no doors, at least, she hadn't come across any as of yet. Another thing that was missing on this level was a scent...any scent at all.

It smelled sterile, as if any trace of an aroma had been studiously washed away. She kept moving watching straight ahead as she walked, turning back every few minutes to be sure she wasn't being followed. But who would even know she was up here if there weren't any security monitors engaged?

When it felt like she could have possibly walked at least half the floor, Nisa thought about turning back. She didn't think there was a doorway here, but she couldn't actually believe that. There had to be a way for a shifter to get above ground. Just because they'd designed this under-ground hideaway to keep protected from the humans didn't mean that no shifter ever went above ground. They did, even though the Faction Leaders were required to approve above ground missions or travel. Nisa knew this for a fact because she often went above ground without approval.

She'd never liked running on the indoor tracks or in the park sectors that had been built to mimic the condi-tions in the Gungi. Since her mother had taken her above ground for her first run as a jaguar, Nisa had craved the scent of fresh air. She loved the rainy nights best, when there was just a hint of a chill and the rain fell against her thick yellow-brownish coat. She was certain that was what her cat needed right now. So she continued to move down what seemed like an endless hallway.

There were still no doorways in sight, but there was a sound. It was faint, but it was there, like someone tapping. Nisa followed it, hoping it would lead to either an answer of where she was or a way out.

The rubber soles of her shoes were perfect as they kept her approach quiet, while the tapping grew louder. She moved faster, her heart beating wildly as she began to feel the noise was being made specifically for her. Did someone know she was here? Were they sending her a message? Maybe that she shouldn't be here or that someone else was coming? It didn't matter, Nisa wasn't afraid. She was curious. As she'd always been.

She was getting closer. Not just because the sound was louder but because a scent slowly began to creep into the air. It was a fresh scent, like rain or morning dew. She kept going, dragging her hand along the wall as she'd been doing in search of the seams to a doorway. Dozens of steps later, none came. Yet she stopped anyway because the tapping had also ceased. A flash of light caught her eye across the hallway and Nisa pounced, following the tiny white dot until her entire body was pressed against the opposite wall, the vibrations from the resumed tapping rippling through her.

"Who are you?" she whispered because she knew there was someone on the other side of this wall.

She could feel them, another shifter, even though she still could not see it. The tapping continued, growing louder and faster until it almost matched the beat of her heart. Nisa turned and pressed her ear to the wall in the hopes of hearing more even though the tapping was getting to the point where her eardrums quivered in overdrive. Her fingers trembled and the sense that something was horribly wrong began to suffocate her. Nisa tried to push away from the wall, but she could not move. It was as if a magnet had drawn her there and was now holding on for her life.

There was a loud thumping and when Nisa was finally able to pull her face away from the wall a cone of light showed the distorted face of a cat on a naked human male's body. She opened her mouth to scream but the sound died as a blast of cold air slammed against her back. The invisible force that had been holding her to the wall finally released her completely and she stumbled back, just as the thing that was on the other side of the wall disappeared. Nisa turned to see where it could have gone and where this frigid air was coming from. That's when she saw it...the doorway.

She ran to it, jumping through the narrow passageway without a second thought.

CHAPTER 4

———◆———

DECAN YANKED HIS SHIRT UP and over his head and then let it fall to the ground beside the heap of clothes he knew belonged to Nisa. He held back a curse as he quickly untied his boots and stripped off his pants. Then, he was shifting, running through the area that was once a national preserve.

She had a head start but it didn't matter, her scent was locked into his senses so that he knew he could find her wherever she was. It was how he'd known she'd left her room.

He had been lying on the bed, arms folded behind his head while he thought about the events of the day. The beginning of his mission for the Assembly Leader, butting heads with Nisa about who was in charge, and the appearance of Kyss. He also needed to contemplate the murders and what that meant for him and his agenda. But all he'd managed to really give deep thought to was, Nisa Reynolds.

Decan had never ached for a female before. Yet, he'd ached as he stood in front of her, wanting with a sickening need for her to reach out, unzip his pants and take him into the waiting heat of her mouth. The second he'd closed his eyes he'd thought of her doing just that and his entire body had hardened, the lion inside roaring its dissatisfaction with the way things had actually turned out. Nisa hadn't undone his pants and licked him until his release burst free. She hadn't stood and wrapped her long legs around his waist, opening so that he could slip deep into her.

And he hadn't done a damn thing about those facts.

Because he couldn't.

She was untouchable and if anyone in this world knew what that meant, Decan should, after all he'd been through.

Rome had made it perfectly clear what this job was about. Sleeping with his daughter had not been listed in the things to do. In fact, the Assembly Leader's final words before he'd left had resonated most with Decan.

"I want my daughter safe. That is the first priority of this mission," he'd said as they stood in his office.

Safe meant untouched by him or anyone else. Decan understood that perfectly. He wished his cat could decipher the meaning of those words.

The four-foot tall, three hundred and fifty pound white lion raced through the path of bald cypress trees that had been battered and still withstood the shift in climate that had plagued the earth in the last years. The trees that normally stood in water, now barely thrived in less than three-feet of water making the path much easier to travel for the four legged beast. Years ago this place would have appeared to be too wet and humid for him to track a jaguar. But not for Decan. He'd been specially trained in tracking. That, combined with all of his shifter senses lent him the upper hand. Now, because of the decrease in moisture in the air, it was much easier to pick up her scent.

Who was he kidding? He'd never lost her scent. He feared it might actually be imprinted on his cat at this point. And that, would be a horrific mistake. For both of them.

She was about ten feet ahead when she turned quickly and doubled back. She knew he was behind her, no doubt, and was trying to lose him. She had no idea who she was dealing with.

Her body was long and sleek, at least five feet. Her coat a perfect pattern of large rosettes and spots. Powerful paws slammed through the water and skittered only when he crossed over to stand in front of her, his teeth bared, head lifted. Her cat roared in response, not backing down, but pressing forward. He stood taller, daring her to try. She did, going up the trunk of a tree and then jumping down so that she was now behind him. The moment he turned she was off and running once more. This time Decan didn't think. He didn't recall any rules or wait for any permissions. He let the lion burst free, taking the lead… in everything. He let the chase go on until she was once again near the doorway to allow her back into Oasis. Only she could not get in through this doorway on her own because she wasn't authorized. She was going to figure that out and be pissed, but for now, he had the upper hand.

His cat circled around her and landed with his front paws on top of the clothes they'd both left behind the bushes that hid the narrow opening. He shifted only seconds before her and was ready for her rage when her shift was complete.

What he wasn't ready for and should have anticipated was the sight of her standing only three feet away from him, totally naked.

"Standing on my clothes is real mature," she spat the moment she was able to.

Decan heard her words but he wasn't really processing

them. She was perfection. He'd thought so when he saw how elegant and powerful her cat looked moving through unfamiliar territory. Now, he knew it went through and through. The human body was just as alluring, from her slim waist to the curve of her hips and the pert breasts he knew would fit perfectly in his hands. If he were stupid enough to touch her. Which, this morning, he would have sworn he was not.

"Move out of my way," she said before coming straight at him. She pressed both her palms on his bare chest and attempted to push him back.

Decan didn't move. He did, however—despite the stark warnings of the man—plant his hands on her hips and lift her off her feet. She opened her mouth to say something, but it was too late, he was already moving them, taking the couple of steps back to the side of the building where the cloaked doorway was and pressed her back against the cinderblocks.

"What—" she started to say.

"Stop," he replied through gritted teeth. "Stop before it's too late."

Her hands were still on his chest, her dark skin against his lighter hue. They both looked down at them simultaneously and she sucked in a breath. She was going to tell him to get his tainted hands off her. To get his act together before she told her father. *Say it!* He willed her silently. *Say it!*

"Stop what?" she asked instead, her tongue snaking out to run slowly over her lips.

"Don't. I'm warning you," he said.

"Didn't you hear?" she asked as she brought one leg up and wrapped it around his waist. "I don't take warnings."

Her other leg was easing around him by then and when they locked at the base of his back, Decan growled.

Nisa growled in return.

His fingers tensed, blunt tipped nails digging deep into

her skin as his cock hardened to a painful length. It was apparent that not only did the lion want inside of her, the man did too. She held his gaze and Decan swore he could see her begging him to do it in the deep depths of brown eyes. But she didn't speak. There wasn't another sound between them.

Instead, his body tensed because he sensed something else. Rogues.

"Fuck!" he yelled and released her. "Get dressed now!"

It took her less than three seconds to figure out what was going on and grab for her clothes the way she was instructed. Decan dressed without looking at her and when she moved to the wall...to the spot her cat had remembered coming out of, he saw the confusion as the palm of her hand did not activate entry.

Instead of providing the explanation she wanted—the one he had no intention of ever giving—Decan pushed past her, holding his right hand up until his claws broke through the skin of his fingertips. With his claws against the wall moving in a series of circular motions the doorway slid quietly open and he stepped aside. She was angry. He could scent it as well as see it, but she wasn't stupid.

Nisa slipped through the opening and Decan followed. It closed behind them and when he turned again it was to a gun pointed at the center of his chest.

"STAND DOWN!" KELLER YELLED TO the six guards that were now standing in the brightly lit hallway.

One had Nisa's back pulled against him, one arm tightly around her waist, the other holding a gun to her temple. Decan pushed the gun pointed at him away from his chest and moved quickly to pull Nisa out of the guard's grasp.

"Don't. Touch. Her." He growled and the guard immediately backed away.

"What the hell, Decan?" Keller grumbled as he walked in front of the guards that were now moving to stand across the hall from the doorway. "First, the doorway alarm was tripped, then the sensors picked up activity around the perimeter. Where the hell were you and why didn't you use the proper exit and entry points?"

Nisa hadn't pulled away from him, a fact he was supremely thankful for because he would have hated to grab hold of her the way the guard had been doing. But if that's what it took to show them that he meant for his warning to be taken with deadly seriousness, then that's precisely what he would have done. She stood beside him, tucked under his arm as if they were joined...but they weren't, he reminded himself. She was just his assignment. Nothing more.

"Not now," he told Keller, because Nisa did not need to hear this conversation.

"Decan—" Keller began, his nostrils flaring.

"Ten minutes," Decan said interrupting him. "Give me ten minutes and I'll meet you in the lodge."

There was a moment of tense silence as the lion and the cougar refused to break eye contact.

"Ten minutes and then I'm coming to find you...again," Keller snapped.

Decan didn't reply, but moved away, walking Nisa down the hall to stop in front of the elevators.

"What's going on?" she asked, but still remained close to him.

"Not now," he said again, his teeth clenching.

The elevator doors opened and Decan ushered them inside, but the moment they closed Nisa moved to the other end of the car and fired off a round of questions.

"What the hell is this place? Who is Keller Cross? And why did I just feel like we were being hunted in a place you said was secure?"

Her t-shirt hung off one shoulder, the baggy pants she

wore were twisted and her tennis shoes were untied. But all Decan could see when he looked at her was the endless stretch of soft mocha skin enhanced by the delicious curve of her hips, her ass and her breasts. As his body tightened in response to that thought, the unmistakable stench of rogues still permeated his senses, forcing his lion to react.

"I told you I would take you out for a run," Decan replied. "It slipped my mind so I'll apologize for that. But you had no business going up there on your own. It was reckless and stupid and you should thank me for coming to your rescue."

A part of him sensed the words he'd just said were wrong, but they were already out by that time and the low rumbling sound of her cat disagreeing wholeheartedly with what he'd just said, echoed throughout the car.

"I did not need to be rescued!" she countered. "I picked up the rogue scent out there just like you did. And I've never asked permission to leave Oasis—"

The second her lips clapped shut Decan nodded.

"Right. You've never asked permission but you've been leaving regularly. I know because each time in the last six months that you've done so, I've been there. Watching you. Making sure nothing happened while you were out disobeying one of your father's staunchest rules. So yes," he stated evenly. "You need to be rescued, from yourself!"

Her mouth opened, then closed again as she struggled for words. Decan was fine with that. The less she talked, the easier it was for him to think. Actually, no, that wasn't right. The elevator door opened and he reached for her. She backed away and he cursed. He wanted to explain, but knew it wasn't possible, so he grabbed her arm and pulled her off the elevator.

She yanked free the moment they were in the hallway on the floor where their rooms were. He didn't try to hold on to her, which he easily could have, instead he let her walk ahead of him. Trailing behind her, even while she was quiet, wasn't easier. His gaze immediately went to the sway of her ass in those ridiculously huge sweats. He'd seen her wear them before during the training sessions she lead back at the Assembly Headquarters. While most of the other female shifters wore the more form-fitting training gear, Nisa always wore something baggy. In the beginning Decan had thought she was hiding her body, but then he'd seen her in full guard gear and changed his mind. That uniform fit her every curve to perfection. He'd lost count of how many days he'd wished he were the material of her tank top so that he could hug her full breasts in the same way. She could be such a bundle of contradictions.

He was so deep in that thought that he hadn't seen her stop in front of her door, so he bumped into her.

She turned immediately and stared up at him.

"Now that I know stalking is apparently a part of your assignment, you don't have to prove that point by literally being on my heels," she quipped.

Her brow was furrowed, shoulders set stiffly. Anger was even an alluring scent on her, like something sweet baking. It tickled his senses to the point that Decan was reaching out to touch her when he probably should have been running to get away from her.

"I'll apologize for yelling, but not for trying to keep you safe," he said as his hands closed around her arms.

His action had been slow, his fingers wrapping gently around the bare skin of her biceps. She didn't look down at his hands, but he knew she was letting the effects of their contact sink in. He knew because he felt it too. It was similar to the way it had been when they were outside and he'd put his hands on her. Like a lock clicking open they stood still and waited to see what would happen next. He was as powerless to stop it as she was, even though he was certain that a part of both of them knew just how a big a mistake this was going to be.

She tilted her chin upward as if she'd heard his every thought and Decan sighed as his cat pressed forcefully against him, begging for the extra connection.

He gave in because in the space of those few moments there was nowhere for him to run. Besides, was not an option when both his body and his cat were in sync. He brushed his lips over hers first, tentatively, trying to test the cat and the man to see if they were both certain. In the next seconds his tongue was pushing past her lips, taking every bit of her taste and groaning into a kiss that he knew would change everything.

Her arms went around his neck and she pulled him closer. Decan wrapped his arms around her waist, holding her tightly against him as their tongues continued to duel. His cat was on full alert standing at attention and hearing the low, but undeniable call of hers. Decan stilled because this had never happened before. Not with any other female he'd been with. It was so strange, he had no idea how to react.

Fortunately, Nisa did. She deepened the kiss, letting her hands slip down to his shoulders where her nails dug through the material of his shirt to prick his skin. Her body moved against his, the curve of her breasts along his torso, in a sensuous motion that had a low growl rumbling in Decan's chest. He pushed her back against the door and she lifted a leg to glide up the side of his, wrapping it seductively around his waist. His hands moved down to grip her ass, squeezing as he melted into the kiss. Her lips were soft, her tongue hot and wet against his. And her scent, it filled every part of him, enticing him, goading him, forcing him.

Decan's hand was moving before he could even consider what he was about to do. His fingers trailed along the elastic waist of her pants, dipping lower when he came between them. She moaned. The sharpened edge of her jaguar's teeth nipping his lower lip as his pressed lower, moving down to cup her bare mound. Yes, it was bare, free of any hair at all, and Decan wanted to roar his intense pleasure at the thought. She was warm here also and wet, damn it all to hell, she was so fucking wet. His fingers slid easily between her plump folds, grazing the tight bud of her clit before moving further to find the spot he needed. He hadn't even been aware of the search, but his cat had, and Decan had to tear his lips away from hers to let the deep purr of satisfaction echo throughout the hallway.

Immediately following were three chimes that pierced the haze of desire that had been about to take Decan to a place he was certain he shouldn't tread. Wanting to be thankful for the interruption but instantly hating Nisa's reaction to it, he pulled his hand from her. She had already lifted her head to the sound, flattening her palms on his chest as she prepared to move away. He did it for her and did not say a word when she turned from him and entered her room.

Gritting his teeth as the door closed, Decan once again let his claws extend and used them to trace a code over the door's control pad, to lock her inside. She would hate that she could not get out and no doubt let him know about it the moment he returned. But Decan didn't care. Now, more than ever, he knew that not only did he need to protect her from her own recklessness by going above ground unescorted, but he also had to keep her safe from what was happening around her that she had no clue about.

CHAPTER 5

———————

"ARE YOU OUT OF YOUR mind? What the hell were you doing out there with her?"

Keller didn't waste a moment, jumping right in and making his feelings absolutely clear.

Decan had just walked into the small, dark room where he knew they would be meeting. It was the only room in the entire bunker that was not monitored by cameras or audio. He moved slowly, pulling out a chair and taking a seat before responding.

"I've got it under control," Decan replied and ignored the look of disbelief on the cougar's face.

"So you knew that rogues were less than twenty feet away from pouncing on both of you while you—"

"I said I've got this!" Decan interrupted.

"They're looking for her," Gold said, his deep voice breaking through the tension.

"Rome said the threat was down here," Decan spoke to his longtime friend. "He was certain they were below ground."

"Doesn't mean they're working alone," Gold continued.

"You need to get her dropped off as quickly as possible. She's jeopardizing our entire mission," Keller insisted.

Decan stared at him directly. "She *is* the mission," he said coolly. "For now anyway."

Neither Keller nor Gold spoke. They were most likely as confounded by Decan's words as he was. Decan had known Keller for ten years, since Decan's return to Oasis. He and the cougar had shared a similar experience above ground and had both vowed the vengeance on the same human. Gold, on the other hand, was the same age as Decan. They were neighbors in Houston, only nine years-old, when Gold's parents were killed in a train crash. Maura Canter had announced at the double funeral that Gold would be moving in with them and Jalil had known better than to argue. Decan had been cool with the new arrangement, preferring to have a surrogate brother, over his sisters any day. A year later when their home in Houston was almost burned to the ground as the humans hunted a cheetah shifter who had taken refuge in their cul-de-sac, Decan was sent to live with his grandparents and Gold, who had gone into his shift early and attempted to attack one of the human police, was taken underground with rest of the Canter family.

Now, the three were together, with a job to do. Nisa was interfering with that job.

"This is not what we planned," Keller insisted.

"I don't need you to tell me about the plan," Decan told him. "I know what the plan is because we've talked about nothing else for I don't know how long."

"It has to be the priority, Decan," Keller told him. "You know what happens if we don't succeed."

"We will succeed," Gold interjected again. "We have the best cover now to not only get into the Central Zone headquarters, but to also get above ground."

Decan looked at his old friend standing at his full six-feet four-inches. Gold was a big guy, tall and bulky with eyes the bold color of his name. He spoke in a deep voice with a slight southern twang and fought like the vicious white lion he could so quickly shift into.

"How is that?" Keller asked then, turning his attention to Gold.

Decan knew why Keller was really pissed at him and if he let himself think long and hard about it, he'd be angry with himself as well. But he wasn't going to do that. Forward movement was the way he liked to proceed. Looking back never did anybody any good.

"There's a big function above ground day after tomorrow. Every member of the Ruling Cabinet will be there, along with some other international players. We can put somebody in position to infiltrate the Cabinet and feed us the information we need for the final leg of our plan," Gold told them.

"How do you know about this?" Keller asked.

"Who do you plan on sending to infiltrate the Cabinet?" Decan spoke simultaneously.

Gold folded his beefy arms over a massive chest that pressed almost violently against the material of his black shirt.

"The answer to both questions is Kyss," he said.

Keller shook his head. "Who the hell is that? More baggage you've picked up?"

Both of those inquiries were directed at Decan, who was getting tired of Keller's tone and attitude. The cougar definitely lived up to his reputation of being all smiles and charm with the females, and a perpetual ass with anyone else.

"She found us," Gold said. "But I've had a chance to check her out a bit since we've arrived here. She's not registered in the database. But there are twin cheetahs who are. Their family goes straight back to Brazil. The mother of the twins had a sister who gave birth twenty-nine years ago. There's no record of the baby and none of these cheetahs are listed as residents in any of the bunkers here. I suspect they've been living in the caves down here for whatever reason. The interesting part—which I was able to get from Kyss—is that they go above ground. A lot."

"Without permission like someone else, I'm guessing," Keller stated.

Decan didn't even look at Keller. "We need to know more about her before we include her in any of our plans. For all we know she could already be a mole for someone else," he said to Gold. "And furthermore, it's a ridiculous and unrealistic rule to think you can tell shifters where to go and when."

This wasn't the first time he disagreed with one of the Assembly Leader's rules, but he was careful to never voice those opinions, outside this circle of three.

"Containment has been Rome's answer since the Unveiling," Keller added.

"He tried it the other way and more shifters died," Gold said. "But we shouldn't have to be friendly with those who refuse to befriend us."

"They're not all like that," Decan said.

"No. But we don't always have the luxury of time to figure out which ones are open to our kind or not," Keller reminded him.

"I agree," Decan replied, before looking pointedly at Keller. "Which is why we should continue on to the Central Zone in the morning."

"So you can drop off the Assembly Leader's daughter and head above ground to continue the surveillance you've put on hold for the past six months." It was a statement. Not an order because Keller knew it was futile to ever speak to Decan in that tone. Still, he hadn't formed it as a question either, probably because he didn't want Decan to think he had a choice. Decan knew he didn't.

He'd fully committed himself to their quest. He wasn't backing down now. Even if his lion was threatening his sanity with the instant heat and draw to a female he should not give a damn about.

Before Decan could reply his comlink buzzed from its place on his left wrist. He immediately looked down at the screen to see an incoming call. Already carrying the guilt of things he hadn't shared with Keller and Gold, Decan decided to answer the call using the speaker function. Keller and Gold knew nothing about the Assembly Leader asking Decan to assist Jace Maybon with the search for Cole Linden. Considering the sensitive nature of the search and how many members of the Shadow Shifters had spoken out against using their limited resources on continuing the search, Decan was fairly certain Jace wouldn't mention it on this line.

"Good evening, Faction Leader Maybon," he said as he looked up at a shocked and suspicious Keller and Gold.

They both knew to remain silent as they listened.

"Good evening, Decan. I wanted to check on your location and get your ETA for tomorrow," Jace Maybon stated.

Jace was the wild card of the FLs. The brash and opinionated owner of one of Los Angeles's largest talent agencies. At least that was how he used to be known. Since the disappearance of Cole Linden, Jace had been somber and just on the brink of going completely rogue in order to find his friend. Decan could easily relate to that type of dedication and simmering rage. He carried his own scars and had personal goals to assuage them. So he spoke in his normal tone when replying to the FL.

"The Everglades," he told Jace. "Leaving first thing in the morning. Should get to you by nightfall."

"Good," Jace replied. "We've had an interesting development that I want you to follow up on immediately."

"Yes. I'll only be there a few days and then I'll be heading back in this direction," Decan lied. Something he'd been doing a lot of lately.

"Change in plans," Jace told him. "Get here as soon as you can and I'll give you the details. And check your vehicles when we disconnect. The tracking devices must not be working because we're unable to see your location on any of the positioning maps."

The call was disconnected before Decan could reply. He had no intention of telling the FL that the trackers had been disabled on each of the vehicles before they even entered into the Florida area. Not to mention the fact that this bunker and a thirty mile radius were protected by a power grid that not only supplied electricity and heat to this facility, but also kept any unauthorized devices from working while on the premises.

"So they've been trying to track you," Keller said as he sat on the edge of the heavily glossed wood table.

That, six chairs and a mini-bar were the only furniture in this room. That's the way Keller had designed it. Minimal and private. It was what their team needed.

"We figured they would, that's why we dismantled the tracking devices before we got close to the bunker so they wouldn't receive a scramble signal," Gold stated.

"She never even bothered to check," Decan said as he flattened his palms on the table and leaned his weight on the furniture. "She was so busy trying to figure out why the bunker wasn't on her maps that she never noticed the light had stopped blinking on the dashboard and no doubt somewhere on that board she carries around like a detachable body part."

"But she's going to figure it out soon, isn't she?" Keller asked. "She has a reputation of being too intelligent for her own good. That's why you need to get rid of her as soon as you possibly can."

That was much easier said than done, Decan thought as he pushed back and nodded. "We're leaving at four.

Set your alarm," he told Gold who replied with a wry chuckle.

"You think getting up early is going to throw her off the scent of the lies you're force feeding her?" he asked.

Decan stopped at the door and looked over his shoulder at both of them. They had no idea that he was also keeping something from them.

"I think I've been running covert operations for a long time," he told them. "So having the little lady as cargo for the time being is no big deal. We're still on track to finish what we started. Nisa Reynolds has nothing to do with that."

He seemed pretty confident as he stepped through the door and heard the almost imperceptible click when it slid closed behind him. But as Decan walked down the winding hall toward the room where Nisa was sleeping, he wasn't so sure.

She was inquisitive. And she was sexier and more enticing than he'd thought she would be up close and personal. That was a combination he'd never faced in all the covert ops he'd worked during his time in the US military.

She was unexpected, he concluded as he approached her room and unlocked the door. But she wasn't going to stop him. Not her, the Assembly Leader or Jace Maybon were going to stop the events he'd set in motion. He wouldn't allow them.

N ISA HAD KNOWN HE WAS going to come back. She didn't know how or why, but she'd known.

Another shower hadn't eased the ache that was firmly planted between her legs. Nor had it washed away the feel of his hands on her. She could look at each spot on her skin that he'd touched and recall with absolute accuracy the sensations that had gone through her body at the time. Especially as his fingers had slipped deep inside of her. Never, in all her years of pleasuring herself, had Nisa felt the way she did when Decan's fingers penetrated her. Even now she wanted to sigh with the intensity of that memory.

But she didn't.

Instead she lay on her side with her back to the door, staring into the darkness of the room. She'd already searched the space earlier and knew that there were cameras and audio wires all over the place. So as much as she could, she kept the lights off. Even when she was in the shower she'd been in the dark. Apparently this was a place where they felt they needed to watch everyone doing everything. That was all well and good, it was their place not hers. But she wasn't going to be watched or photographed, or whatever their intention was. And she wasn't going to run back and tell her father that someone under his supervision had even expected her to. No, that's what they were certain she would do. Which is why Nisa was doing the exact opposite.

It was also why she'd kissed Decan so wantonly. Because each time he looked at her he saw the Assembly Leader's daughter. A task to mark off his list of things to do. Well, Nisa wasn't going to be so neatly compartmentalized. True, it shouldn't matter what Decan thought of her or wanted, or didn't want from her. He was simply escorting her to the Central Zone. Nothing more.

Yet, Nisa knew that was a lie.

She couldn't explain exactly how she knew, but she did. There was something more brewing steadily between her and that lion shifter. Something she admitted only to herself that she'd never felt before. Or had she? In the past few months her body had felt differently. The way she touched herself feeling more inadequate each time. She'd tried to brush it off as simply being tired after working so hard and long on getting the holodeck up and running. Now, she wondered what it all meant.

She wondered about so many things.

Decan and everyone in this place were working hard to keep a secret from her and most definitely her father. Nisa was going to find out. What she was going to do with the information when it was hers, she wasn't quite sure. But she was going to find out.

There was no sound to the lock disengaging but she'd sensed him on the other side of the door moments before it opened quietly. It was a warming that began slowly in the pit of her stomach whenever he was near and then her cat, sliding slowly against that warmth as if it had been waiting for it, forever.

She brought her knees up closer to her chest, her hands pressed between them, head sinking into the thick soft pillow. She wore shorts and a tank top with socks on her feet because the cement floor, although smooth and glossed, was cool and unfamiliar to her bare feet.

He moved slowly, almost predatorily as he approached the bed. Her tank top rode up her back with her latest movement and she felt the heat of his gaze against her skin. He stood there for endless moments and Nisa willed herself to remain still. He was watching her and she was thinking of him. It was a strange sensation, one which had her biting her bottom lip in consternation. This wasn't a predicament she'd found herself in before. It didn't mean that she couldn't come up with a way to get through it. To the contrary, her mind was already working to figure this out.

"Get some sleep," he said finally, his voice low. "We're leaving early in the morning."

"Since I'm sure you've locked both of us in here this time, I guess there's nothing to do but sleep."

That wasn't what she should have said. She'd told herself that she was over him locking her in this room like she was some uncontrollable child. So maybe she wasn't over it, but she hadn't intended for him to know that.

"You should take your own advice," she continued quickly and turned over to lay on her back.

Her next move took a little thought but managed to feel totally natural. Nisa stared directly at him as she extended an arm and patted the pillow beside her. "Leading requires a clear head. Rest works wonders for a busy mind. My Uncle Baxter used to say that to me when I was a little," she told him.

Baxter was the Overseer who had been with her father and her father's family for years. He was a human who had come to the United States with his assigned shifter family. His job was to watch over them as they made the transition into the human world. To keep them safe and to report back to the Elders and the Seer of the Gungi on their status. He'd turned eighty-nine last month, celebrating his birthday reluctantly with the four-tiered chocolate cake Nisa had directed their baker to prepare for him. Next to her parents, Baxter held a huge chunk of her heart.

"I'm not a child," Decan replied.

That admission hadn't been necessary. Nisa knew he wasn't a child. He was a full grown shifter. One whom she was undoubtedly attracted to. She wondered if that were the reason she'd invited him to sleep beside her. No, it wasn't. She believed in keeping her enemies, and those she hadn't quite yet decided whether or not to trust, close.

"And yet, the rest theory, would probably still work," she quipped. "Come on. I'll stay on my side of the bed. I promise I don't bite."

That brought a chuckle from him. The sound was quick and momentarily startled her. It wasn't until she felt the bed give beneath his weight as he sat on the other side and leaned over to remove his boots that she realized it was because she liked it.

Following her advice it only took him a few seconds, of which he used to pull his shirt over his head and lay back on the bed beside her. Nisa was surprised by how close he was. Maybe this bed was smaller than she'd thought. She attempted to roll over again, but immediately felt his arm going around her waist to pull her back against him.

When her back was spooned against his front and she was once again biting her lip at the new development, she felt the sharp nick against her neck.

"I'm not making any promises about not biting," he whispered as his tongue licked over the spot where his lion's teeth had scraped along her skin.

That was when the first slither of doubt etched along her spine, sending a warning echo to her brain. What the hell was she doing? And how was this going to end?

This wasn't going to be good.

It couldn't be.

The clicking he'd already connected with dread sounded loudly and every muscle in Decan's body went on instant alert. They were coming for him. Again.

There were five of them this time. They never came alone. Not after the first time. The time that had ended with him sinking his teeth into the human's throat and crushing his windpipe.

They would attempt to hold him down again. No doubt resorting to the drug he detested because no matter how big and strong they thought they were, they were no match for his shifter strength. That, among other things, was what they feared most. That the shifters were an elite species, one that could wipe the humans out at any moment. Despite his upbringing and their tribe's teachings, Decan wasn't so sure that was a bad idea.

"Stand up and face the wall!" the first one yelled.

They wore all green, a darker tone from the military fatigues he'd been used to seeing when he was a soldier. It had been four years since then, he knew because he'd been keeping count using his claw to scrape each day along the concrete walls that surrounded him. He didn't move when they commanded. He never did. And they were too afraid to touch him. Scared that his shifter DNA would rub off on them. Idiots.

"Up! Now!" the man yelled again, this time using a baton to poke into Decan's ribs.

If he pressed the button at the other end, electric volts would shoot through the baton and ravage Decan's body. It was painful and only served to anger the lion that had already been awakened inside of him. To avoid the worsening of this scenario, if at all possible, Decan stood slowly this time, but he did not turn his back to them. He would never voluntarily turn his back to another human again. That was what led him here in the first place.

He looked directly in the man's dark eyes without blinking and stood with his hands at his sides, fists already clenched and at the ready. He'd fought them each time they'd come to him since that first night, because he wasn't an animal to be caged and mistreated, regardless of what they thought.

"Get the chains, tie him to the wall," another one behind the first man suggested.

Decan heard the chains but did not take his eyes off the one standing in front of him. He was the leader. The way in which he stood with his legs slightly spread, the baton in one hand, his other resting atop the gun at his hip. He didn't wear any stripes or other military commendations, which didn't surprise Decan. The world had changed since he'd served. In fact, it had changed since the Unveiling. There was an air of lawlessness now with law enforcement officials and these militant goons who dedicated all their time and attention to one issue: the Shadow Shifters.

"He broke through them the last time," another—smarter human—had replied.

"Do it!" the second man yelled.

The leader held up a hand to impatiently stop the noise behind him.

"If he cooperates there will be no need for chains," he said while keeping his gaze on Decan.

Then he boldly stepped closer.

"Do you understand that, cat?" he asked in a voice full of disdain. And carefully masked fear.

"If you tell me what I want to know, I won't beat you like the worthless animal you are."

Decan didn't move or reply. The beatings didn't scare him. And he wasn't going to pull that gun out and shoot him until he was certain he was dead. Because they needed him for something. Decan hadn't figured out what, but their impatience was growing, which meant his resistance was getting to them. Decan couldn't find it in his heart to be a bit sorry about that fact.

"Now, where is your leader? Where is Roman Reynolds? Where is the one setting all the fires?" he asked, baring his crooked teeth.

He'd been to Oasis in the months after his honorable discharge from the Marines. Visiting with his family had been a delight. Seeing the place in which all of his kind had been forced to live was not. Oasis was Roman Reynolds' idea. Decan did not agree with it.

Decan did not reply.

The question came one more time. When he still remained silent, the leader gave a nod and the four that had been standing eagerly behind him, came forward with their tasers and batons and yet another battle had begun. All the while his lion remained unseen. Decan had given them that pleasure and eventually pain before. He'd sworn never to do it again. He could fight them just as long and fiercely in his human form. That was something else they hated. His resilience and his strength. They hated it because they couldn't match it. And he hated them because—according to the laws of the Ètica which still bound the Shadow Shifters regardless of their new circumstances—he was not supposed to kill them. One slip was enough to have guilt choking him on a daily basis. Another, might kill him. If these hate-filled humans didn't manage to do so first.

Hours later she came to him, as they always allowed her to. The prostitute who had glimpsed his Serfin tattoo the night he'd hired her, and had immediately called the Outlaw Task Force.

The group of law enforcement officials—or hunters were more like it—were formed to search for and dispose of any and all shifters. Armed guards had kicked in the door and crashed through the windows of the hotel room where Decan had asked the woman to meet him. They'd used some type of gas to knock him out before carrying him to the secret Shifter Isolation Camp located in the deserts of Arizona.

"Easy baby, Marlee's right here," she would say as she climbed over him, sliding down until the already slick walls of her pussy grabbed his cock and held on until he could not contain his release any longer.

Decan's eyes shot open. He was lying in a bed. Not on the cold cement floor of the SIC where he'd been held for nine long years. The air he breathed was free of the stench of sweat, smoke and sex. He still wore his pants, but his chest was bare and his shoes were off. He inhaled deeply and exhaled slowly in an attempt to calm the man and beast that had not experienced this particular dream in a long time. Not since a new scent had begun to fill his senses upon waking. The new scent wasn't just in his memory this time. It was close and it was real. Each time since the quarterly meeting six months ago—the day he'd first seen Nisa—he'd awakened from the dreams of Marlee riding him to a thunderous climax, with the Assembly Leader's daughter's scent permeating the air.

Tonight was no different. No, that wasn't correct. It was different because he had more to go with just her scent. He'd kissed her and he'd touched her. He didn't need to close his eyes or fall asleep to recall the feel of her tongue against his and the moist heat that surrounded his fingers as they'd pressed deep inside of her. The memories were fresh and potent and they were the reason his cock was rock hard at this moment. Not the dream and certainly not anything that happened in that dream. Marlee had never solicited this type of desire from him. And no matter how many times the idiot humans running the SIC thought they would be the first to claim a human pregnant with a shifter's seed, they were wrong. There had never been any fear of Marlee becoming pregnant because a Shadow Shifter could only reproduce with its *companheiro*. And Decan was certain that Marlee was not the woman he was destined to be with for all time. There was no such woman for him.

As if she knew he'd been thinking of her, Nisa moved. Her arm falling over his waist, her leg settling between his. Her breath was warm against his arm and for an instant Decan considered moving so that he could have her head lying on his bare chest. He would hold her tight and revel in the idea that she was so close and at the moment so unguarded with him. But that wouldn't last. He knew that and thus decided it was futile to even try.

Decan let his eyes close slowly as he tried to clear his mind of her and focus on tomorrow and the next day. But her hand moved again, this time lower on his abs. It was warm, or was that just him? Her fingers were still and then they weren't, curling so that the sharp tip of her nails scraped over his skin. The quick jolt of pain should have taken him to that dark place where he came out swinging and asked questions later. Instead, this time, it did the opposite. It warmed him until he almost forgot everything else.

The low hum of his cat vibrated through his body and as if it were speaking directly to her cat, she pressed closer to him and moaned. Her nails moved like spikes down his stomach and over the buckle of his pants. She cupped his erection and squeezed. Decan growled.

In the next seconds he was moving, flipping her over and onto her back. If she looked startled when her eyes opened and she stared up at him, he dismissed it. The lion and its need were in charge now and he was following its lead, pushing her shirt up until her breasts were bared before him. His mouth covered a nipple while his palm flattened over the other breast.

She held the back of his head, her fingers going into his hair, nails scraping his scalp. He sucked hungrily, totally enamored by the tight nipple and the soft malleable flesh. But it wasn't enough. With both hands on her breasts now, Decan went lower, tracing a heated path down her torso with his tongue. His mind was on one thing claiming this scent that had been taunting him once and for all.

Nisa, apparently had other ideas.

With her hands still on his head she pushed him away, and rolled from beneath him while his scrambled mind struggled to catch up.

"I'm not sure what you're used to, but I'd prefer my partner have me on their mind when they're with me," she snapped and pulled her shirt down to cover her breasts.

"What?" he asked, the fog clearing slowly from his mind.

"My name is Nisa," she replied and slipped off the bed.

She was pulling at the blanket and Decan had to hop off the bed to keep her from yanking it from beneath him.

"I know what your name is," he replied.

"Good," she said before tossing the blanket at him and walking toward the door. "Tell Marlee I said hello. And if you want to keep an eye on me so that I don't go sneaking above ground again, do it from the floor outside this door."

At his silent confusion, Nisa used her claws to disengage the lock on the door and waited for him to walk through it.

When had she figured out how to do that? It didn't matter, Decan Canter did not sleep on floors, not since his time in the SIC—the worst time of his life. And he had no intention of leaving her alone tonight. He clinched his teeth and kept the curses to himself. He'd wanted her.

Nisa. Not Marlee. And yet, the name of the woman who had almost killed him, had somehow managed to save him from making a grave mistake. Sleeping with Roman Reynolds' daughter was not smart. It could only lead to more disastrous occurrences in Decan's life. After being tortured and held against his will for nine years, Decan was ready for some semblance of normalcy. Facing the wrath of the Assembly Leader was definitely not normal.

With that resolved in his mind, Decan dropped the blanket on the bed and walked around to the other side. He grabbed his boots and his shirt and stopped in front of her near the door.

"Your name is Nisa and you're the Assembly Leader's daughter. You're a job and nothing more. I forgot that for a moment," he told her.

"And you're an ass. I'll be sure to remember that from now on," she said tightly before closing the door behind him.

CHAPTER 6

———◆———

NISA MOVED QUICKLY.
The fact that she'd found herself alone after she'd showered and dressed at three-thirty the next morning was not a mistake. Decan Canter was not a shifter who made mistakes. From what she'd been able to research on his family and his time with the military she'd surmised as much. And when she'd lay in that bed thinking throughout the night she realized that every step he made had been deliberate.

There were still questions running through her mind as she'd left the room and made her way to the lowest level of this bunker to where they'd parked their vehicles. Where had he been for the last nine years? He'd only showed up in Oasis last year. His prints and body scan were still logged into ViceSecure from that day. Their internal backup spanned ten years. The master board, however, housed every bit of data from the day of Oasis's inception. That was located on the holodeck back at Assembly Headquarters. All she had now, was what was stored on her portable board, and while that had given her the shape of the shifter she was dealing with, it didn't fill in all the spaces.

How and why had Decan stayed above ground for so long and why was he back now? More importantly, why was her father placing so much trust in a shifter they knew hardly anything about?

All these questions masked the biggest anomaly where Decan was concerned. Nisa shook her head as she approached her vehicle and dropped her bag to the ground beside the front tire. The memory of last night, hell, the last twenty-four hours still burned in the back of her mind. Why had she let him touch her? Because she'd been drawn to him. Her and her cat had felt the heat permeating between them from the first seconds he'd walked up behind her back at Assembly Headquarters. Nisa had been trained to put down any shifter who dared to get out of line with her personally, by Lead Guard and Seer Eli Preston. In addition to sharing their knowledge in technology and security, Lead Enforcers and her uncles, Nick Delgado and X Santos Markland had continued her education by rehearsing all the warnings they wanted her to tell any male shifter bold enough to approach her. Her Uncle Baxter had given her all the history instructions she'd ever need on how female shifters handled suitors. But it had been her mother who had taken her to the side after her first shift and then again when she'd turned eighteen to talk to her about men, the *calor*, and finding her *companheiro*. The latter two Nisa had tried to dismiss because it had been more than awkward hearing her mother speak of such things, but she'd paid particular attention to the differences between the male and female Shadow Shifters. She'd been doing that all her life. Yet, none of her teachings or personal observances had prepared her for this shifter.

Or the strange things she could hear and feel when he was around.

As she knelt down beside the Tracer and pulled her board from her bag she recalled what happened last night.

His hands and mouth had felt so good on her. He was everywhere she'd ever imagined the right man would be when she allowed him into her bed. Her body quivered in anticipation of his next move and her cat had lay in wait for the moment it could finally receive this type of sexual release. Then there'd been an interruption, voices sounding in her head, scenes flashing in her mind. The name Marlee spoken loud and clear in Decan's voice. Only, Nisa wasn't totally sure he'd actually said it, not at that moment.

When he'd stood to answer her accusation he'd looked perplexed. His body was taught with arousal but there was something else present in that room. Something Nisa hadn't been able to ignore. The stench and force of the lies between them. It had angered her, and made the confusion of what the hell was going on, more prevalent. She hated it all because it made her feel like she wasn't in control. And Nisa needed to be in control. For once in her life, she needed to feel like everything she did and said was of her own accord, for her own purpose.

She'd needed him to leave and he had. Then she'd begun to think.

He wouldn't tell her where they were and there was no record of this place on any of her maps. He was lying about who Keller was and why they were there. And when she'd been researching him on her board she'd noticed her secure link to the holodeck at Assembly Headquarters was disconnected. That was why she'd dressed and left her room extra early because she wanted to see what else was different now that they'd stopped at this place.

The tracking system on the Tracer was disabled. The power signal located just behind the front tire was off, and when she tried to access the Tracer's control panel via her master controls on her board, they were disengaged as well. She moved quickly to the other vehicle, typing the codes into her board only to discover that this one had been disabled as well. Cursing, she stood and was startled when she turned and came face to face with the alluring cheetah that had joined their traveling party.

"Good morning, sexy," Kyss spoke as she reached a hand out to touch Nisa's hair.

Nisa didn't move as she chastised herself for not picking up the shifter's scent and letting her sneak up behind her.

"Good morning," she finally muttered and then stepped around her.

"What are you doing out here so early?" Kyss asked as Nisa continued back to her Tracer.

Nisa stopped in front of the door handle on the driver's side and used the pad of symbols embedded into the steel to punch in her access code. She'd half expected the code not to work since it was clear that someone had tampered with the vehicles. But the locks disengaged and she opened the passenger door on the driver's side first.

"I'm getting ready to leave," she replied and lifted her bag from the ground to toss onto the back seat.

"Without our fearless leader?" Kyss continued as she came around to lean against the driver's side door.

Nisa closed the back door and replied, "He's not my leader."

Kyss smiled. "Oh? Then tell me, Nisa, who are you looking for to lead you?"

"I don't need anyone to lead me," Nisa stated evenly and reached for the front door handle.

Instead of Kyss moving—which would have been the acceptable action—the cheetah reached out, clasping her hands to Nisa's waist and pulled her close. To keep their faces from colliding Nisa lifted her hands, planting them on Kyss's shoulders and held her head back.

"What are you doing?" Nisa asked, wariness circling in the pit of her stomach.

Kyss licked her bottom lip and continued to smile. Her palms had splayed out so that her fingers now grazed the sides of Nisa's ass.

"I'm trying to get an idea of just how much leadership you actually need," Kyss told her. "From the rapid beating of your heart and the low rumble of your cat, I'd say you're ready for full submission. And I'd be more than happy to help with that."

Nisa could only blink at the cheetah's brashness. Then she managed a smile of her own.

"If you'd be happy to continue breathing, I'd suggest you take your hands off me and never presume that I'm open to anything other than information you can provide on the Ruling Cabinet murders," she said in an icy tone.

When Kyss hesitated, Nisa easily pulled out of the cheetah's grasp, being sure to push her back against the vehicle at the same time.

Kyss chuckled and flicked the long tail of her hair over her shoulder.

"What? Decan's not sharing secrets with you yet?" Kyss asked and moved away from the door as Nisa had continued to stare at her expectantly.

"Just tell me what you know." Nisa insisted as she pulled the driver's side door open.

She had no intention of discussing Decan and what he did or did not say to her with this female.

"I know what I said I knew." Kyss talked as she opened the other door and sat sideways on the back seat right next to where moments ago Nisa had placed her duffel bag. "Lial was at the scene of the last murder."

"Gillian Peterson, niece of Aldo Peterson, senior member of the Ruling Cabinet, was killed three nights ago in a hotel room in Houston," Nisa stated as she recalled what she'd read from the human media sources. It was easy to tap into their global internet system. The trick was doing so without leaving any footprints back to the ViceSecure link that supported all the Shadow Shifter intelligence. She'd managed it easily on more than one occasion. This last time had been the first that she'd been searching for information about a murder.

"They want us," Kyss said. She was sitting with her elbows on her knees while she stared down at her black painted nails. "They act all scared because they know we can shift into a three hundred pound cat at any minute and rip their throats out. But really, that shit turns them on."

Nisa was now sitting in the driver's seat, the door still ajar, hands resting on her lap. She could see Kyss through the rearview mirror.

"I went to this club once. You might know it since your Auntie Caprise used to dance there. It used to be called Athena's. Actually, it still is even after all this time. Of course it's under new ownership. Some sleazy old dude. Anyway, humans are still just as basic as an always horny shifter. These two guys saw my tat," she paused and then looked up to the mirror to stare directly at Nisa.

"It's on my inner thigh. You can see it too if you want." Kyss winked.

Nisa tilted her head and quirked her lips. "No thanks."

Kyss shrugged. "Your loss. So, moving on. After they saw the tat they got all hot. I mean, their cocks were just about bursting through their jeans they were so ready to get inside me. I'd been hitting a three day dry spell so I figured what the hell. We go back into one of the rooms there and the guys are naked in like five seconds. But before I could even take my shirt off they were asking me to shift for them. They wanted to know what it felt like to have a big sexy cat licking all over their body. Wanted to see if that would get them off."

Nisa gasped. She'd meant to remain straight-faced and stoic, but Kyss's candor took her by surprise.

"It did," Kyss continued with a nod and a grin. "Faster

than even I thought it would. So yeah, they're interested in us for all sorts of reasons. Gillian Peterson was just like those hard-up jokers at the club. She loved getting laid by a cat. Lial had been giving her exactly what she wanted for the past few months, for a hefty fee I might add."

"She was paying him to have sex with her?"

"She was financing her own brothel," Kyss said. "Lial and a gang of other Serfins were all too happy to give those uptight socialites exactly what they wanted but couldn't get from their starchy human guys. That's probably how he ended up in Gillian's hotel room."

"Why would he kill her?" Nisa asked.

"I didn't say he did," Kyss replied.

"No. But you are saying too much," Decan announced, irritation clear in his tone as he reached into the back seat and yanked Kyss out.

Nisa had felt his approach, but she hadn't cared. She wanted to know what Kyss knew and she was fairly certain that if she asked Decan he wasn't going to tell her.

"I was just answering your girlfriend's questions," Kyss replied and looked up at Decan with pouting lips. "I want to ride with you."

Nisa watched as Kyss's hand trailed a path from Decan's shoulder down his torso, to just above the buckle of his pants because that's when he grabbed her by both wrists and pulled her up until only the tip of her boots touched the ground.

"You'll ride in the second vehicle. You're gonna keep your mouth shut and your hands to yourself," he told her.

Nisa wondered what she was seeing. She was pretty sure that Kyss had just made a very sexual overture toward her. And now she was clearly tempting Decan, for the second time. As much as she normally believed that she loved unraveling a puzzle, this chick and what was going on in her mind wasn't something Nisa wanted to explore. With that thought she pulled the driver's side door shut and started the Tracer's engine. When she'd tossed her bag on the back seat, she'd put her board on the front passenger seat. It was powered up and when she started the Tracer, the vehicle's diagnostics report came onto the screen. The tracking system had definitely been disabled by someone who knew how to hack into her system.

"What do you think you're doing?" Decan asked when he had to go around to the passenger side door and open it because Nisa had locked the driver's side door.

"I'm getting ready to drive to Houston. If you're coming you should climb in."

He was irritated. She didn't have to look at him to figure that out. "I told you this was my mission," he said.

"And I'm not arguing that fact. That doesn't mean that I can't drive my own vehicle. If you get in," she said and reached for the board, "we can get moving."

She slid the board down into the compartment on the door so that he couldn't see the screen. Decan knew that the tracking system had been disabled. He'd had to since he wanted to keep reminding her that he was the leader of the mission. If she asked him why, he wasn't going to tell her. Or at least he wasn't going to be honest with her. The aroma of his lies always lingered just beneath that other very alluring scent he carried. The one that was like a direct communication link to her cat.

He surprised her by waiting only a beat and then getting in. But not before giving a nod to someone outside of the vehicles—probably the Serfin guard named Gold that had joined this group along with Decan. This shifter had a history in Oasis, one that was a bit turbulent but not so much that her father refused to let him be a part of this mission. Either that, or Decan had some very special reason for keeping Gold with him and he'd somehow been able to convince her father that this was a good idea. That was something else for her to contemplate.

Only one day in and this mission was off to a turbulent start. All her brainpower and maneuvering was to go into effect in the Central Zone where she could work to impress Faction Leader Maybon. She was also fairly certain that coming very close to having sex with Decan Canter was not on the agenda either, and yet, as he sat beside her and she prepared to pull off, the way he'd touched and kissed her, the path he'd made down her body last night, almost to the point of kissing her...was all she could think of.

"YOU SAID YOU KNEW I was sneaking above ground alone before." Nisa stated as she drove through the final stretch of tunnels.

In less than an hour they would be at the Central Zone Headquarters. Then he could drop her off, hear what Jace Maybon wanted to tell him about the search for Cole Linden and get the hell out of there. There'd already been one glitch in his plan. He didn't want to adjust for anymore.

And Nisa was definitely a glitch.

"Is that how you usually let women know you're interested in them?" she asked.

She'd been talking for the last half hour, but he hadn't really been listening. In fact, he'd been trying his best not to get any closer to her than he already had. Even through words. But this last question had him swearing.

"What are you talking about?" he asked as he stared over to her.

She shrugged. "I'm just asking if that's the way you normally pick up women."

"I don't pick up women," he said.

"Well, not if you go around stalking them first. That's certainly not romantic at all."

"And I don't do romance," he continued, ignoring her previous statement.

"Oh. Well, yeah, you don't have to convince me of that fact. You definitely suck at romance," she quipped.

"I don't—" he began and then paused to clench his teeth tight enough to possibly break them. Instead it gave him the few seconds he needed to regroup. "I don't have to convince you of anything. In addition to watching you sneak out at night, I saw the way you cut down any shifter that showed interest in you. The baggy clothes during training sessions, practically staying arm-in-arm with your pal Shya or locking yourself on the control deck to work for endless hours, all the shields you love to employ."

"I'm not denying them," she replied, even though he'd caught the quick tightening of her hands on the steering wheel. "I haven't had a lot of experience with the opposite sex, in that way."

That's not something Decan wanted to know. Actually, he did. It made him feel a hell of a lot better than thinking of another shifter with his hands on her.

"It's not a big deal," he mumbled and then looked out the window.

The tunnels here were tinted an electric blue color, signifying they were approaching what was considered royal territory in Oasis. The perimeter surrounding each of the zone headquarters were colored passageways to help document where they were in their underground haven. They did not use street or highway names as were helpful to traveling above ground. Down here, they relied on the maps of the tunnels which were programmed into the control board in each of their enhanced vehicles. The lighted passageways were an added notification method.

"Of course it's not," she stated. "I mean, it only leads to the continuation of our species."

Sarcasm was one of her favored shields as well.

"That's not all it leads to," he said before rubbing a hand down his face.

"Have you ever been in love, Decan?"

He definitely did not want to answer that question. But Decan knew she wasn't going to stop just because he wanted her to. Besides, she could be asking him deeper questions—like why the tracking system had been disengaged, or revisiting the inquisition about Keller and the bunker where they'd spent the night. None of which he wanted to answer either. So with reluctant resolve, he figured he'd have to settle for this topic of discussion, no matter how uncomfortable it was making him.

"No," he replied. "Have you?"

"No," she answered.

"Well, you've got plenty of time for that," he said, hating how bitter the words tasted in his mouth.

"I'm not looking forward to it," she told him and turned the vehicle down a narrow passageway. "I mean, I know that some shifters are very focused on finding a *companheiro* and living some type of happy life thereafter. But I have other plans."

Curious, Decan looked over at her again.

Her hair was a riot of bouncy dark brown curls. Silver clips gripped the top of her ear and her Topétenia tat was just beneath her right lobe. The jaguar drawing was long, stretching along the skin from the end of her ear, down to almost the start of where her neck spanned out to her shoulders. It was surrounded by colorful flowers and spirals which, to someone not paying attention, might think was just an exotic floral design. But Decan saw the cat, he saw the pulse of her heartbeat vibrating through the primal creature and his heartrate increased.

The heat started then, moving down his neck, spreading throughout his torso and lower, until the hardening of his cock was inevitable. This was insane. He was just looking at her and she was fully dressed and still, there was something undeniably happening between them.

"And those plans don't include any type of pleasure?"

he asked, his hands going flat on his thighs.

Why couldn't he stop this conversation? Why couldn't they talk about something simple, like what the Central Zone Leader would possibly serve them for dinner?

"I know how to take my own pleasure," she replied.

She'd said that as nonchalantly as she may have answered when someone asked her name. As if it were perfectly normal for an attractive twenty year old to be responsible for her own pleasure. To be clear, Decan wasn't against anyone bringing themselves release. Especially not a Shadow Shifter because their genetic make-up made sexual urges so strong and intense that they could not be ignored as a human probably could. So Nisa could bring herself to climax. That was fine. But the pleasure he wanted to give her, and no doubt would receive himself from doing so, was something he knew she'd never be able to match.

"Do you?" she asked and the look that was most likely meant to be innocent landed on him. Decan almost exploded.

She'd looked over to his face and then, as if she'd known something was amiss, her gaze had dropped to his groin. His erection was unmistakable and she did not instantly look away.

"I always do what is necessary, Nisa," Decan replied through clenched teeth.

"Oh," she said and then dragged her gaze back to the passageway ahead. The blue light from outside did not penetrate through the dark tinted windows of the vehicle, so it felt as if they were cocooned, wrapped in privacy just in case.

Decan wanted to refute any "just in case". There was none. There was only this mission. But his body was saying something totally different.

"What do you want to do right now, Decan?"

"Don't ask me that," he groaned.

"I want you to tell me," she said. "I've never heard anyone say it to me before and I know you won't sugarcoat it because you don't do romance."

But that's what she deserved, wasn't it? She was the Assembly Leader's daughter so she should have a jaguar shifter born from a family that her parents approved of, giving her every dose of romance possible. That wasn't him. Decan, the lion and the former prisoner, should not be the one touching her or thinking about pleasing her.

"What do you expect me to say?" he asked as his head fell back against the seat rest, eyes closing and his fingers tingling.

He was resisting the urge to free his erection and stroke it in lieu of being able to sink inside of her. His thoughts drifted again to her mouth surrounding his length, sucking him deep and strong, but that had him growling, his claws trying to break through his skin.

"Tell me what I could do to make you feel better," she said.

Her voice was so low he'd barely heard her. So naïve he wanted to scream with the joy of being the one she chose to ask this. It was the best privilege for any shifter. Just not him.

"Nisa," he said and then let out a whoosh of breath that he prayed would give him some clarity. "I shouldn't have touched you before. Shouldn't have kissed you, or anything else. You are a job."

"I am a female shifter who could have just as easily driven myself to the Central Zone without you. You're older than me, yes. More experienced, obviously. But I'm not a child and neither am I a fool. I know when I'm feeling intense arousal and can see that you're having as difficult a time with it as me. So I'm asking you a question and all you have to do is answer."

That's all he had to do.

"Put your hand on me," he said, eyes still closed, claws digging into his thighs as he'd tried desperately to hold on.

He could feel her even before contact was made. Warm and enticing as she cupped him, squeezing with her fingers the way her mouth would when his length was freed. Painful as the heated iron was slammed against his skin. The smell of burning flesh filling the air and making him nauseous. Echoes of cheering in the back of his mind as they tried to break him, to kill the man and the beast. Blood, warm and putrid as the lion was unleashed taking a life with no regrets.

The vehicle jolted and came to a sudden stop. Decan's eyes opened quickly to see that they had come only inches from crashing into the steel doors leading into the Central Zone Headquarters. He looked down and was startled by his fingers gripping Nisa's wrist. Her hand was just inches from his erection. The look on her face when he turned to her was filled with confusion, shock, and disappointment.

CHAPTER 7

———◆———

THE MAHOGANY MULTI-PANED DOOR OPENED by lifting from the floor to the ceiling. Nisa and Decan stepped inside. Their booted feet fell on gray marble tile that stretched the length of the circular shaped room. About fifteen feet from where they stood, black tiles created another circle on the floor. More gray marble filled this circle and surrounded an intricate black and silver shield design with each of the Shadow Shifter tribes' insignias set in its center. This design marked the entrance of every zone headquarters bunker throughout Oasis.

Black columns stood tall around the two curving stairways leading down from the upper level. That's where Nisa and Decan looked to see Faction Leader Jace Maybon and a female shifter descending the stairs slowly.

For just a moment Nisa was nervous. This was the moment she'd been waiting for since her father had suggested she might be able to help bring some stability to the Central Zone. She'd met Jace Maybon before as he and her father were close friends and the Faction Leaders met with the Assembly Leader several times a year. So it wasn't nervousness at seeing him, or being in this lavish facility that was causing her hands to shake slightly. No, that was caused by the shifter standing next to her.

Decan had told her to touch him and Nisa had wanted to. Oh, how she'd wanted to. The bulge in his pants had looked so big and intimidating. Yet, she hadn't been intimidated at all. She'd been ready. There was no doubt in her mind that sex with Decan would be drastically different from any of the things Nisa had done to pleasure herself. And damn if she wasn't counting on that fact.

Now, however, she was simply trying to keep a lid on her sexual frustration while she met with the Faction Leader.

"It's always a pleasure to see you, Nisa," Jace spoke as he came closer and reached for her.

Nisa easily went into his arms for a hug. "It's good to see you again, too," she replied, holding back the urge to call him Uncle Jace. This was a business visit, not a friendly one.

All of the FLs had been there when she was born and they'd all played a part in her upbringing so she'd grown up feeling as if they were all her family. All of them except Cole Linden.

"And you're Decan Canter," Jace said after releasing Nisa and turning his attention to where Decan stood beside her.

"Yes sir," Decan answered and accepted Jace's extended hand.

"Let's go over here to the conference room," Jace suggested when he took a step back. "Then I'll let you two get settled."

Jace had already taken a step away when the woman that was with him cleared her throat. As Jace turned back she shook her head and stepped forward, extending her hand to Nisa first.

"Hello, I'm Amelia Sanchez, Pacific Zone Executive

Assistant. It's a pleasure to meet you Ms. Reynolds. I've had a chance to meet your parents and am not surprised at all by how beautiful you are."

Amelia may have thought Nisa was beautiful, but this woman was stunning with her olive hued skin and raven black hair. Her eyes were exotic, her accent reminiscent of Magdelena, the Seer, who had been born and still lived in the Gungi rainforest in Brazil.

Nisa shook her hand and smiled. "Hello Amelia. It's a pleasure to meet you as well," she said.

"And you too, Mr. Canter," Amelia continued. "Jace...I mean Faction Leader Maybon, has told me a lot about you."

She was shaking Decan's hand now and Nisa was looking at the lovely woman and wondering how long she and Jace had been co-workers...or rather, friends. She was certain that look Amelia had just tossed Jace's way when he'd obviously forgotten to introduce her was one only two people who were very comfortable with each other would share.

"It's nice to meet you, as well," Decan told her as he shook her hand.

Then everything Nisa had been thinking about Jace and Amelia vanished in a jolt of aggression that seared through her. The feeling was so potent Nisa had to take a step back. She felt as if the room was spinning and lifted a hand to her forehead as she closed her eyes and tried to steady herself.

"Are you alright?" Jace asked.

He was immediately by her side, concern clear in his voice.

"Yes. I'm...ah...I'm fine," she replied and managed to look up at him and offer a tentative smile.

Jace was not smiling. In fact, his frown had creases forming in his forehead as he turned his attention to Decan.

"What happened before you came here? Was she hurt?"

Jace fired the questions at him.

"No," Decan answered, but did not look at Nisa. "She was not hurt. And our trip here was uneventful."

Considering she hadn't forgotten the reported bunker they'd stayed in, or the strange shifter who had been tapping on that wall trying to get her attention before she'd gone above ground without permission, Nisa remained silent.

"Let's move into the conference room," Amelia said and took Nisa's hand.

Nisa followed the shifter's lead, crossing the entranceway and stepping into a room after another door opened upon their approach.

This room was all glass that offered views out to the crater filled walls that surrounded it. There was a glass and steel table in the center of the room with matching chairs and white carpet on the floors. Nisa took a seat as she continued to rebound from that strange feeling she'd just had. Jace and Decan came in and the door closed behind them. Once they were all seated at the table, Jace immediately began.

"First thing tomorrow morning you'll meet with Amelia and Marco, one of the Central Zone Lead Enforcers," he said to Nisa. "They'll be with you in the security room to walk you through all that's been going on here and issues specifically related to the Central Zone that VeriSecure doesn't cover. Decan, you and I will meet privately to discuss an event I'd like you to attend the day after tomorrow."

The moment he said that Nisa sat up in her chair and squared her shoulders.

"It's late but we can have some food brought to your rooms since you've been traveling so long tonight," Jace continued. "I'm glad you could make it here as quickly as you did and I'll be sure to let the Assembly Leader know."

He'd looked at Decan as he said that and Nisa felt irritation take over the spurt of anger she'd felt only moments ago. Was he really giving Decan the credit for simply driving her from one place to another? She could have done the same on her own.

"I know it's late but I really don't see the point in putting off the discussion of the anniversary gala the Ruling Cabinet members will be attending day after tomorrow," she stated evenly and was rewarded with the combined looks of shock on the face of every person in the room.

"Especially since we know that Lial Johansen, the shifter we think is now leading the Rogues, will be there."

The last was spoken just to make sure they knew how much she now knew. Of course none of this information had been shared with her by the people she trusted. No, they'd preferred to keep things like this from her. But now Nisa knew. She knew a lot and she wasn't about to let them talk and plan around her again.

"How did you hear about that gala?" Jace asked.

"Yes," Decan added. "How did you hear about it?"

"Not from either of you," she announced. "But that doesn't matter. I'm guessing that this is the reason Decan was sent here with me. I was the cover so that none of the rogues that have been planted down here in Oasis to keep an eye on what we're doing could report back to Lial that you're planning to corner him and take him down."

Nisa had learned all of this last night as she'd sat in that room, searching on her board. It had taken her an unusually long time to find some of the information, but the minute she'd searched Gillian Patterson's murder, familiar names had begun to pop up. For instance, Agent Dorian Wilson, who was a human FBI agent had been present at some of the meetings her father and the other FLs had attended with a human named Wilson Reed, the last president of the United States. Two years after the Unveiling, the human world took a turn for the worse. Wilson Reed was accused of aiding and abetting the

Shadows and subsequently assassinated. After which time, instead of having the Vice-President assume the role as Commander-In-Chief, as was the well-documented protocol for the human democracy in this country, a group of young radicals being led by former congressman Ewen Mackey used fear and intimidation to destroy the remaining government. Ewen Mackey became the leader of the Ruling Cabinet, a group devised to not make fair and legal laws for the country, but to use the humans' fear of shifters and his promise to eradicate them from their country as a way to gain control.

"We're not having this discussion," Jace immediately stated.

He stood and was about to push his chair under the table and probably order her to leave the room, but Nisa continued.

"Yes. I think we are," she stated. "When my father said you needed help bringing this zone together I knew he meant something beyond what was going on here in Oasis. Your problem isn't just that you have unreported shifters somehow getting inside and going out without anyone knowing. It's that you fear Lial has infiltrated, not just your security here, but also your intelligence. You want me to go in and create an impenetrable cyber shield the way I did at Assembly Headquarters to protect your classified files. That's fine, I can do that. But not without telling you first that if Lial has gotten into your files and has shifters down here working for him, then your problem is much bigger than you think and a new computer shield isn't going to stop him."

There, she'd said it.

While Nisa had been chatting up Decan on their ride here, she'd also been rehearsing how she was going to let her dear Uncle Jace know that she was on to the real reason she'd been summoned here. Before leaving Assembly Headquarters she'd begun tracing the electronic footprints left on the Central Zone's security system. Whoever had gotten into their system had also created a doorway so that these unlisted shifters could enter Oasis. And once the trio of cheetahs had stopped them in the tunnels with their information, Nisa presumed they were unlisted as well.

Decan wasn't saying a word, but she knew he was pissed. The first thing he was going to ask her when they were alone, was why hadn't she told him this before now. Her reason would be, because telling him all she'd been able to find out wasn't going to get her the job as Central Zone Faction Leader.

Jace cursed and ran a hand down the back of his head, while Amelia sat back in her chair and attempted to hide a smile.

"What I didn't understand at first was why the files that were tampered with were such a big deal. They were just notes from someone named Blaze Trekas and most of them were written in another language. I didn't have time to translate them, but I plan to."

"No," Jace said as he sat down again. "You will not translate them and you will not do anymore research into Lial, the Ruling Cabinet or anything else. You are here to mimic your holodeck from the Assembly Headquarters to ours. That's it. Fuck! Rome's going to lose his mind when he finds out you've been digging into this. And then, he's going to want your head and probably mine for not stopping her!"

The last was said to Decan, who had just sat forward, letting his elbows rest on his thighs as he glared at Nisa.

"She's not going to research anymore about this topic," Decan said slowly. "Not one more word."

Nisa ignored both of them. "I'm going to do whatever I can to protect us. If Lial is working with the Ruling Cabinet who has been killing Shadows for years, then I'm going to be a part of stopping him. So we might as well

start with the gala. What are you planning? You're sending someone up there aren't you? Who is it?"

There was silence and then Nisa's gaze narrowed on
Decan.

"This is why you were here all along. You came so that
he could brief you and you could go above ground and
try to stop Lial. Was that also part of the information Kyss
brought to you? She said she picked up Lial's scent at the
scene of Gillian Peterson's murder. Were you wondering
why he would kill the family members of the Ruling
Cabinet if he was working for them?"

She had so many pieces moving in her mind, some
of which she'd put together, but others that were still
dangling out in space. This morning when she'd gotten dressed she'd felt rejuvenated because she'd found so
much information that had begun to make sense. Now
that the information was out, she wasn't sure she had it
figured out after all.

"I think it's been a very long night," Amelia began.

When Nisa was ready to speak over her, Amelia simply nodded in Nisa's direction and continued. "This
discussion will come from clearer heads if we take this
up tomorrow morning after breakfast. Now, Nisa, I will
show you to your room."

As far as being handled went, it was one of the smoother
scenarios Nisa had watched. Actually, it was along the lines
of how her mother might have handled the situation. Jace
was clearly irritated and Decan, well, Nisa could smell
the waves of anger rolling off him and had to admit that
she wasn't looking forward to their confrontation. The
one that would come tonight, the moment he guessed she
was alone. So, in an effort to retain any allegiance with
the two male shifters, Nisa stood. She looked to Jace and
offered him all she could by way of an apology.

"I can help," she told him. "I know the role you and my
father would like me to play in all this and I accept that,

but only if I'm allowed to help in other ways as well. I've been trained for this and I know there will come a time in this investigation that you will need a skill that I possess. I'm just trying to speed up the process."

"Get some rest," was Jace's simple reply.

Decan had not spoken another word before she left.

"You're a feisty one," Amelia said as they boarded an elevator and went down to the floors where the sleeping rooms were located. "I should have guessed since Kalina is a very spirited jaguar and Rome, well, he's Rome."

Nisa only smiled in response because she wasn't certain what to say to that remark. She didn't like when people presumed to know her or what type of shifter she was, solely based on her genetics. They had no idea how different her thoughts were from her parents, and she wasn't about to tell this one either.

"Listen, I'm sure you have some sort of plan formulated in your mind," Amelia continued when they stepped off the elevator after traveling two floors down.

"But allow me to offer a piece of advice."

Amelia stopped and turned to Nisa, blocking her path.

"Don't push your way in," she told Nisa. "Male Shadow Shifters are genetically trained to protect the female. Whether the female believes it's necessary or not. So if they think you're in danger by getting involved in this investigation, they'll do whatever is necessary to keep you away from it."

"I don't need protection," Nisa stated. "I've been training since I was four years old. I'm ready for whatever this investigation may bring."

"Are you Nisa?" Amelia asked. "Are you ready to stare down the barrel of a human's gun and realize that your life is over in that instant? Or, are you ready to fight a rogue until one of you is left dead? Because that's where this particular investigation is leading."

Her words were meant to make Nisa uncomfortable

and possibly to frighten her. Nisa didn't budge.

"And that's why my father didn't want me involved because he doesn't think I can handle myself?"

Amelia shook her head. "I'm not even going to put myself on the line by daring to insinuate what the Assembly Leader is thinking. What I will say is he wouldn't have sent you here, knowing what's going on in the Central Zone, if he didn't think you could help."

"And that's what I plan to do," Nisa countered. "I want to help."

"I was in the room during the last call between your father and Jace. Rome's idea of help in this instance is you sitting behind that holodeck and working your magic there."

"That's ridiculous when I can be of use in both places."

"But you can only stay alive in one," Amelia said.

Nisa sighed.

"I won't be kept in a corner. I know how to handle myself." She raised a hand when Amelia was about to say something else.

"And no, I'm not being stubborn and totally dismissing my father's feelings for me. I respect and love him and Uncle Jace, too. I know they're only looking out for my best interests. But this is my life. What good is it if I can't live it the way I want? If I can't live it to help my people?"

To Nisa's surprise Amelia smiled.

"And that's where my advice will help. Don't push your way in. You have information, use it to show them you're an asset. And then use it to hold over their heads if necessary."

When Nisa only stared quizzically at her, Amelia turned and continued walking down a long hallway. She stopped in front of a door and then turned to face Nisa again.

"Get some rest and be ready to meet with them tomorrow. They'll try to shut you down. Make sure you have something that stops them from doing so."

"Something like what?"

"Something they don't have. Leverage," Amelia told her and then walked away.

Nisa went into the room and immediately pulled her board from her bag. Amelia was working alongside Jace which in itself was a questionable feat. Every Shadow Shifter in the Assembly knew that Jace Maybon only slept with females. He didn't work with them, nor did he commit to them in any way. The mere fact that Amelia was—even under the executive assistant title—acting as Jace's second in command, was big. It was very big and Nisa respected the female's position, as well as her advice.

So she was going to find that leverage and first thing tomorrow morning when she met with Jace and whoever else attended, she was going to be prepared to present them with an offer they could not refuse.

Her life depended on it.

"WHAT DID YOU TELL HER?" Jace asked the moment Nisa and Amelia were out of the room.

"I didn't have anything to tell her," he replied, because that was the correct answer.

All that Decan knew about the Ruling Cabinet and Lial Johansen, was information he'd obtained on his own and through working with Keller and Gold. He had never discussed any of this with the Assembly Leader. Nisa, on the other hand, could have overheard a conversation between her father and his FLs, because there was definitely truth to what she'd said. The things Decan hadn't known were confirmed by the look on Jace's face right now.

"My assignment was to bring her here to help you with tech issues you were having in this region and to talk to you about a lead you have on the Cole Linden search," Decan said, being careful to keep his voice level and his heart rate steady.

Any one of these could give away the fact that he was lying. The FL would instantly pick up that scent and undoubtedly question him further. The ability to hide scents and restrain his cat was a hard won effort, which Decan had been extremely thankful for over the years. It was also the one that was going to allow him to finally put an end to the threat against all Shadows living above ground.

Jace was now standing, rubbing a hand over the lightly trimmed beard at his chin. Shadows didn't show the same signs of aging as humans, so even though the FL was approaching his early fifties, he had no gray hair and no wrinkles on his face. His body was still fit in gray slacks and white dress shirt. His skin tone was a little darker than Nisa's, his hair cut low, eyes dark and assessing. Decan had done his research on this Shadow, just like he had on the other FLs, the rogues, and every member of the Ruling Cabinet. Jace Maybon could be fair. He could also be vicious.

"I'd planned to talk to you about that tomorrow at breakfast," Jace said as he turned to face Decan.

The FL leaned back against a black lacquered table with two long rectangular shaped lamps on each end.

"The murders surrounding the family of Ruling Cabinet members are concerning. Bas was planning to take one of his teams above ground to investigate in the upcoming weeks," he told him.

Decan only listened. In the first two years after the Unveiling, Rome's plan for the Stateside Shadows was to continue to work amongst the humans and to prove to them that not all the Shadows were dangerous. He'd even proposed to then President of the United States, Wilson Reed, that Shadows who could not abide by the country's laws, should be punished just as the human offenders. Albeit with some modifications because a man or woman who could shift into a three to four hundred pound cat wasn't going to be easily contained in a cell with the general population. President Reed had gone along with Rome's proposal, at least in the beginning. Then the President's wife had been involved in a rogue attack at a museum. She'd died before he could get to her. The directive to kill all Shadows upon sight had come from Reed's Vice-President because Reed was inconsolable. Reed's Vice-President was Taggert Mackey, Ewen Mackey's uncle.

"Faction Leader Perry was going to investigate whether or not a Shadow was committing the murders?" Decan asked even though he thought he already knew the answer.

Everyone thought a Shadow was killing those humans, Shadows and humans alike. Kyss's announcement that she'd picked up Lial's scent at the scene of the last murder added to that assumption. But Decan wasn't convinced.

"Yes," Jace answered. "He and his team were going to question some of the Shadows still living above ground and then, because a few members of his team were younger and had no previous ties to a life above ground, they were going to attempt to get closer to the cabinet members to see what they could find out."

"And then what?" Decan asked because to his knowledge Rome and the Assembly hadn't done enough to protect the Shadows above ground.

They hadn't done enough to fight for all of the Shadows' right to live safely above ground. If he were to gain the FL position for the Central Zone, his first act would be to bring them up from the underground. They didn't belong here. Not on a permanent basis.

There were some Shadows still living up there, but the Assembly Leader openly chastised them for putting their families and the remaining Shadows in danger by tempting the humans. It wasn't a stance Decan would have thought a leader like Roman Reynolds would ever take, but it's precisely what he'd done for the last twenty years. Decan planned to put a stop to it, even though doing so would most definitely anger the Assembly Leader and those who faithfully followed him, including Decan's father.

"If it's a Shadow committing the murders, than we will deal with him or her. It's our place to punish our own. If it's a human, then we make sure that information gets into the right hands and we walk away."

"What would be the right hands?" Decan pressed.

Jace stared at him a moment. He was no doubt sizing him up, trying to see if Decan could actually be trusted. Decan let his palms rest on his thighs. He stayed seated in the chair he'd taken upon entering the room. Keeping eye contact with the FL, he focused on breathing evenly and thinking about his own plans for the Shadow Shifters' future. Those were true and honest thoughts for Decan. So were the thoughts that always circled back to Nisa.

In the months he'd spent at the Assembly Headquarters learning all that he could about Roman Reynolds and his motives for what he thought was the right thing to do for their people, Decan's mind had betrayed him by focusing way too much on Nisa. He'd known it was a problem then and probably should have foreseen the situation he found himself in now, but again, he couldn't tell the Assembly Leader that he would not accept this assignment. Especially since this assignment put him in the perfect position to claim his personal revenge.

"There's an FBI agent that we've known for a long time. We trust him and he trusts us. That was the new development I wanted to speak to you about," Jace said. "He'll be at the gala and he'll be looking for you."

This was getting more interesting by the moment.

"Why?" Decan asked.

His cat was restless, pacing with irritation that Decan had just now accepted was because of the separation from

Nisa. The cat needed to be near her, while the man still attempted to fight that entire scenario. Decan lifted an arm and let it rest on the table beside him because he needed to move, to take some type of stance against the beast that prowled inside. It was a simple movement, but one he hoped would be enough. The last thing he needed was for the FL to pick up on any agitation within him.

"Because he's been working with Blaez Trekas to find Cole," Jace told him.

The words seemed solemn and hefty in the silence of the room. Decan wasn't certain how he should proceed.

This seemed like a good place to start. "Who is Blaez Trekas?"

"He's a wolf shifter. They call them lycans. Cole sought help from Blaez and his pack not long after the Unveiling. Then there was a fire and Cole was gone again."

The one word brought man and cat in alignment. The lion woofed and the man sat forward in the chair. It recalled a fire, one that had killed many, humans and shifters.

"And now the FBI agent and the lycan are working with you to find this Shadow. Why? What's so important about him that he must be found and that the search for him brings so many from different sides?" Decan asked.

From the moment Rome had mentioned this search for Cole, it had been the lowest issue on Decan's list of priorities. This Shadow had been missing for twenty years. Either he couldn't come back to the life he knew or he didn't want to. Either way, Decan had better things to do with his time and efforts than to spend it trying to find him. Still, these additional facts concerning the Shadow's disappearance had him curious.

"Cole was my closest friend. We fought alongside each other and governed together with Rome and Bas. I know he's alive and I want him found. If the lycan and the FBI agent can help me do that, then that's what will be done. Rome said you were the one to bridge the connection between those above ground and us. He said your extended time above ground and in the human military would work to our advantage should the time arise. Well," Jace said with a nod. "The time has come."

That it had, Decan thought as he slowly stood to his feet. The time when he would have to decide whether his own personal goals outweighed a path that might assuage his father. He wanted to answer and to be clear on where he stood at the same time, but something stopped him.

She was on the move.

CHAPTER 8

———◆———

NISA PAUSED JUST BEFORE TOUCHING the control panel that would open the door leading above ground.

"How is it that you know what I'm going to do and where I am?"

She spoke quietly without turning to face him.

"And why do I feel you when you're near as if you are a part of me?"

Decan didn't want to answer either of those questions. Partly because he wasn't totally sure himself and also because he might be afraid of the answer.

"It is unlike anything that I've ever experienced before and as hard as I try to go back and recall any anomaly related to being a shifter that would possibly explain how this is possible when we've only known each other such a short time, I cannot come up with any."

She didn't have an answer and she didn't like that. She wouldn't like not knowing something. The sound in her voice was almost sad. Decan did not like that.

"Let's go," he said simply and reached around her to

disengage the locks on the door.

As the wall pulled back providing a seamless opening Nisa slipped through first and Decan followed. As with all the doors leading above ground, they stepped out into a forested area with trees instantly surrounding them. The climate above ground had changed significantly in the years the Shadows had been underground. This led to a decrease in the human population in more than sixty-five percent of the once occupied areas. Big cities had dwindled to look like ghost towns, vegetation growing through concrete walkways, trees sprouting and maturing through abandoned buildings. Deserts were filled with dwellings created amidst sandstorms. Vehicles now possessed larger tires able to navigate the many different terrains that had evolved and to move at speeds greater than the shifters that the humans chased on a daily basis.

Managing to ensure that each of their doorways were protected from sight and scent had been a huge feat for the Shadows, but as the above ground world had changed, so had the underground one they'd created. Their technology had advanced significantly under their private and unsanctioned lifestyle. They'd been able to not only amplify their own transportation systems, but create new weapons and protections against the elements and the humans. It was a new world, Decan thought, as his booted feet trampled over old branches and debris. A world that the Shadows deserved to live in openly.

He walked only a couple of steps ahead of Nisa affording her the only amount of privacy he could. The chuffing sound of her cat signaled she'd shifted and seconds later Decan shed his clothes and did the same. She brushed past him in a slow motion that signaled she was open to him walking with her.

Decan would guess this wasn't what a human would call a normal sight—a white lion and an exquisite yellowish brown jaguar. They moved at an even pace, large paws pressing into the earth while mature trees provided a canopy of protection. It was well past midnight and all was dark. Where there used to be sounds of night creatures echoing throughout forested areas at this time, now there were sounds of the unknown. Not just wildlife, but whatever else lurked in an atmosphere that had been cloaked in mysterious weather anomalies and increased solar activity.

Moonlight broke through the thicket of trees creating dramatic slashes of light through the total darkness. Nisa's coat looked golden whenever she walked through the light, fading into the darkness mysteriously as she moved past it. She was a glorious creature to look upon, the strength in her legs and flanks apparent. The pride and fierceness set in the way she held her head high and stared straight ahead as if there were nothing out there that could frighten or conquer her, was astounding. And entrancing.

Decan could not stop watching her. Of course his cat was keeping all its senses on alert because he knew that danger could appear at any second. Still, he never took his eyes off her. She wanted to run long and hard, to cover miles and miles of territory in an attempt to exhaust herself of all her worries. It was what she'd become accustomed to doing. Decan could admit that the act in itself was helpful. If she weren't who she was and the world weren't what it was now, then there would be no concern.

He knew this terrain. There was a creek toward the south. Coming up close to her he made a grunting sound and then took the lead, running through the maze of trees at a speed that allowed his mind partial freedom. She followed close behind, not willing to let him have too much of a lead. They ran far and fast until his paws touched the cool water first. He shifted and submerged himself beneath what he knew in the light of day would be a clear spring beneath an eighteen foot waterfall. At night the place was dark and shadowy, the atmosphere a thick humid haze.

Decan loved to swim. He enjoyed the feeling of weightlessness and being surrounded by the powerful element. When he finally came up for air, lifting his hands to drag them down his face, his eyes opened to see her not five feet in front of him. She'd shifted as well and had also submerged herself in the water. Now she was upright with everything from her shoulders down under water, her head tilted back, arms raised, hands squeezing water from her hair. She looked exotic, like a vision from some surreal dream, as water rolled off her arms, dripping from her elbows and spotting her face. Her lips parted as she sucked in air, eyes opened to mere slits, and as if summoned, luminescent moonlight rested over her, casting her dark hue in an ethereal glow.

He was speechless. Breathless. Motionless. For endless moments as even the lion inside him remained still. In awe.

"You stare a lot," she said without turning to him.

"You're something to stare at," he replied.

"I'm sure you've seen plenty both above and underground," she continued and then lay back on the water to float.

"Not like you," he told her truthfully as he closed some of the space between them.

There was a need to be close to her, all the time that Decan didn't feel like fighting at the moment.

"You've seen the world. Both worlds and you chose to come back underground. Why?"

"I have something to do there," he admitted.

She didn't break her stride and Decan stayed close, treading water.

"I do too," she told him.

"But you like coming above ground," he said extending his arm so that he could touch her fingers with his own.

She did not pull away at the contact.

"I feel like I belong here," she told him. "You could say I'm the child that wants exactly what her parents tell her she can't have."

There was a hint of humor in her tone, but when she continued, Decan knew just how serious she was.

"Actually, I'm the woman who wants more. I want what we should all have without fighting or compromise. It's an intense feeling, one that I've always known I would act on...damn the consequences."

"Damn them, huh?" Decan asked and laced his fingers with hers, holding on as if he thought with her admission she might swim far away from him.

She turned then, just slightly so that water sloshed over part of her face.

"We should not be prisoners, hiding underground to appease a world of fools who are too afraid to realize that man and animal have co-existed for a very long time," she told him.

"They've co-existed as man being the ruler and ani-mal—"

"Being smart enough to let man think he's ruling them, but still commanding our space and killing man when he reached beyond our boundaries," she continued his statement.

Decan couldn't help but smile because she thought a lot of the same things he did.

"This is dangerous," he said after a time.

"Being above ground where the humans that hunt us might easily come upon us," she said and then shrugged. "I guess it is. But it's also living."

Again, Decan agreed.

"I was referring to this thing between us," he added.

She stilled.

"I shouldn't want you," he admitted. "But I do."

"Okay," she whispered and let him pull her toward

him. "I guess I'm not supposed to want to be touched by a lion. But I do."

And touch her he did.

Decan found her other hand, lacing his fingers through hers as her body aligned with his beneath the water. At first he held her hands under the water, then he lifted them until her arms were above her head, her head tilted back slightly.

"I like touching you," he whispered. "Far too much."

His fingers slid slowly down the length of her upstretched arms, gliding along her soft skin similar to the way rivulets of water had as well. When he continued down, keeping his fingers only on her, touching the curve of her breasts, she let her arms fall down, hands going to his shoulders.

"It is a delicious temptation," she said. "One I never imagined existed."

"The things I want to do to you will probably surpass your imagination as well," he admitted as he cupped her breasts.

The weight of them in his hands was intoxicating and Decan wanted to close his eyes and simply continue touching her. But he knew that wasn't a good idea.

"Try me," she told him and leaned in closer to kiss his shoulder.

Her tongue moved in circles over his skin, her fingers gripping him tighter. This belonged to him. Her touch, the soft whisper of her words, the warmth of her tongue, it was all his. Decan knew this because it felt more right than anything he'd ever thought would in his life.

"You're...this isn't... we can't," he finally managed, the words ragged in his throat.

She paused and looked up at him. "Not one thought I've had since I was fifteen was what it should have been. I know who I am and what was expected of me. But I also know what I want."

She kissed his chest, moving from one hardened nipple to the other, taking the tight buds between her teeth and biting down until Decan could do nothing but let his head lull back and groan. She was acting like a woman who knew what she wanted. Regardless of the facts—she was the Assembly Leader's daughter and eleven years younger than him. Her mouth was hot on his skin, her nails scraping along the insatiable creature resting just beneath the surface.

"You don't know what you're doing," Decan continued as the struggle became harder.

He became harder. The moment she wrapped a leg around his waist and rubbed her bare center against the length of his arousal.

"It's okay, Decan," she whispered and lowered a hand between them to grasp his cock, rubbing him along her swollen folds. "I'm not looking for a joining or anything so permanent. I believe in fate and things happening for a reason. You were selected to bring me here," she continued, gasping when the crest of his cock rubbed over the tight bud of her clit. "You were selected to bring me... pleasure."

That word, in her voice...Decan wanted nothing more than to sink deep inside her at this very moment.

"If that's what you want," he replied without contemplating whether he should or what would happen if he did.

He moved a hand to the base of her neck, then up to bury his fingers in her soft, damp hair. He pulled her head back roughly, aroused further by the surprised look in her eyes and the quick lick of her tongue over her lips. He stared at her mouth, visualizing how delicious his cock would look moving in and out of it. On a hungry sigh Decan slammed his mouth over hers, his tongue thrusting deep into her mouth as her nails dug into the skin of his biceps. He kissed her until the warning bells were silenced in his mind. Until his lion was roaring with need and he thought he could hear her jaguar responding in turn. It was the strangest thing, and then…it wasn't. He'd heard stories of cats knowing their *companheiros* before the human part of the shifter figured it out. It was an instant recognition causing the animals to be immediately drawn to each other in ways that the human sometimes could not explain. The bond was strong and tended to take over anything else.

Decan had certainly believed in the *companheiro connection*, he just didn't believe he would find one, not after everything he'd been through. Hell, he didn't even know if he wanted one.

The sound of Nisa moaning just before she sucked his tongue deep into her mouth, had Decan giving up on any of those thoughts. All he could manage was the here and now.

Tearing his mouth away from hers wasn't easy, but it was necessary. She looked up at him in question and he said only one thing, "I've got you."

She looked like she trusted those words and when he lowered her back into the water, she went willingly. He stretched her body out the same way she'd been when she was floating and then quickly moved around her once more, until he could lift her legs and place them on his shoulders. Her bottom lip now caught between her teeth, Nisa stared up at him while moving her arms under water to stay afloat. Her nipples poked through the water's surface. His cock throbbed at the sight and his hands tightened on her calves.

"I'm not an easy shifter," he said, his voice gruff. "When I take, I take it all."

"Take me," she told him, her eyes blinking and changing to the golden hue of her cat. "Take me, now."

Decan pulled her up even closer and almost smiled when he realized she was in tune with his thoughts. He lowered his head and touched his mouth to the waiting heat of her pussy.

She tensed and whispered something incoherent just as he used his tongue to separate her folds. Letting his hands fall, Decan placed them at the base of her back for further support. The action also brought her closer, an effort his cat greatly appreciated as he flattened his tongue and licked her from her clit back to her entrance, delving so deep inside her, she squirmed in his arms. Her scent was everywhere now, sifting quickly through his nostrils, over his tongue, slipping down his throat. His cat purred at the delicious bliss unfolding. The man pressed his face further, until he felt as if he might be drowning in her.

She arched her back, moving her head from side-to-side, causing ripples in the water as he continued. Licking and thrusting his tongue inside of her, sucking and enjoying. Her thighs convulsed as Decan pursed his lips and pulled her clit into his mouth. She trembled all over and when he figured her climax had completely taken her, Decan shifted, moving so that he could hold her upright in his arms once more. He kissed her again, letting her taste herself on his lips. Letting his senses attempt to return to normal. She'd tasted sweet and felt like a slice of heaven as she'd thrust her hips to meet his ministrations. He held her tightly against him, keeping his eyes closed so as not to let the outside in. That would be a mistake, he knew. The questions, the warnings, the reality of how badly he'd messed up was waiting for him the second he opened his eyes. So he kept them closed, kept his hands on her skin, his tongue rubbing languidly against hers and he enjoyed.

For once in Decan's thirty-one years, he enjoyed being with a woman. With this woman.

WHAT DID ONE SAY AFTER that? How was she supposed to act now that he'd...or rather they'd...?

Decan's reaction was to hurry them back to land and shift. It was quick and bewildering. Almost as fast as he'd finally ended their kiss and moved them through the water. For a second Nisa wondered if he'd scented danger, but when she let her mind go clear long enough to try and scent something on her own, she came up with nothing. So this was officially his reaction to the undeniable pleasure he'd just brought her?

Okay, well she would simply follow suit. For now.

She shifted and they ran back in the direction they'd come until they were once again at the entrance to Oasis. She moved faster this time, dressing in the leggings and t-shirt she'd worn and slipping on her shoes. Decan was just pulling his shirt down over his head when she turned around to face him.

"You don't have to try to figure out a way to tell me that this changes nothing. I already know that. We'll go inside and to our separate rooms and I'll be at breakfast with you and Jace in the morning," she told him.

He let out a breath as his hands fell to his side. "We're in no position for these types of changes. And I'm not sure you should attend the meeting tomorrow."

Nisa nodded. "The changes I want to make will require me to attend that meeting."

When he was going to say something else, she raised a hand to stop him.

"As you probably know from watching me all those months, I'm pretty tuckered out after a run. So this is where I leave you," she said and then turned to open the access door. Because, unlike the one last night, this was one she could open.

She didn't want him to say anything else, didn't know how she would react if he did. She'd told him the truth.

She wanted him. He'd given her a bit of pleasure as a pre-amble? Or as a parting gift? She wasn't certain. However, what she was clear on was that she would not stand there and beg for more, no matter how much she wanted it. Pride was oftentimes a bitch.

He followed her through the door and stuck right behind her as they moved to the elevator and then she went to her room. Nisa did not speak to him again, nor did she turn to look at him. He'd given her something no other man had given her. Sure, she'd mastered providing her own orgasms by the time she'd turned sixteen, but this time was totally different. Never had she felt the pleasure traveling so fiercely through her entire body. And while her virginity was still intact, she felt like the super orgasm was enough. Right?

Even if it wasn't, to her cat's dismay, it was all they would have because Decan was clearly intent on only doing his job from this point on. She was too for that matter, so madam cat would just have to deal with that. Nisa was adamant about that fact as she kicked her shoes off and dropped down onto the bed, thrusting a pillow firmly between her legs in an attempt to quell the still throbbing need.

CHAPTER 9

———◆———

"I WANT YOU TO ATTEND THE gala and take the meeting like we discussed," Jace spoke after they'd had breakfast.

"There's a Croesteriia who we came across in the tunnels. She has information about the murders. I can take her with me," Decan said before Nisa had a chance to speak.

He was trying to keep her quiet. They all were.

Nisa had been first in the dining hall, already filling her plate from the buffet when they'd all come in with shocked and worried expressions on their faces. She'd taken a seat at the table and had eaten that food as if it were the best in the world. Her decision to continue with her original mission had been solidified when she'd finally fallen asleep last night. Whatever was going on between her and Decan was secondary. And whatever Jace said to try and stop her would fail dismally thanks to her early morning research efforts and a phone call from Shya.

"We met," Jace announced. "I made it a point to meet with everyone from your team last night. Kyss is an interesting character."

"One who has a problem with boundaries," Amelia immediately added.

Nisa knew exactly what Amelia was referring to and again wondered just how long Jace and Amelia had been "friends". There was a definite connection between them. Not like she'd seen between the joined shifter couples at Assembly Headquarters. The ones that Nisa called her aunts and uncles, shared a much closer bond. One that was instantly noticeable by their fierce protection of each other, and their shared scent. The *calor* was the scent that engulfed *companheiros* once they'd mated. It was distinct to each couple, but the basic spicy aroma was a telltale sign that the two were a couple, which equated to no poaching on either side or things would get rough pretty fast.

There was no scent between Jace and Amelia, yet there was something, Nisa was certain of it.

"She possesses an interesting ability to obtain information," Jace continued. "That's all that matters."

"And how do we know we can trust her?" Nisa countered.

She'd been sipping from her piping hot cup of tea as she sat back in her chair listening to the conversation that flowed around her. Now, she set the cup on the black lacquer table and waited for their response.

"You said she can get information," Nisa continued when the silence remained. "The holodeck I created is comprised of virtual docks that gather around one central source. The main databases are kept on the central source. Specific information pertaining to the corresponding zones in the US and the different branches internationally, sprout from the central source like branches on a tree. Central Zone does not have a complete holodeck infrastructure—that's why I'm here now—but it has the central source and a few docks dedicated to this zone's operations. There was only one dock compromised. One which was clearly marked classified and contained an access code with the faction leader prefix."

She paused, letting both hands rest in her lap now, her back straight, her gaze zooming in on Jace.

"The dock that contained classified information on all the Faction Leaders and their security hierarchy. That's the one that was breached," Amelia stated evenly.

Nisa nodded, but never took her eyes off Jace. "That's correct. So, whoever broke into that dock knew exactly what they were looking for and how to obtain it. The system is set with alarms to signal hacking at any level. None were sounded. Which means this person had the access code. They got in and they got the information they wanted, on the specific shifters that they wanted."

"What are you saying?" Jace asked, his hands fisting on the table.

Nisa wasn't totally comfortable with what she'd uncovered and she was even less comfortable with the fact that she was delivering this information to a Faction Leader, before and instead of to her father. It was a serious accusation she was about to make. One that even Shya was nervous about as she'd expressed during their earlier phone call. According to her best friend, if something like this was going on and Nisa was the one uncovering it, she would be in danger. No question about it. And if that were the case, the safest place for her would be at Assembly Headquarters behind the security laced steel walls Rome had created and the top level guards that he'd trained. Nisa disagreed. Her place was here and if there was danger it was to all the shifters. She would not hide just because she was the one uncovering the infiltration.

"In the months before the Unveiling there was chaos with Captain Lawrence Crowe and the Comastz Lab attempting to develop a super soldier using shifter DNA. There were casualties and as the unfortunate situation escalated more shifters were lost. In addition to the Blaez Trekas notes, the information that was accessed through the database was on two shifters in particular—Jacques Germain and Cole Linden. Now, who better to have betray the Assembly than another shifter? An unlisted Croesteriia with nothing to lose."

Jace cursed and Decan frowned.

"What do you suggest?" Amelia asked Nisa.

Nisa looked at Amelia and exchanged a slight nod. She'd taken Amelia's advice last night and found the leverage she needed. Amelia seemed pleased with that fact.

"I suggest we do as Decan had the forethought to do earlier. Keep Kyss with us. My father always taught me to keep my enemies close. Kyss definitely has information and can easily get more. For us, or from us. Until we figure out which way she's more likely to swing, we keep her at our side. It's much easier to dispatch a threat that's in arm's reach, than searching one out," she said.

"True. And if she goes to the gala someone can watch her to see who she speaks to, watch her move and listen to her conversations. So that we know everything she does," Amelia continued.

"Exactly," Nisa added. "We also need the element of surprise on our side. The members of the Ruling Cabinet would never expect. Someone they've never seen before."

"They don't know I'm a shifter," Decan told them.

Nisa looked to him in surprise because she had been referring to herself.

"The reason I was able to stay above ground for so long after the Unveiling was because they thought I was human," he continued.

Amelia crossed her legs and rubbed a finger over her chin.

She wore white today, a skirt that barely touched her knees, a silk camisole, waist length jacket and yellow five-inch heel sandals that made her legs seem never ending.

Her hair was pulled back into a tight bun, diamond studs sparkling at her ears.

Nisa nodded in his direction. "You were honorably discharged from the US Marines six years ago. After that time—"

"After that time," Decan interrupted, his brow furrowed as he sat up and leaned closer to the table. "I went to a place where there were some humans who assumed they knew. They died. No one that will be at that gala tomorrow night knows who or what I am."

"Which is why Rome knew you were the one for this job," Jace continued.

His anger held a potent aroma, one that alerted her cat and had feelings of protectiveness riding close to worry. Dismissing the feelings quickly, Nisa cleared her throat.

"Then we'll both go," she announced. "They don't know who we are so they won't be expecting us."

"You do not know how to handle them," Decan countered. "I was trained to do what I do above ground. You were not. Once they realize who and what you are, they will attempt to kill you."

"One," Nisa stated as she met his glare, "I am not a helpless cat. I've been tactically trained all my life. I can defend myself. And two, we would have guards, just as my father assured I had guards to accompany me through the tunnels."

"This is not what you were trained for," Decan insisted.

"But it is what I'm prepared to do," Nisa stated.

"It is what will be done," Jace finished the dispute. "I'll assemble the guards myself. Decan, you be prepared to speak to them and go over some tactical scenarios in preparation. Amelia, you and Nisa go over the floorplan of the hotel and all the players scheduled to be present."

Nisa knew not to look triumphant, no matter how much her feet wanted to tap a happy dance along the white glossed floor. Instead she gave Jace a solemn nod and stood when he did, in preparation to leave the room.

"Nobody else is to know about this," Jace stated. "No other family members or friends. No one. Do you understand, Nisa?"

Jace knew how close she and Shya were. He knew that because of the shifters they'd been born to and the specific dangers each one had faced growing up, that they had a special bond, a trust that could not be matched. If Nisa's knowledge and this assignment put her in danger, telling Shya more about it would rope her in as well. Nisa wasn't on board for risking her friend's life, especially not after Shya had been fighting so hard to live.

"I understand," Nisa told him.

Amelia went over to say something to Jace, and Nisa headed for the door. Decan was right behind her, grabbing her arm to stop her departure.

"You have no idea what you're walking into," he said through clenched teeth.

"And I'll never know until I walk into it," she replied. "I can do this, Decan. The question is, can you?"

"You know damn well I'm better trained for this than you are. They're humans, Nisa! They will kill you the second they see your eyes shift."

"I'm not an idiot, I don't plan to walk into the room purring and growling, Decan."

She pulled away from him at that moment because the spot where his fingers touched her skin were on fire. She barely restrained a hiss of relief when he dropped his hand and did not attempt to touch her again.

"I know what I'm doing," she reiterated when he continued to stare angrily at her.

"You don't," he insisted. "But I do. And I don't plan to let you out of my sight for one minute."

"Is that so?" Nisa asked with an arch of a brow. "Then I'd suggest you get your horny cat in line. If it's growling and moaning every time you touch me now, it might be the one to give us away."

He looked as if he doubted her words, as usual. Nisa tried not to be offended, anymore. He didn't trust her training, just like her father. She was going to prove them both wrong.

"WHAT THE HELL ARE YOU wearing?"
Decan asked the moment she opened the door. He'd come to her room earlier than they were scheduled to leave for the gala because he hadn't been able to find a moment alone with her since Jace gave out the assignments at breakfast yesterday. It was late into the evening by the time Decan had finished with all the impromptu training sessions and the private briefing with Jace. Then Gold had appeared at his door and when he'd finally left, Decan had convinced himself that going to Nisa's room at that time of night wasn't going to end well.

It probably would have ended with him on top of her or some other version of him being buried deep inside of her. Which on the surface may have sounded—and most definitely would have felt—good, but would only further complicate this situation.

"It's called a dress," she replied and attempted to move past him.

"It looks like you don't know what size you wear," he continued, ignoring her sarcasm and concentrating instead on the slip of black material they were referring to. Clasping his hands at her waist he pushed her back into the room and stepped inside with her. Kicking the door closed behind him he looked at her once more as she huffed.

"Really?"

"Yes. Really," Decan replied when she pushed his hands away from her.

The hem of the dress was so high up her thigh, it rode

a fine line between immediate arousal and should be prohibited for fear of producing a cardiac event. Thick straps wound behind her neck, leaving her shoulders bare. The same material hugged her generous breasts, but left the stretch of skin between her breasts and almost to her navel bare.

"You're practically falling out of it," he snapped.

"Good," she replied and cupped her breasts, moving them in a motion as if to lift them higher. "That's the intention."

That wasn't necessary, Decan thought. Not at all. They looked high and plump and tasty without any effort. She offered him a brilliant smile and Decan's teeth clenched tightly.

"We need to go over the ground rules."

Because he'd be damned if he was going to walk into a room full of human males who would no doubt be gaping at her. Until they found out she was a shifter and then they would be pulling their guns and aiming to kill her. Decan was prepared to kill in either instance.

Nisa surprised him by backing up and leaning against the desk across the room. She folded her arms over her chest and crossed her legs at the ankles. The action drew his attention to the strappy sandals she wore with her neatly painted toes peeking from the black leather. She'd done something different with her hair too. It was twisted back on one side leaving fluffy curls to lay neatly on her forehead and in the back. Her lipstick was a dark burgundy color, and her eyes looked bigger, sexier with the make-up she'd applied there. In short, she was breathtaking and Decan was struggling to keep it together long enough to say what needed to be said to keep her safe.

"Go," she prodded with a nod when he was still standing there quietly.

She smelled of pure confidence and sex. Yes, she was aroused. No matter how cool and collected she appeared, her body would always give her away, especially to him. There was some consolation in knowing that this nagging urge wasn't one-sided. However, it didn't make it any easier to accept.

"We'll arrive at the party separately. It's better if nobody gets their first glimpse of you with me," he said.

He'd come up with that on his own. Jace had insisted Nisa stay with Decan, but that wasn't going to happen. No way was he putting her in the type of danger that would fall upon her if any of the humans found out who he was.

"Gold will stay with you. You think whoever accessed those records is a shifter, so you'll be checking for any other shifters in the room. Use your comlink to snap a picture of them if you can and run it through the database. Keep a mental list of each one you spot and we'll do deeper research on them when we return."

"What are you going to be doing?" she asked.

"I have a meeting with Jace's contact," he told her.

She nodded.

"So, no matter what I bring to the table, you're still determined to keep me out of what you're really doing."

Decan was wearing slacks, a black button front shirt and black jacket. Together they looked as if they were in mourning. Or they were a couple working an undercover case for some covert agency in a blockbuster movie. Both scenarios had him frowning.

"You have your assignment and I have mine," he told her. "That's how it's been since the beginning."

"Oh right, you and my father decided you would come along with me as a sort of bodyguard, when really, you were coming here to what? Help them find Cole? Is that what you are? Some type of shifter investigator? Is that why there's no record of you beyond articles of birth and contact information for the members of your tribe?"

He'd slipped one hand into his front pant pocket as she

was talking, but at those last words he stilled once more. He told himself she couldn't help it. She had an inquisitive mind. The records on her—the ones marked private and kept in one of those classified docks on the holodeck which he had access to as a Senior Enforcer—said she'd been that way since she was a little girl. She'd done everything early, walked, spoke, even shifted. Always in a hurry and always looking for the answers. He wanted to admire that about her, to revel in the fact that he was inquisitive as well. But he couldn't because in Nisa's instance, her natural persona might be what got her killed.

"I am not at liberty to discuss my job with you."

"Then what about the rest? Are you not at liberty to tell me anything about yourself other than your name?"

"You know something else about me," he said.

One elegantly arched eyebrow lifted as she asked, "I do? What's that?"

"You know that I like the taste of you and that I spent all last night dreaming of when I could put my mouth on you again."

She'd been prepared for a quick retort. Something snappy. Another question maybe. A criticism of him and his assignment. Something. Anything, other than what Decan had said. That caused her lips to snap closed tightly, her arms sliding slowly down to her side. She didn't speak when she pushed away from the desk, but walked slowly, taking deadly sexy steps to the bed where she picked up a small purse. She continued until she was face-to-face with him.

"That was fun," she spoke when she looked up at him. "But I'm guessing you've done better."

She lifted a finger then, running it over his bottom lip before dropping her hand once more and walking around him. He wanted to curse. No, he wanted to grab her and toss her hot little ass on that bed. If she felt like being sassy then he'd spank her until she thought better of doing so again. Or maybe he'd give her smart mouth something to wrap around so that no more stinging words came forth. Either, or, would suffice, because the basic truth was that Decan wanted to spend his night inside of her, deep and long, hard and wet. Then she'd know better than to push him.

"Are you coming?" she asked from behind where he still stood.

She'd opened the door and was walking through when Decan finally turned around. He closed his eyes and took a deep, steadying breath before following her out.

This job was turning out to be a big mistake. One, Decan wasn't sure he'd rebound from, no matter how many times he'd done so before.

CHAPTER 10

⸺◆⸺

THIS WAS THE WORLD NISA did not see often enough. It was the place her father had been sure to keep her away from.

Upon emerging from a different door that had led into yet another heavily forested area, Nisa, Gold, the two Central Zone guards, Jordin and Zion, climbed into a black vehicle that had been waiting for them. The top of the vehicle lifted slowly, revealing six captain's chairs. Once inside, Gold waved his hand over the shiny silver steering wheel and Nisa watched with wide eyes as the entire front dashboard came alight in a neon green color. It resembled her holodeck with its screen-like appearance and different modes of control. He reached an arm forward and touched a button on the screen. Seconds later there was a clicking sound and Nisa felt herself being forced back against the seat. While she could still move her arms and legs, the rest of her body was momentarily stilled as she suspected the automated seat belts were engaged.

She hadn't seen any wheels on the vehicle when she'd

first approached but now she heard them as they began to move, the spheres screeching over the dirt terrain. They traveled quickly even though there was no sign of motion except for the flash of lights along the cityscape as they moved further away from Oasis, deeper into the human world. Nisa tried not to ogle the fluorescent light. The blue, pink and white that seemed to glow from every building. The sky was pitch black, something she'd noticed on the times she'd come above ground. Her mother used to talk of clouds and stars, a sky filled with emotion when she'd lived above ground. Yet, Nisa had never seen any of that.

They traveled over a narrow bridge with its towers and suspension cables fashioned in a bending curve which gave it an animated feel. The water beneath was also dark with reflections from the buildings and bridge above making it look like a glittering pool of gems instead. Coming off the bridge they rounded a corner and continued down a long street with more buildings and vehicles. But none as opposing as the one at least fifteen hundred feet ahead. It was a slender building, tall—at least one hundred stories—but flat like an envelope. Frosted white beams formed the main structure of the building, with iridescent windows on both of its flat sides. That's where they were going, Nisa thought. Or rather she felt it. Her cat was alert, her body poised for whatever came next as the vehicle they were in came to a stop directly in front of the building.

They each stepped out and for endless seconds stood on the sidewalk looking up at the building.

"What's the plan again?" Zion, the six-foot seven-inch tall jaguar shifter asked.

He was a lanky guy with brown hair that was spiked to one side. Jordin stood next to him and answered his question when everyone else remained silent.

"We get in, sniff around and get out with more information to take back to the FL."

She was a much shorter guard, coming in around five-feet three or four inches. Her jet black hair fell in heavy waves around her shoulders, cupping a pretty face with a hint of make-up that showcased her Korean heritage.

"All while keeping Nisa within our sight," Gold added.

He was standing close to her, so it took almost no effort at all for him to touch her elbow and begin to lead her toward the door. Golden Harris was a six-foot tall, two hundred and thirty pound white lion with eyes so gold they actually appeared to glow. A fact which would certainly be a dead giveaway to his shifter status, which is why he wore dark framed glasses with brown slacks, beige shirt, bow tie and brown jacket.

As she walked through the glass doors that had automatically slid open for them, Nisa looked back to make sure Jordin and Zion were with them. It was habit. She didn't want to lose sight of any of her team this evening, so she'd been committing everything about them to memory. Zion had bent his arm and Jordin had slipped hers through it so that they moved like a couple on a date. Jordin wore all black like Nisa—a cropped jeweled top that bared the creamy skin of her midriff and a sheer jeweled skirt that hugged her hips and legs down to its short train. Black silk shorts worn beneath the skirt were the only thing that kept the outfit classy. Jordin sported deep red lips and walked like a runway model, while Zion wore a collarless charcoal gray jacket over a heather gray shirt and darker gray slacks. The pair looked young and hip. Not animalistic and deadly.

A glass elevator took them up to the fifty-first floor, where they stepped out onto a silver specked floor. Gold led them toward an entryway where he paused and reached into his inside jacket pocket to pull out an envelope. A man wearing a white suit and standing in the doorway accepted the envelope and after looking at it gave Gold a nod. They continued inside, moving into a large room flanked in candlelight and yards of sheer white material draped from the ceiling. There were long tables covered in crystal dishes, tall centerpieces filled with water and flashing lights inside. And the people, there were hundreds of people. Humans.

Nisa took a deep breath and attempted to act like this wasn't a big deal. But it definitely was. She'd never been around so many humans before in her life. She wondered if they could smell the cat in her. Of course not, humans didn't have a heightened sense of smell the way Shadow Shifters did. They wouldn't be able to tell just by looking at her that she wasn't one of them.

With that thought in mind, Nisa walked with a little more confidence, smiling as men and women looked at her, giving slight nods by way of greeting. She'd been so busy doing this and taking in every aspect of this world that she felt she'd missed, that she hadn't noticed the cheetah until her scent filled Nisa's nostrils. Nisa paused and turned around just as Kyss was lifting a hand to touch her hair.

"You made it," she said. "I've been waiting forever for you to get here."

"Why?" Nisa asked. "I didn't know it had been confirmed that you were coming."

She hadn't been told that Kyss would be here. Sure, she'd been the one to tell them that they should keep suspected enemies close, but nobody had bothered to confirm final plans with her. Kyss's original reason for showing up was to give Decan information on Lial and the murders. Nisa still didn't trust that was Kyss's only goal here, which was why she planned to keep an eye on her.

"Oh yes, I'm always on the job," Kyss continued and then shifted her attention to Gold. "Hey big guy. How's it hanging?"

Gold did not reply but continued to move his head as if

he were looking around the room.

"Not speaking to me tonight?" Kyss asked when he declined to respond. "That's cool. We ah…did enough last night."

She'd said that as she rubbed a finger over the skin beneath her bottom lip. Nisa tried not to think about what Kyss was referring to. She didn't want to concern herself with who the shifter slept with. Still, she would have thought Gold would have been smarter than to fall for Kyss's charms.

Said charms that were now wrapped in hot pink sparkly shorts that rode so far up her legs they could have been considered underwear and a white halter top. Her shoes were pink also, with straps that wound in a crisscross fashion all the way up to her knee. Her hair was once again in that long straight tail that swung dramatically each time she moved.

"There's someone over there I need to see," Gold told Nisa. "Come with me."

"No," she replied. "From here I have a view of the entrance and all three of the side doors that could be used as exits. You go ahead. I'll be right here when you finish. Unless who you're going to see has something to do with us finding the rogues in this room."

Gold didn't immediately answer, but stood still looking at her. Contemplating what he should do, no doubt.

"Look, I'm just gonna stand right here and Kyss is going to stand here and keep me company. You do trust Kyss don't you?" she asked with an arch of her brow.

Kyss had folded one arm over her chest and brought the other one up so that she could dip the tip of a shiny red fingernail between her teeth. She was looking at Gold like they'd definitely done some things last night so she was basically daring him to say he didn't trust her now. Nisa wanted to shake her head in disgust, but she'd been feeling her own bouts of lust lately so she decided not to judge anyone else who had the opportunity to scratch that persistent itch.

"Stay right here," he said evenly. "Both of you. I'll just be over there."

He pointed to a crowded glass bar where two bartenders were creating drinks in fluorescent colors. It was only about ten feet away from where they were standing.

"Fine," Nisa said because, yes, only about ten feet away. He was acting as if he were leaving her on another planet.

Gold did not speak again, but walked away after looking in Kyss's direction. The second he was out of earshot, Kyss moved closer to Nisa.

"Good job," she whispered in her ear. "He doesn't have a clue that you were trying to figure out how to get away from him the moment you stepped into this room."

Nisa wasn't going to insult either of them by denying that fact. She did want to roam on her own. Jordin and Zion had walked in their own direction once in the room and a part of her had detested the idea that she had to stay with a chaperon.

"I can see more without him breathing down my neck. Besides, having anyone guard me that close is ridiculous considering nobody in here knows who I am," she said.

"I agree," Kyss stated. "And I see something we can do to occupy ourselves while he's away."

She was staring straight ahead, to where a man dressed in a gray suit was standing. He looked like he'd just stepped out of a boardroom meeting with his neat yellow tie and carefully pressed white shirt. His head lifted and the quick smile that ghosted his lips said he knew they were staring at him.

"That's Graham Parker. He's second in command to Ewen Mackey in the Ruling Cabinet," Kyss said just before snagging two neon green drinks with limes stuck to the side of the glass.

She handed Nisa one and despite not knowing what it

was, Nisa lifted it to her lips for a sip.

"No one in his family has been targeted," she said with the glass blocking her mouth just in case Graham could read lips.

"Correct. He and Mackey are the only two of the eight members who hasn't had anything happen to one of their family members," Kyss continued, holding her glass up in the same position as Nisa. "We should go talk to him."

"Why?" Nisa asked.

Kyss was actually taking a sip of her drink now, so Nisa answered her own question.

"Because he's the second in command. So if anyone in the Cabinet was working with a shifter, either it was him, or he would know who it was. Add to that his family's been safe, and he looks like the one," she said.

Kyss lowered her glass and smiled brightly. "Let's go."

Nisa didn't think twice. Well, yes, she did because that was her nature. She thought that going over to speak to Graham Parker was harmless because again, he had no idea who she was. Kyss didn't look like a shifter and there was a room full of people. All they would do is talk and sniff because if Graham was working with a shifter, the scent would stick to him like lint.

"Hi darlin'," Kyss spoke the moment they were close enough.

Nisa easily dismissed the accent Kyss had adopted and smiled as Graham looked from Kyss to her.

"Hello ladies," he said and lifted a hand to smooth down his goatee. "Are you alone this evening?"

Kyss had already moved in, to the point that she was now standing right beside him. "We're together, silly," she said and then giggled. "And we're trying to figure out how to have a good time at one of these things. Everyone in here looks so stuffy."

Nisa watched her working. This was how the cheetah was able to get so much information. She was practically leaning on Graham now, bending just enough so that her halter top gaped open, giving him—and Nisa, for that matter—an unfettered view of her bare breast. Graham did what Nisa suspected any man would do, he looked.

"What type of fun are you interested in?" he asked and lifted a finger to trace along the bared skin just an inch or two away from Kyss's breast.

"That depends," Kyss replied and tapped her glass lightly against her chest so that condensation from the glass rolled down her skin.

Nisa was doing good holding her shock at bay until Graham leaned down and licked the droplet of water before asking, "Depends on what?"

Over his head Kyss winked at Nisa.

"Whether or not you have a friend for my friend," she answered.

Graham stood up straight then and looked at Nisa. "Sure," he said and licked his lips. "I've got lots of friends. Just let me get my keys and we can get to that fun."

Kyss pouted and stomped her foot. "I don't like waiting."

"Oh no," Graham said and laced an arm around Kyss's waist, pulling her up close to him. "I won't keep you waiting, sexy. Stay right here."

He kissed the tip of Kyss's nose and Kyss let her hand fall down to grip his crotch.

For a man that was being bold and brash that motion clearly caught him off guard as his cheeks blushed bright pink and he giggled like a fifteen year old boy.

"Be right back," he told her and then turned to move hastily through the crowd.

"What the hell are you doing?" Nisa asked the moment he was gone. "We were just supposed to pump him for information."

"Look," Kyss told her. "This is your first mission. I've been doing this a long time. We'll get the information we came here for and probably more. You just need to follow my lead."

"Your lead is heading to that man's bed," Nisa said.

"Of course," Kyss told her and shrugged. "That's where you get all the juicy information."

"That's not part of my plan," Nisa told her and started to walk away.

Kyss stopped her by grabbing her elbow.

"No. Your plan was to waltz in here, ask a bunch of questions, have someone give you all the answers and then you go back to headquarters and replay it for Jace. He'll be in your debt or impressed by your skills and then he'll name you Central Zone Faction Leader."

Nisa didn't speak. She didn't want to confirm what Kyss had said, and she couldn't deny it.

"That's both naïve and selfish. People are dying, Nisa. And whether or not they're humans who want us dead, they don't deserve to have a shifter killing them because a human is directing him to do so. I believe in a fair fight. Always," she said.

"Sex is off the table," Nisa replied. "That's where I draw the line."

Kyss rolled her eyes. "Right, you're saving yourself for your *companheiro*. Okay, that's fine. I'll do all the leg work. You smile, look sexy and listen well."

That's exactly what Nisa found herself doing fifteen minutes later after they'd taken a ride on an elevator with Graham and entered a room two floors down from the gala.

"My friend likes ropes," he'd said as he insisted Nisa climb up onto the bed so that he could tie her up.

The look she'd given Kyss at that point clearly stated something else that was off the table, but Kyss had only nodded her head as if to say, "shut up and do it". She didn't have to do what this cheetah told her. Nisa was a Senior Guard and Kyss was an unlisted shifter with no real allegiance to anyone or any cause. She'd also gotten them into a private meeting with the Ruling Cabinet's second in command. Kyss had been right, Nisa wanted to crack this case for Jace. She wanted to prove herself to him, Decan and her father. So she lay back on the bed and allowed her wrists to be tied to the headboard, and her ankles to the bottom posts.

For the first few moments after that Nisa had stared up at the ceiling thanking the heavens that Graham Parker couldn't tie a knot to save his life. If she wanted out, it would be easy enough, so she relaxed against the bed and listened as Kyss talked.

"You're with the Ruling Cabinet aren't you?" she was saying as she pushed Graham's jacket down his arms.

When it fell to the floor Graham took her by the shoulders and pulled her up to him. He lifted her until only the tips of her toes touched the floor and kissed her. The kiss looked rough and greedy. Nisa wondered if it were painful too because his fingers were digging into Kyss's arms and from the way he was moving his head and making an annoying sound he was trying to eat her face. Nisa wanted to close her eyes but she didn't because she'd caught a scent.

It was definitely animal.

So there was another shifter here besides her and Kyss. She looked to the door and then to the wall on the other side of the room that was all windows. Both appeared to be closed, so where was the scent coming from?

Seconds later the door opened and Graham released Kyss from his hold. He was smiling as he stared at the three who came in. Two men and one woman.

"Here she is," Graham said. "Isn't she everything I said she was? Both of them. Look! Look!"

The man was excited, again, like a young boy. The other two men, well, their eyes had darkened instantly as they looked at Kyss with her partially bared breasts and

Nisa with her legs and arms spread wide.

"Oh yes," the female of the trio said. "Both of them."

She didn't hesitate but walked over to Kyss and grabbed the back of her head. This kiss was different from the one Nisa had just witnessed. The woman moved slower, tracing her tongue over Kyss's lips and then diving deep when Kyss extended her tongue for a duel. Graham backed up and took a seat in a chair. He spread his legs and Nisa watched as he unzipped his pants. She turned away when one of the men touched her breast. He didn't smile as he looked down at her, just squeezed. She didn't smile either and she tried like hell not to puke all over the red satin comforter.

"Watch them," he directed Nisa as he continued to massage her breast.

Nisa did as he said because to keep looking at him was making her cat rage. If she didn't have to see him and didn't have to acknowledge that he was fondling her, then the cat would remain calm. At least she hoped so.

Looking forward didn't really help. The other man had come to stand behind Kyss and was now backing her up until he could sit in a chair. He pulled Kyss down on his lap, her back facing his front. His hands immediately went to Kyss's breasts while the woman used her hands to grab Kyss by both knees and spread her legs wide.

"Before this goes any further, I like names," Kyss said. "I'm Kyss. Like the hot one we just shared."

The woman in front of her smiled and moved her hands slowly up Kyss's thighs.

"I'm Lora," she said. "He's Jack and the one back there who's going to be in charge of your friend's orgasm is Patch."

"Now that we're all acquainted," Jack said and reached up to grab Kyss by the chin, turning her face so that he was just inches away from her mouth. "Let's get down."

Nisa tensed at his words. Her fingers clenched and when

Patch leaned in closer to rub his tongue along the rim of her ear she had to bite down on the temper, restrain the cat and keep her head. Remember those names. This place. This scent.

It was definitely animal, but it wasn't Patch. As he'd touched her and leaned in closer she'd inhaled deeply, wanting to connect the scent with a body. But it wasn't this one. So where was it? Where was this animal and what type was it? She couldn't tell. Nisa knew all the Shadow Shifter tribe scents. This wasn't one of them, which meant it wasn't a cat.

"I should get my camera," Graham said.

He couldn't get anything since both his hands gripped his rigid cock as he watched Kyss with the others.

"Ewen would love this," Graham was saying as he stroked himself harder.

"Where is Ewen?" Nisa asked. "Maybe he could join us?"

Maybe he had the other animal scent on him? Nisa didn't know but whoever had that scent, it was driving her cat wild. It wanted out and it wanted to fight. There was a threat near.

"Nah," Graham said and licked his lips, spittle dripping from his mouth. "He's taking care of business tonight. Shifter business."

Kyss moaned loudly then and Lora rubbed her hands between Kyss's legs.

"He should be here handling this business," Kyss whispered.

"Yes," Nisa added. "He should."

She was saying the words, but her body was also moving to the side in an effort to get away from Patch's touch. It felt dirty. And she felt disloyal.

"He's gotta give that funky animal new instructions," Graham said, his hand slipping up and down his cock as he'd already started to ejaculate. "Disgusting business.

Not like this...ahhh yeah, just like that..." he sighed and jerked and pumped into his fist.

The scent was closer and Nisa's incisors grew longer. Her claws broke through the skin of her fingers.

"Shit!" Patch yelled.

She looked at him then, her eyes wide, but not as wide as his. He'd climbed over her at some point and was now staring down at her...and the first remnants of her cat.

"Shifter!" he yelled again. "She's a fucking shifter!"

DECAN SAT BACK AND TRIED not to turn his nose up at the stench of the wolf.

He hadn't been surprised when Blaez Trekas had walked up behind him in the crowded room. He'd come here looking for the man and he'd found him—all of him. Now, they sat across from each other, neither fully trusting the other but knowing they had a common cause.

"Lial Johansen is working for the Ruling Cabinet," Blaez said without formalities or menial chit-chat. "Or at least he used to be."

Decan could appreciate the get in and get out mentality. He wasn't one hundred percent comfortable in this room, with all these humans. Possibly because he didn't trust that small part of him that had been vying for revenge for the last five years.

"If he's working for them, why would he kill their family members?" he asked.

"I think you know the answer to that question," Blaez answered.

Blaez Trekas was bald. He had tattoos going down his neck and probably everywhere else. But he was wearing black slacks and a white dinner jacket. He looked like a billionaire. A strong lycan billionaire.

"What I know is that humans are dying and shifters are being blamed for those deaths. If Lial is the killer then he should be taken down. If not, then we need to prove that before this war between us escalates even further."

Decan couldn't believe he was saying that. The words were necessary he told himself and then took a cleansing breath just in case the wolf could sense his dishonesty the way another cat shifter could.

"Lial isn't here tonight," Decan continued. "And neither is the FBI guy, Wilson."

"And neither is Cole," Blaez replied. "So you can report that to Jace Maybon."

"I'd rather find out why a Shadow Shifter came to you in the first place. How did he even know who or what you are?"

Decan wasn't buying this connection that seemed to have just surfaced. Rome had told him that Jace had a new lead on finding Cole. Then, when he'd met with Jace last night, the FL had spoken of an arranged meeting with Blaez Trekas. How and why was the communication between the Shadow Shifter and the lycan so casual?

Blaez sat back in one of the lounge chairs surrounding the small glass-top table. He shrugged as he asked, "He didn't tell you?"

"All I know is that you told Jace you had a lead on Cole's whereabouts. How you knew Cole was even missing or how to contact the Faction Leader of the Shadow Shifters to tell him this, is a mystery to me," Decan told him.

A mystery that he'd like to solve before he moved any further.

"I'm not a fan of keeping secrets from your pack," Blaez replied and leaned forward to rest his elbows on his knees.

"Shadow Shifters don't have packs," Decan told him. "We're a community of feline shifters fighting for our place in this world."

"You're a species on the run." Blaez corrected him. "We all are. The humans fear us because they can't control us."

"And you want to change that? You want to help the

humans to accept us?"

Blaez shook his head. "Not in a million years. But I'm not running or hiding. I did that before. It didn't work. So here we are."

"You've seen Cole?" Decan asked.

Blaez nodded.

"Maybon showed up at my door years back. My home wasn't easy to find so I knew instinctively that things were about to get worse simply because he—a Shadow Shifter—was there," he said.

Decan listened. He sat facing the entrance and each of the exit doors. His senses were on high alert for any species other than human in this room. So far he'd only picked up the scent of the wolf sitting across from him. Satisfied with that he waited while Blaez continued.

"We'd watched in horror on television as the Unveiling unfolded, so as Maybon told us about his missing friend we sympathized with him. My mate offered to help."

"Your mate?"

Blaez gave a wry smile. "Our pack works a little differently than your so called democracy. Anyway, Kira was able to locate Cole in the southwestern region. My pack went out and found him."

"But you didn't tell Jace?"

"Cole did not want us to."

"So where is he now?" Decan asked.

"That's what we need to find out," Blaez told him.

"Wait, you said you found him, but now you don't know where he is? How is that possible?"

"In the beginning Cole asked us to help him and we did so, for years."

Decan wasn't sure if he was believing this. The wolf's words matched what Jace had told him, still Decan felt like something was off.

"How did you help him?" What could you and your pack do that Roman Reynolds and the other Faction

Leaders couldn't?"

Blaez smiled and nodded at the woman who then appeared at the table with fresh drinks. Decan didn't offer a smile, but instead inhaled deeply as a secondary check. They hadn't ordered any drinks so why was she replacing them? He glanced around at that moment, spying small groups of humans together talking, and more guests arriving even though the gala had been in full swing for at least an hour now. What he didn't see or sense was Nisa, Gold or any of the other shifters that were supposed to be here working.

"We could still move around above ground without detection," Blaez continued when the woman was gone. "After the President's tirade and eventual death the entire world knew who and what Roman and his friends were. That's why he had to close his firm and go underground."

"But they didn't know Cole because Cole had gone missing the night of the Unveiling," Decan said.

He remembered the years when he'd entered high school and armed guards stood at the doors of the school watching every student enter and exit. It was like that everywhere he went. Guards filled the streets looking for any signs of the shifters—namely, the reported leaders of the species, Rome and his friends.

"We worked with Cole tracking down Reed's killers and making sure a shifter named Boden and all of his rogues were dead."

Decan knew that name. Boden Estevez was the rogue Topétenia shifter who along with Captain Lawrence Crowe were responsible for unveiling the shifters to the world.

"Then, a year ago there was a fire," Blaez continued.

Decan tensed. There was a fire a year ago at the SIC in Arizona. It came after the explosion and it had nearly killed him.

"We were in Sedona," Blaez was now saying. "In the

area near where Sebastian Perry's resort used to be. Cole had sensed a large group of rogues there. The fire started before we could find them. And when it was over, Cole was gone."

"Gone? Where?" Decan asked and then he paused.

White hot pain speared through his chest. His hands trembled and the lion inside roared. He stood so abruptly his knee hit the table and his glass tumbled to the floor. Blaez stood as well. His eyes flickering an intense blue for a second before returning to normal.

"Nisa," Decan whispered.

"Death," Blaez said.

CHAPTER 11

NISA JUMPED FROM THE BED swinging her arm so that her claws swiped the man named Patch across the side of his face for a second time.

"Gun!" Kyss yelled from across the room.

Nisa ducked in time to have bullets cracking the bed-frame behind her. She crawled on her hands and knees, teeth bared just before she jumped on one of the humans who had burst into the room. Her teeth clamped down over his wrist, sending the gun he'd just fired to the floor.

Adrenaline pumped through her veins, the instinct to fight for her life pounding against her skull like a brick. Her cat was ready to kill. It would be so easy to shift and take them out quickly, but she refrained. It was hard, but she did it and the next human that aimed a gun at her was rewarded for his efforts by her jumping on him, knocking him to the floor, her claws digging into his chest as she leaned her face into his and roared with all the ferocity she possessed.

That's when she heard the glass breaking and more roars filling the space. She looked up in time to see a black wolf with bright blue eyes landing on the floor before charging the human that had the bad luck of standing closest to it. Kyss was lifting her leg to kick a gun out of one man's hand, while reaching behind her to sink her claws into the stomach of another.

Nisa growled as heavy rope wrapped around her neck and yanked her head back. Her hands went to the rope as she tried to break free. The person on the other end was strong, pulling her so that the heels on her shoes broke as she was dragged across the floor. She managed to turn around just in time to see the tall bulky guy who thought he'd caught her. Her teeth bared, she roared once more before yanking on the rope so hard the guy lost his footing and tumbled toward her. He was just about to fall on top of her when a blur of white flashed before her eyes, and a roar like none she'd ever heard before vibrated throughout the room.

The man hit the wall with a sickening thud. He appeared dazed momentarily, to be followed by the spurt of blood from the quick and efficient bite to his throat. Nisa had only a moment to gasp before the new arrival turned to her, a man's body with the lion's face.

His hair had gone completely white, his eyes like glaciers. The beard was longer, blood dripping from his teeth as he glared at her.

"Decan?" she whispered before being pushed to the side as he charged another human.

Kyss came to her then, helping her up off the floor as the white lion and the black wolf finished the last two humans in the room. An eerie silence fell over the space as Nisa came to her feet, her claws and teeth retracting.

"Your shoes are fucked," Kyss said glibly.

Nisa looked down and kicked what was left of the sandals off her feet.

Footsteps approached and seconds later Keller and Gold entered the room.

"They're coming," Gold announced.

"There's a back elevator. Let's go!" Keller insisted and moved to touch Nisa's arm.

Decan roared so loud everyone stilled again.

His face was normal now, his hair back to its black and white streaks, but his eyes, they spoke clearly of rage and Keller immediately dropped his hand from Nisa's arm. Decan moved first, coming toward her and scooping her up in his arms. Nisa wrapped her arms around his neck. A part of her wanted to say something, to tell him she could walk, or to stop being so grouchy, but the words didn't surface. Something inside held her tongue and kept her still in his arms as they followed Gold out of the room. They all boarded the elevator and stepped out into the darkness of the parking garage. In seconds three large vehicles pulled up and Decan moved them toward the first one.

"We need to lay low, at least for tonight," Gold said.

A man she didn't recognize came from around the other side of the vehicle holding what looked like one of the human's bloody jackets around his waist to hide the better part of his nudity.

"I'm on your comlink," he said. "I'll send you the address of a place to stay."

Decan nodded and then looked to Gold and Keller.

"First thing in the morning," he said. "That's how long you've got to come up with a damn good reason for why you weren't with her."

Keller shook his head. "We were doing what we came here to do. Babysitting wasn't part of the deal."

"This is my operation. Whatever I say needs to be done, gets done!" Decan yelled.

"It was Mackey," Gold said. "We had him."

"I don't give a damn! She could have been killed!" Decan continued.

"It's been a really fun night, but I'm kinda hungry and

tired, so can we wrap this up and reconvene in the morning?" Kyss asked from where she leaned on the second vehicle.

Nisa had never felt as out of place as she did at this moment. She was barefoot, in a shifter's arms and remaining totally silent. How the hell did she get here? And where was the Nisa Reynolds that swore she could handle a mission on her own?

"First thing in the morning," Decan repeated and then yanked the passenger side door open and deposited Nisa into the seat.

She immediately slid to the side and familiarized herself with the dashboard controls of this foreign vehicle. Decan slammed one door and then the other as he climbed into the driver's seat.

"Sit back," he told her.

Nisa paused and then decided to do what he'd said. There would be time for her to speak her mind, soon.

The vehicle took off quickly, moving even faster than the one that had brought them here in the first place. They drove through the city, into the almost pitch blackness of territory unknown to her, before finally coming to a stop. Decan stepped out and before he could get to her door Nisa got out on her own. Her feet landed on a grassy surface, and she looked down to see long blades of grass passing her ankles. Decan walked in front of her, going up the steps of what appeared to be an old wood house. Vines wrapped around the railing of what used to be a porch. Ivy stretched up the front walls like fluid arms and circled around the windows and roof so that the wood barely showed anymore. The place looked more like a grass hut now. He opened the door and waited while she entered, before closing it again. She followed him to the back of the dwelling where he opened another door and walked them down a flight of stairs.

Here, there was light and furniture and warmth. She

almost sighed in relief at the sight of a small bathroom and a shower stall.

"Go ahead," he said, his voice seemingly loud in the closed space. "I'll be here when you get out."

Nisa didn't know what was happening to her. She was actually standing there searching for words. There was so much to say to him. So many questions and so much to tell him about what she and Kyss had learned about the Ruling Cabinet, but she did not say a word. She simply turned around and walked into the closet-sized bathroom.

D ECAN WATCHED HER.
Leaning against the doorjamb after opening the door, he just watched.

Her body was tight in all the right places, plump in the others. There was power in her legs, her calves moving up to her thighs. Her arms were long and strong as she lifted them over her head and let the spray of water hit her sides and her back. Soapy lather ran down her body in silken stretches that made him jealous all over again.

Wasn't that how he'd felt as he'd run from that ballroom and headed to the elevators to follow her scent. Someone was touching her. They were feeling her and taking what was his. The sensation had quickly turned to rage when he'd seen the rope go around her neck and knew the human had planned to kill her. Now, Decan was back to not knowing what the hell he was feeling where she was concerned. Actually, that wasn't true. The bulging in his pants said he was definitely aroused and the sheer reluctance to letting her out of his sight again had him standing there while she bathed and watching like some perverted stalker.

"It's a good thing I'm not modest."

He heard her words and blinked when he realized she'd

shut off the water and stepped out of the shower stall. Naked.

"The towel is behind the door," she continued.

He nodded and moved further into the small room so that he could push the door closed enough to pull the towel off the wire hook.

"Thank you," she said when he handed it to her.

"You're not modest around me," he told her. "Because you know there's no need."

She'd bent over and began rubbing the towel down her legs. Standing again she tilted her head as she stared at him.

"You have no idea what I know," she replied.

"You know there's something between us. It's been there since the moment I first saw you."

"Well, since you technically stalked me for about what? Six months? Without me knowing, then I'd say I had nothing to do with that, so how could I know anything."

"But you felt it. That day as you packed your Tracer. You didn't startle when I came up behind you because you knew I was there," he said, keeping his gaze leveled on hers.

Yes, he enjoyed looking at her body and yes, they were only about three feet apart and he figured he could just reach out and touch any part of that body he wanted to at the moment. But he wanted to look into her eyes, to know what he was feeling was reciprocated. Decan had no idea why that was so important to him now. It had never been before.

"I knew someone was there. We were packing to leave. I had a team," she said.

"You wanna know why I watched you all those months?" he asked as he took a step toward her.

She wrapped the towel around her body and tucked it beneath her arms. "Why?"

"Because I knew," he whispered. "I knew there was a

connection."

The *companheiro connection.*

He'd known and yet he'd tried to resist it. To ignore its lure and implications. He did not want a mate. The years he'd been a captive in the SIC had shown him the dangers of being a shifter. Of mating and possibly creating more shifters. No. He would not be a part of bringing new life into such a volatile world.

"Each time I tried to leave Assembly Headquarters, I was brought right back. When I wanted to go in the opposite direction of where I knew you would be. I ended up just feet away from you once more. I was drawn to you and you were to me."

She shook her head. "I didn't know you were there."

"Didn't you?" Decan asked and this time he did touch her.

He grabbed her by her waist and lifted her to sit on the small vanity.

"Didn't you feel me?"

"No," she whispered, her voice just a little shakier than it had been just seconds ago.

"Not physically," he told her and then touched his fingers lightly to her temple. "Mentally."

"You see, the *companheiro connection* is stronger than the physical hunger of mated shifters," he continued, letting his fingers slide down her cheek. "It's a mind, body and soul connection that very few shifters experience before the lust takes over."

"There was lust," she said and licked her lips. "All those months I wondered why it was getting stronger. Right from the start there was lust between us. It's only grown in the short time we've been together."

He nodded.

"And again, the mental."

Decan lowered his face to hers, he touched his forehead to hers and closed his eyes. "That night you thought I called you by another woman's name," he said quietly. "I didn't. Not verbally. You knew that name because you pulled it out of my mind. You used our connection to see a part of my past I wished I'd never lived through."

She gasped.

"You're the only one that's ever been able to do that," Decan continued. "Just you, Nisa. Just. You."

HIS HANDS WERE ON HER knees now, pushing them apart.

Nisa swallowed. And she did not speak.

Well, to hell with that, she was tired of playing like she didn't possess a coherent thought, or logical vocabulary.

"I heard you say her name," she told him. "You said Mar—"

He leaned in and touched his lips to hers at that moment. His tongue moved slowly against hers and damn, hers followed its direction as if it were made for that reason alone. In seconds she was tilting her head and leaning into the kiss. Her eyes were closed, his hands warm against her skin.

Marlee.

She heard the name and was about to say something to him, but then she realized he was still kissing her. His hands were moving steadily up the inside of her thighs but his lips were most definitely still on hers, his tongue stroking against hers in a fashion designed to drive her crazy with desire.

"Marlee is the one who called the Outlaw Task Force on you. She's the reason you're locked in here now."

The words continued and she reached up, grabbing hold of his wrists and then with all the force she could muster, pulled her mouth away from his.

"Who? What? I don't understand," she told him.

"I don't either," he whispered. "Not totally anyway. I

just know that there are some shifters who experience this, while others do not."

"No," she said and shook her head. "I'm just a shifter. My job is to fight and design computer systems. I'm not—"

He kissed her again and Nisa felt like he was doing so to keep her quiet. She didn't like that, but she didn't stop him either. This time she lifted her hands to cup his face and when she was absolutely breathless from the kiss, she pushed his face away from hers.

"Why can't we simply be attracted to each other? I'm a virgin, but I don't wish to be any longer. Let's just get this over with so we can both start thinking straight again," she said.

"Nisa?"

"No," she repeated, shaking her head once more. "Just this," she continued. "Just you and me and just this."

For a few nervous moments Nisa thought he would deny her. She thought all his talk of *companheiro connection* and body and soul was going to send him running. It was too serious—all that talk about connecting and committing. She didn't want it. Not tonight anyway. Not after what she'd just been through.

With his hands on the top of her thighs, Decan's thumbs brushed over the sensitive skin of her pussy. She sighed with relief, her eyes closing slowly before opening again.

"Is this what you want?" he asked.

His voice was husky, his eyes a crisp clear blue that seemed to cut right through her. To the parts of her that no one had ever seen before. Nisa dismissed how uncomfortable that made her feel and instead pulled his shirt so that the buttons popped off. He'd obviously removed his jacket while she was showering. That was just fine with her.

"This is what I want," Nisa said and pushed the shirt down his arms in an effort to convince him and herself.

He had to move his hands from her in order to totally remove the shirt. Nisa did not like that but it gave her time to ditch the towel that was hindering her from feeling the touch of his skin directly on hers. She'd been craving that touch since he'd held her in the water. His mouth had been so hot on her then, even with the cool of the water on her back. He'd unbuckled his pants and was pushing them and his boxers down his legs when she grabbed him, pulling him to her as she locked her legs around his waist.

"Yeah," he groaned and buried his fingers in her hair. "This is what I want too."

Pulling her head back, he kissed her roughly this time, his teeth brushing over her lips sending a quick slice of pleasure/pain through her body. The unfamiliar sound that escaped from her must have been a green light for Decan because his nails scraped along her scalp as he sucked hungrily on her tongue.

She ran her fingers over his strong shoulders, up and down his bare back, pausing with a gasp at what she felt.

"What?" she asked in a breathy whisper.

He went totally still. So much so that if Nisa hadn't felt and heard the quickened thumping of his heart she would have thought he'd died in her arms.

"It's nothing," he said.

But as he spoke he'd moved away from her mouth, dropping a chaste kiss on her shoulder.

"It feels like something," she said still moving her hands over the parts of his back she could reach. "It feels like a lot of something."

"You feel better," he told her. "Every part of you feels so much better."

As if trying to prove his point, Decan let his fingers slip from her hair down to her shoulders. He massaged her there and whatever thoughts Nisa had before his magical fingers had done the magical thing that relaxed her totally floated away. When his mouth touched the spot where he rubbed, she moaned. His kisses were lethal. The tiny bites that just barely pierced her skin were sinister. Her breasts felt full all of a sudden, her nipples hardened to a painful point.

He must have sensed that change in her as his kisses moved slowly—tortuously so—down her chest until he'd taken one tiny bud between his teeth. The other nipple was now between his fingers as he tugged and licked, then sucked and cupped. Nisa arched into him, her head hitting the small circular mirror above the sink.

"Yes," he whispered over her skin, "you feel better than everything, Nisa. Better than I could have ever imagined."

She'd taken her hands from his back to grip the sides of the vanity. It was small and she was certain it wasn't built to accommodate her sitting on it and Decan doing what he was doing to her while she was sitting on it. He was taking full advantage of the fact that he now had unfettered access to her very naked and very sensitive body.

She'd closed her eyes to the sensations his mouth was sending through her body and so was barely aware of the fact that he seemed to be moving lower and lower. Until the second his fingers touched her pussy, separating her plump folds and his tongue flattened over her clit.

"Why does that feel so good?" she sighed and curled her toes. "I had no idea it would feel that good."

He moaned over her, licking every inch of her and making deliciously naughty sounds while doing so. Cracking her eyes open Nisa looked down to see the top of Decan's head, framed by her thighs. It was a gorgeous sight, one she knew she'd never forget. Just as she would not forget the angry slashes she could now see crisscrossing his back. The sensation of being filled and the trembling of her thighs cleared the thought from her mind and Nisa bit her bottom lip to keep from screaming out.

"Oh no you don't," Decan said gruffly and tilted his head back to look up at her. "I want every sound. Every pleasurable moan, every bit of your release."

She sighed and shook her head because he was moving his fingers in and out of her as he spoke. In and out, deeper and deeper he went, faster and faster Nisa felt herself falling.

"Give them to me," he urged and licked his lips before dipping his face back down to her dewy folds.

He licked and pumped her. She bucked and moaned, feeling as if she were going to explode at any moment now. He continued, whispering instructions for her to "let go" and "give it all to me" and Nisa simply floated on the pleasure. Her body had begun to move on its own, her hips jutting forward and pulling back with the ministrations of his fingers. Her pussy creaming as he sucked on her clit and licked her plump skin. So by the time he pulled away from her, and fit his body between her legs, Nisa was about to explode.

She literally felt as if she couldn't take another prick of pleasure. Surely if she did she would tumble over the ledge she'd been precariously perched on since the moment he'd walked up behind her.

"Look at me," he commanded.

She did.

Her eyes opened wide, her lips parted as she panted.

"Give it all to me, Nisa," he told her once more. "I want it all."

"Yes," she said and nodded. "Yes, Decan."

His name came out in a strangled cry as he thrust his complete length inside her.

She screamed his name then, and tore her hands away from the vanity to clap hold of his shoulders. There was stinging pain that was instantly replaced by pleasure that started somewhere deep inside of her and bloomed to every corner of her being. He was thick and long and completely filling her.

Nisa hadn't realized her legs had fallen from around him, but Decan had. He wrapped them around his waist once more, clasping her ankles as he pulled her closer, nestling himself deeper inside of her.

"We've been connected from day one," he said and pulled out of her slowly. "Now, it's official."

Nisa heard his words but didn't have the strength to figure out what they meant. All she knew was that he felt good. Every part of him, every movement, and every word he spoke. It all felt good. So very good she rode along with him. Stroking and pumping, moaning and hissing, until her entire body trembled, her teeth clenching together and the cat inside roared loud and long.

Decan pumped faster. He leaned in and let his lion's teeth glide along the line of her shoulder. His hands were now gripping her bottom, his nails digging painfully into her skin there.

"It's done," he whispered again, just before his teeth sank deep into her flesh.

Nisa cried out again, the pleasure filling her and the pain...awakening her.

CHAPTER 12

———————

DECAN WOKE WITH A START, the dream having pulled him in instantly, bending him to the point where it threatened to break him once more.

How many nights would he dream of his time in the SIC? How many times would he relive the most horrific years of his life? Forever, was his answer. He would never forget and thus would never stop trying to take Ewen Mackey and his band of killers that called themselves the Ruling Cabinet down. They were not rulers. They were anything but because they cared about no one but themselves. Working with shifters to kill other shifters all in the name of keeping humans safe. But Decan knew there was much more to it than that. He knew it and so did Keller. Together they had to bring them down. There was no other way for the shifters to be safe, whether above or underground.

She wasn't in the bed with him.

That was the next jolt that Decan's system didn't need.

He sat up looking around the dark space. They were still in the basement of the cabin that Blaez said they could use. Decan hadn't bothered to ask the lycan how he knew of this place or who it belonged to. He'd only taken the directions and found the key in the location that had been given. They couldn't go back to Oasis tonight because any one of them could have been followed. So they'd split up. Keller, Gold and Kyss were at a hotel while Jordin and Zion were at a campground that a group of protestors used when they weren't walking back and forth in front of the Ruling Cabinet's headquarters in downtown Houston. Those protestors knew more than the other humans gave them credit for. If anyone had truly decided to listen to them, they would know exactly where the majority of the Shadow Shifters were hiding and how to get to them. Luckily for the shifters, everyone thought the group of sixteen to twenty-somethings, were just troublemakers looking for attention instead of finding a job like the rest of the human world. The problem with that philosophy was that there weren't many jobs to be had, unless one wanted to be a shifter hunter. Most large corporations and just about all of the small businesses had shut down years ago. The human's economy was in shambles. Their homes, what was left of them after the months of hurricanes in certain areas, blizzards simultaneously in others, looting, fires…you name it, and this civilization had seen it.

It was a totally different world from the one Decan had been born into and even more different than anything Nisa could have imagined.

Tossing his legs over the side of the bed, Decan stood and inhaled deeply. He followed the scent which led him up the stairs and into the front room of the cabin. That's where Nisa stood, off to the side as she peaked out the window. It was dark in the house and outside so if there were a human out there, they had no chance of seeing them. But Nisa could see out. So could Decan.

"I didn't know it would be like this," she said quietly.

He took another step toward her but thought better and stopped. If he got too close he'd want to touch her and no doubt take her again. The need to be inside her had not been satiated with one time. He'd known it wouldn't.

"My father said if we came above ground without supervision we would be killed. He and Uncle Nick told me and Shya that every day of our lives."

"They wanted you to be afraid," he said. "Fear should have kept you obedient."

She chuckled wryly.

"You don't know me or Shya. We are the direct opposite of obedient."

"But you're smart," Decan told her. "Because you never let your father see how disobedient you were being."

"Why didn't you tell him you knew I was going above ground?" she asked without turning to look at him.

"It wasn't my place," he answered.

"But you followed me. Why?"

"I've been taught to protect. In the military, my parents, my cat. Protect our kind, protect the innocent, protect my *comp*...everyone," he finished and cleared his throat.

Decan knew what had happened between him and Nisa. He knew exactly what they were to each other now. He knew and he hadn't decided how that was going to play out yet. So, for now, he wasn't going to speak the word. Not that refusing to speak it would make it any less so.

"I've been taught to hide," she told him. "To sit in an underground prison and hide."

"You were tops in your tactical training. Eli Preston thinks you're ready to be elevated to an enforcer."

She shook her head.

"My father will never allow that. Just as he never allowed me to travel with any of the guard teams that went above ground in search of other shifters in trouble."

"He's been taught to protect what is his." Decan couldn't believe he was defending Roman Reynolds' motives.

The Assembly Leader had chosen to hide and he'd made the entire species do the same. It was disgraceful. Keeping them locked underground as if they'd been the ones to start this war. Sure, Blaez had said that Rome had no other choice. That he was trying to keep them all from being hunted and brutally murdered, but none of Rome's new regulations had been there to save Decan when he'd been captured. The one that saved him had been the one that set that fire at the SIC. That fire had changed Decan's life forever and now, he wasn't going to follow the leader as easily as he'd been taught. Because this time, the leader didn't have a clue what it felt like to be tortured and taunted just because of who he'd been born to be.

"But I'm not his," she said. "I belong to myself. So shouldn't I have some say in what I will do with my life?"

She was right and she was wrong.

Nisa Reynolds did not belong to her father. She now belonged to Decan. He wisely did not say that to her. She was no more ready to accept their fate than he was.

"You don't know what's out there, Nisa. You have no idea how dangerous it is for shifters now."

"It's dangerous because we hide. We don't know what's up here because we're stuck down there," she said, her voice raising slightly as she finally turned to him.

Her eyes were glowing. The cat's eyes. Her stance was confrontational, her scent...mesmerizing.

"It would be just as dangerous if you were above ground," he told her because it was true. "My parents let me stay and continue my education. Then I decided to go into the military."

"Why? You could have come to Oasis and begun your training there. But you wanted to stay above ground. You felt you were more needed here."

Decan shook his head. "I felt it was beneficial for me to know everything I could, about both worlds. The shifters that stayed above ground had either been found and killed or knew how to hide in plain sight very well. I could hide better than anyone. It kept me alive."

Until it almost killed him.

"How did you do it? Can you teach me?"

"Teaching you will not change your father's mind."

"Not teaching me will not stop me," she countered.

And Decan knew she was right. He knew just as surely as the *companheiro calor* was now lingering between them, that Nisa was going to go above ground more and more. She felt she had a place here. That she could do some good. Was it so different from what Decan was doing? Could he really stand with the others who would hold her back?

On the other hand, could he stand losing her if something happened?

It wasn't a matter of love. No, Decan didn't think he was capable of that. But she was his *companheiro*. That was an unbreakable bond. Or so he'd heard.

"Let's get some sleep," he told her. "We'll head back to Oasis in the morning and give Jace our report."

"But you will not teach me? Once I'm back at Oasis, your job is done and you will walk away."

She sounded so certain. Very irritated by her own words, but still sure that they were true.

Decan closed the space between them, lifting his hands to cup her face when he was close enough.

"I won't be walking away from you, Nisa. Not tonight and definitely not tomorrow."

Not forever.

Those two words lingered in his mind, but instead of speaking them Decan kissed her forehead. When she brought her hands up to circle his wrists, he kissed her temples. She tilted her face up to him and he kissed the tip of her nose.

"Open your eyes," he whispered and she immediately

did as he asked.

Her cat's eyes were staring up at him. Decan blinked until his lion's eyes could respond.

"I won't walk away from you."

She nodded slightly at the commitment he'd not only made to her as part man, but as the fierce beast that lived inside.

Coming up on her toes she kissed him this time. Touching her lips lightly to his and whispering, "Thank you," before wrapping her arms around his waist and pressing her body into his.

Decan held her close as they stood in front of the window. He wrapped his arms tightly around her and breathed in their now shared scent. On a ragged exhale he kissed the top of her head and was just about to lead them back downstairs when he sensed something beyond the window.

Turning his head ever so slightly and being careful to only open his eyes a slit so that the brightness of the lion's eyes did not alert anyone to their presence, he looked out. His training on restraint came in handy because what Decan saw would have definitely frightened Nisa. She would have reacted to that fear defensively and been ready to go out and fight. But Decan knew this was different. The eyes staring directly back at him were not eyes he'd ever seen before. They weren't the eyes of any Shadow cat, and they did not resemble the eyes of the wolf he'd seen tonight.

This was different.

And it was scary.

It was meant to be scary, he decided, because its next step was to kill.

"ARE YOU OUT OF YOUR fucking mind?" Rome yelled after Jace's excuse.

Jace didn't cower. Instead, he stood tall—albeit a relatively safe distance from the Assembly Leader—and stared him in the eye.

The distance was only safe because Kalina had positioned herself so that Rome would have to push her out of the way to get to Jace. That was a shame because at the moment Rome wanted to wrap his hands around the neck of a man he'd called friend for the better part of thirty-five years.

"You said finding Cole was our priority," Jace continued.

"At the expense of my daughter's safety? Are you really going to stand there and try to sell me that load of crap?"

"Rome," Kalina said, placing a hand on his arm. "Let him speak."

He didn't reply. He didn't give permission, nor did he deny it. He simply stood there trying to bite his tongue because words were quickly leaving his mind. In that instance the only thing left would be the physical and Jace Maybon was definitely not ready to receive what Rome had kept stored for anyone who dared to threaten his daughter's life.

"She knows, Rome," Jace stated. "She knew that someone broke into the files and obtained the confidential information on Jacques and Cole. She said it had to be someone with the access codes, meaning it had to be a shifter. She knows every shifter in that database. Not sending her up there to look for the culprit would have been unconscionably stupid."

"No, Jace," Rome said in as even a tone as he could manage. "You're simply vying for the unconscious aspect. She's my daughter and I expected you to keep her safe! Not send her into the arms of danger! That is not acceptable. None of this is."

"What I think he's trying to say, is, where is Nisa now, Jace?" Kalina asked.

Jace cleared his throat and admitted, "We don't know."

It was Nick who stepped in front of Rome this time, blocking the path to Jace. "You gotta come better than that, man. This is his only child."

"She's with Decan," the guard that Rome recognized from being with Decan back at headquarters, said.

"Decan will keep her safe," he continued.

"What's your name?" Rome asked as he turned all his attention to the one that seemed to have some answers for him.

"Gold, sir," the guard replied.

"Okay, Gold. Where is Decan?" Rome asked.

"I don't know—" Gold began.

Rome was already shaking his head.

"I mean that I did not have the location to where he was going. Last night, that lycan said he had a place for Decan to go that would be safe. I figured Decan took the information," Gold continued.

"But you haven't heard from him since then?" Nick asked.

"No. But that's not unusual. Decan knows better than to make too much outside contact. Especially above ground. We all knew to get back down here as soon as it was safe. For us," he said looking toward a cheetah sitting in a chair with her legs propped on the conference room table.

"It was safe at first light because mostly everyone in the hotel was still asleep. We were able to get out undetected and we took two vehicles to get back to a doorway down here. We used the underwater entrance," Gold said proudly.

Rome couldn't bring himself to say that was smart. He was still too pissed off that his daughter wasn't here to give any type of commendations for good work. Especially not to Jace.

"You sent them all up there and what did you get out of it? Nothing. They were run out of the gala without finding any more information about the murders or the shifter that betrayed us," he told him.

"That's not true."

Every head swung to the door that had slid quietly open as Nisa stepped through.

"We received confirmation from Graham Parker that Ewen Mackey is working with a shifter. Why he would have that shifter killing for him? We don't know, but at least now we are certain that a shifter is doing the killings," she said looking directly at Rome.

Never in all his life did he think he would love so unconditionally and as deeply as he did his only child. She was, as Kalina had stated before, the best of both of them. She was also the future. Nisa was everything that Rome had worked for so hard to accomplish in these last twenty years.

Inside, he breathe a sigh of relief that she was alive and well. Outside, he was still pissed. The muscle in his jaw twitched and his gaze narrowed on his child. Her mother, however, was across the room in seconds, wrapping her arms around Nisa and pulling her into a hug that looked as if it might suffocate her.

"I'm fine," Nisa whispered to her mother.

"I know," Kalina said as she pulled back and looked in her daughter's face. "You are capable and knowledgeable and you're fine. But you are also my daughter, so allow me the time to fuss and assuage the worry."

Nisa smiled into her mother's hazel eyes. She'd never seen a female as beautiful as the woman standing in front of her at this moment. Everything that Nisa aspired to be was inspired by this person.

"Whatever you say, First Female," Nisa said using the term that shifters not related to Kalina called her.

Her mother smiled and did that tilt of her head that had long since served as a warning to Nisa.

"Yes, she's fine," Kalina stated. "Sassy as ever. And

you?"

Kalina was looking at Decan who had remained close to Nisa as they'd entered. He'd remained close to her since lifting her into his arms last night. Nisa wasn't complaining, but she wasn't thinking too hard on that fact either. What it meant, what anything about last night between the two of them had meant for that matter. Now, just was not the time.

"I am fine, First Female. Things did get a little rough last night, but I can assure you and the Assembly Leader that once the situation was under control, I kept a close eye on Nisa. She was not injured in any way," he told her.

His voice was stilted, almost as if he were nervous for some reason. Probably because her father's jaguar eyes had appeared and a low angry grumble was coming from where he stood.

"Then I thank you," Kalina said, ignoring her mate and approaching Decan. "For taking such good care of my daughter and of yourself. I know that the Assembly Leader thinks highly of your abilities."

"As do I," Jace interrupted. "So, if we can move to another conference room, I believe the leadership needs a debriefing from Decan."

"That means they're kicking us out," Kyss said to Nisa.

She swept her legs from the table and stood. Today she wore a gray one piece outfit that molded over her slim curves and a waist length yellow jacket. Her yellow polka dot boots came to her knees and this time her hair was wrapped in a messy bun and piled atop her head. Nisa momentarily looked down at the dark blue jeans and fuchsia off the shoulder blouse she'd thrown on in the ten minutes Decan had given her to run to her room and change. They'd left that cabin as soon as Decan thought it was safe that morning, but he'd insisted they take a very long route to find another entrance into Oasis.

"I'm not leaving," Nisa said and looked directly at her

father who had yet to say anything to her. "I was a part of this mission. I should be present for any debriefing that takes place."

Jace folded his arms over his chest and looked at Rome. Gold wisely remained silent while Kyss looked thoroughly entertained.

"Shya came with us," Nick offered. "She's in one of the guest rooms and I know she's anxious to see you."

Nisa gave him a knowing look. "Shya can wait until after the debriefing, Uncle Nick."

"She does have information that could help," Decan said and Nisa almost took a step back toward him.

It had been that way all morning. He kept close to her and she felt an overwhelming need to get even closer to him. It was weird and took a great deal of strength to resist as they stood in the room with so many people.

"We all have information that can help," Kyss continued. "The guy that was all hands, groping me like a horny teenager, he told me that Ewen Mackey was there last night and that he'd had a meeting with his shifter friend that's why he hadn't been seen at the gala."

Jace turned to Kyss. "So are we thinking that the shifter that's working for the Ruling Cabinet—"

"Lial Johansen," Decan injected. "I have it on good authority that Lial was working for the Ruling Cabinet. But that he is not officially working for them now. But Lial wasn't there last night and neither was Dorian Wilson."

"Good authority?" Rome asked. "Whose authority?"

Decan nodded and looked to Jace.

Nisa watched them both, wondering if Decan was going to share with all of them who the person with "good authority" was. She hadn't had a moment last night to ask him where he'd been or how he'd known where she and Kyss were. They'd been talking about and doing other things. Now, it seemed imperative that she know the answer.

"Maybe it's time we all sit down and get things straight," Kalina suggested.

Her mother walked around the long table to take a seat next to the chair at the very head of the table. Jace had been standing next to that chair, but with a nod of his head to the First Female, he moved to take the seat across from her. Nick glanced at his *companheiro* and the Lead Curandero at Oasis, Ary, and then took the seat next to Jace. Ary followed her *companheiro*.

Nisa jumped as she felt Decan's hand at her elbow. When she looked up at him, it was to see his stoic features. His eyes were clear today, his bearded jaw squared. That same face had looked softer last night and in the early morning hours. His beard was softer than she'd figured it would be and her body immediately warmed as she recalled how soft it was when it rubbed against the sensitive skin of her inner thigh.

Nisa sat next to her mother and Decan next to her. Gold and Kyss remained standing, along with the Assembly Leader who everyone now looked to.

Rome moved slowly to take the seat at the head of the table. He rested his elbows on the edge of the table and clasped his fingers together. "Tell me everything that happened last night. What we now know. What we still need to find out. And what our end game is going to be," he said in his deep rumbling voice.

THEY'D TOLD THE ASSEMBLY LEADER everything, Decan thought as he walked out of the conference room.

Everything except where Keller and Gold had been while Nisa and Kyss were with Graham Parker. That was a private conversation, one Decan was going to have the moment he returned to his room.

"Don't you ever scare me like that again," the Assembly Leader was saying as he held Nisa in his arms.

They were standing in the hallway now. The First Female smiling at her *companheiro* and her daughter as they embraced.

"I didn't meant to frighten you, Daddy," Nisa said in a tone Decan had never heard her use before.

Small pangs of jealously speared into him as he saw how Nisa looked up at her father. There was nothing but love and adoration in her eyes. Decan wanted that same type of look for himself. It was silly, he knew. He'd never planned on taking a mate. But here they were and their scent...it was beyond obvious. Gold had arched a brow when they'd walked in and Kyss had smiled knowingly. If the others recognized it, they hadn't spoken a word. For that, Decan was glad.

"Let's have lunch," Kalina said. "We'll get Shya, Nick and Ary and all head to the main dining room for something to eat. You must be starving since you've been traveling all morning."

Decan continued to eavesdrop, not feeling one ounce of shame for doing so. Nisa was a part of him whether he liked it or not, which meant what she did and when she did it was his business. Case closed.

She must have felt the same way, at least a little, because she immediately looked over to where he stood. No, she wasn't asking his permission to have lunch with her parents, but she was wondering what he was going to do. Where he would be while she was with them? She had no idea, he thought. No idea, how hard it was going to be for them to be away from each other now that they shared the *calor.*

Neither of them spoke, mainly because Decan didn't know what to say. Was he really supposed to tell the Assembly Leader that Nisa wasn't going anywhere without him? No, that probably wasn't going to go over too well. Besides that, he had to meet with Keller and Gold. Her parents keeping her busy would actually be a favor to him.

Rome turned, glaring at Decan. The Assembly Leader hadn't asked to speak to him alone yet, but Decan knew a private meeting was coming. He wasn't looking forward to it, but recognized that these were all steps to his future. Even the jagged little edges that pulled him away from the straight path he'd created for himself. Everything was leading to his own personal end game, one that he deserved.

"Let's go," the Assembly Leader said and kept his arm around Nisa's waist.

He moved until Nisa had no choice but to look away from Decan and walk with her father. The First Female, however, stood in place a second or so longer. She looked at Decan with golden specks highlighting her light eyes. Her arms folded slowly across her chest as she tilted her head slightly and continued to stare.

"Have a good lunch, ma'am," Decan finally said because his legs threatened to buckle under the intense scrutiny.

It was one thing to stand strong like any other soldier against their commanding officer, because that was not the time or place to show any weakness. The Assembly Leader expected that of him. But as for Kalina Reynolds, being in her line of fire was not something Decan had ever expected, nor did he believe would be as easy to handle.

When the edge of her mouth tilted in a slow smile, he almost breathed a sigh of relief. But it wasn't until she'd turned and walked away that he let out the breath he hadn't known he'd been holding.

"Bravo," Kyss said and clapped from behind him.

Decan turned his head to look at the cheetah that was now coming to stand in front of him.

"You managed to make it through the first round."

"What are you talking about?" he asked her.

"Oh come on, Decan. You can stop the act with me. Your scent is acrid and has been burning my sensitive nostrils since the moment you and Nisa walked through that door. And if you think her parents didn't sniff out the fact that you'd slept with their daughter...no, you mated their daughter, then you aren't as smart as they give you credit for."

Decan's hands briefly clenched and he rolled his head on his shoulders before speaking. He was not in the mood for her candor.

"Don't you have something else to do?"

She shook her head and grinned. "Nope. I'm stuck here for the time being but nobody really trusts me enough to give me an assignment or invite me to lunch. So, after I finish razzing you about your new mate and her father who may just pummel you for daring to touch his child, then I'll probably head down to the pool for a while."

Decan frowned. "Don't get comfortable here," he told her. "Until you can produce some documents confirming your family and their whereabouts, you're still an unlisted shifter. Most unlisted shifters are rogues. So if you want to keep playing with this team, you'd better come up with some proof that you belong here."

She stepped closer to him, planting her palms on his chest. When he flinched slightly, because her touch wasn't Nisa's, Kyss had the audacity to smile broadly.

"I belong wherever I am," she told Decan. "You should probably start thinking that way instead of constantly searching for your place in this world. It was in the military. Then it was in the SIC. Now you're here. Make the best of it and move the hell on. Your bitterness smells almost as bad as that damned *calor*."

She'd pushed away from him before Decan could do the honors and sashayed her hips down the hallway leaving him to stand there alone. And pissed off because her words had been too close to the truth.

"YOU'RE WAY OFF SCRIPT," KELLER told Decan the moment they were standing in the back of one of the storage rooms.

"Let's just talk about what went wrong last night," Decan said.

He wasn't in the mood to talk about what he knew Keller was referring to. Especially not after is run in with Kyss half an hour ago.

Gold had been leaning against the back wall, one foot flat on the wall, hands at his sides. While Keller had stood with his legs spread, hands on his hips the moment Decan approached. They'd used the secure comlink Keller had provided to schedule this private meeting. So far, after Keller's check of the Central Headquarters bunker, he'd found that this was the only place in the entire facility that had no camera coverage. That was most likely because the only doors down here were magnetically sealed and code and key operated. So the Shadows didn't fear anyone would break into the storage rooms, nor did they think any shifters would come down here to meet and plan what was sure to be seen as the biggest betrayal to Roman Reynolds and his reign in all of shifter history.

"We had a lead on Mackey," Gold stated. "Keller called me and I went to back him up."

"You left Nisa and Kyss," Decan told him.

"They weren't his assignment," Keller cut in.

Decan looked at the cougar with narrowed eyes. "I have a cover here and thanks to me, so does Gold. You're the outsider, Keller. They don't even know you're back from the sea voyage."

"That proves how dedicated I am to this mission. They'll know what I want them to know about me, when I want them to know it," Keller said evenly.

"Nisa's going to figure out how you got into her system and when she does, she's immediately going to zero in on you as a possible culprit in the break-in of those classified docks on her holodeck. So don't get too cocky," Decan said in a tone that was as irritated as he felt.

His shoulders were aching and for a moment while he'd walked down here he'd thought it might be related to carrying Nisa last night. Of course he'd frowned on that thought because there was no way a six-foot five-inch shifter who weighted two hundred and forty-seven pounds and could lift double that amount, should have had any problem lifting a female who weighed no more than one hundred and thirty pounds. Besides, the pain would have begun sooner if it were because of carrying her. It had just begun as he'd left his room and headed this way.

"And she'll be wrong," Keller replied nonchalantly. "Still, by the time she does all that, we'll have achieved our revenge and the Assembly Leader will be so beholden to us he wouldn't dare think of punishing me," Keller said confidently.

Gold smirked and said, "Mackey was on his phone when we caught up with him on the first floor of the building last night."

If there were one thing Decan knew about his friend, it was that he was goal-oriented. Once Gold set his mind to something, there was no going back. Killing Ewen Mackey and bringing down the Ruling Cabinet for what they'd done to his parents, was something Gold had worked toward all his adult life. Decan was happy to be totally on board with helping his friend and exorcising his own demons at the same time.

"And what happened next?" Decan asked, turning his attention completely to Gold.

"The bastard was on the phone planning the next murder," Keller interrupted again. "He never paused in his conversation or even turned to see us as we came up behind him. I could have attacked him right then and ended this!"

And Decan knew that's precisely what Keller wanted to do. Hell, if he walked up on Ewen Mackey he'd want to kill first and deal with consequences later too. Ewen Mackey and his sadistic friends ran the SICs throughout the world. They trapped, caught and caged shifters and then tortured them to get whatever information from them they could before finally killing them. That fire that broke out a year ago, sending everyone in the camps into a chaotic state, was the best thing to ever happen to Decan. It was also the scariest.

"We have to do it the right way," Decan insisted. "It'll be quicker if we had the entire Ruling Cabinet together."

"How are we going to do that? They've no doubt been on guard since their family members were targeted. And after last night, I'm almost positive they won't be leaving the comfort of their homes for a while," Gold said.

Decan shook his head. "No. Ewen Mackey is an arrogant bastard. I heard him too many times in the SIC taunting the shifters and giving orders for unspeakable things to be done to anyone who dared disobey him. He's evil and twisted and of all the people and different species on this earth, he's the one not fit to live."

Which is why Decan was going to kill him.

And he was going to do it in the same heartless way that Mackey had killed Marlee—a knife through his back. Or in Decan's case, the large incisors of his lion piercing through the bastard's spine.

"He's going to continue on as if nothing happened last night. Sure, he's going to up patrols and pick up anyone they even remotely believe is a shifter and throw them into another SIC or kill them right there on the street. But, he's also going to demand his cabinet members come out and continue their own specific brands of torture and disrespect to humans and shifters alike," just to prove his point.

"So when do we strike?" Keller asked. "Full moon's in three nights."

"We're not wolves, we don't need the full moon," Gold stated.

"No. He's right," Decan said. "Ever since that super-moon nineteen years ago, the world has literally been out of whack. The weather, the other beings now surfacing—"

"Yeah, like that big ass black wolf that broke through the window last night. Who the hell was that and how did he know we were there?" Gold asked.

Decan didn't want to say too much about Blaez Trekas, not even to his two closest friends. He felt like he could trust the lycan, but if what Blaez had told him was true and he'd been helping Cole Linden to hunt humans and save shifters since the Unveiling, then there had to be something in that for the lycan. The fact that Cole had disappeared once again in an explosion in Sedona was suspicious. The lycan thought so too.

"The full moon can strengthen some creatures and weaken others," Decan said. "That's what we learned in school."

"They did not teach supernatural shit in the human public school system," Gold quipped.

"No," Decan told him. "That was the class taught by the old shaman in the Serfin complex near San Antonio. He taught me all about other species in this world and in other realms. Most people in the class with me thought it was all a myth, and at first I'd considered it might be. But then I saw that big ass black wolf last night and realized that everything the shaman had said was true."

Gold nodded. "So what now?"

"Now, we go above ground the night of the full moon. We corner Mackey and make him assemble his band of killers and then we get rid of them all. It's that simple," Keller stated.

"And that dangerous," Decan announced. "He's going to be expecting an attack."

"Not if we send him some entertainment first," Gold suggested.

Decan was immediately shaking his head. "Out of the question. We don't know who the hell Kyss is or why she's really here."

"She said she's here to help," Gold said.

Keller laughed. "She helped you get off over and over again, that's about all."

"Shut up!" Gold yelled. "You would have accepted her favors if she'd offered them to you."

"But she didn't," Keller said. "Because she knew she wasn't my type."

"Nobody's your type, that's the problem," Gold continued. "You just toy with all these females, never taking any of them to your bed. It's cruel and unusual punishment."

"It's the way of the world," Keller continued.

"If we're finished," Decan said. "Find out who Kyss really is. I want to know everything about her before we consider bringing her in to this. We'll stay here until the full moon and then we'll take care of this once and for all."

"And then what?" Keller asked Decan. "You think you and your *companheiro* are going to live happily ever after?"

Decan did not respond, but sent a death glare Keller's way insisted.

"Think again buddy. That royal beauty is going to kick your ass so far to the curb when she finds out you not only lied to her, but you betrayed her father and his legacy at the same time. *Calor* or not."

Decan ignored Keller's final words and left the two shifters in the storage room. He was finished with that meeting and finished with hearing input on what was going on between him and Nisa. It was nobody's business but his. This plan had been in place since the moment he'd been helped from beneath the rubble of that collapsed building during the fire. He wasn't about to change it now, not even for a female who caused him physical pain when she wasn't near.

CHAPTER 13

THE MOMENT HE ENTERED HIS room Decan knew he wasn't alone.

The pear scented candles on the dresser, the nightstand and the bookshelf was sort of a giveaway. But it wasn't the only one.

She was here. Her scent—their scent—was stronger than the candles and he eagerly stepped inside, closing and locking the door behind him. The room seemed to be full of her and not just by aroma. Decan actually felt as if the cold and unfamiliar room that he'd been assigned for his stay was somehow warmer now. He knew it was silly, just as much as the pain in his shoulders had ceased the second he'd opened the door. Still, it was no less true.

"What's this?" he asked when she stepped out of the bathroom.

She looked better than Kyss and all her efforts to be sexy and alluring and she was only wearing shorts and a tank top. A very sheer red tank top that allowed him to see her black lace bra without applying any heightened senses.

"I thought I'd bring dinner to you," she said. "You know, since you obviously have something against the dining hall here."

He didn't have anything against the dining hall. But he had tried to convince himself that the pain in his shoulders was because he hadn't worked out in the last few days. He needed to work out and then his muscles wouldn't feel so tense. It had worked, hadn't it? His muscles weren't feeling tense any longer.

And he was no longer thinking about the gym.

"I wasn't hungry," he told her when she continued to stare expectantly at him.

"Well, I am," she said and moved to the bed where she'd spread a blue blanket over the plain white sheets.

A brown wicker basket sat in the center of the blanket. She climbed onto the bed on her knees and reached inside of it to take things out—napkins, paper plates, utensils and food. Sandwiches, chips, drinks. Decan walked closer to the bed.

"I was told we should have a date," she talked while she worked. "That's what normal…I mean humans, do right? They go out on dates and then talk about stuff."

"Stuff?" he asked and rubbed a hand down the back of his head.

She looked up at him, smiled and then shrugged. "Yes. Stuff. I tell you about my life. You tell me about yours."

"You're the daughter of the Assembly Leader and a Topétenia shifter. Your mother is a beautiful and compassionate leader. Your father is a deadly black jaguar who leads with conviction. You like to sneak above ground and run wild through the forest. Your cat is as breathtaking as you are," he said. "Is there something else I should know?"

"Ah," she said and shook her head. "I don't think so."

Nisa smiled again and Decan resisted the urge to climb onto that bed, push all the food to the floor and strip her.

After the stripping there would be moaning, and clawing, and yes, more pleasure than he'd ever known.

"But what about you?" she asked. "All I know about you is that you were ten years old when your parents left you above ground to go to school. You have two sisters and you grew up with Gold."

Decan shrugged. "That's all there is to know."

"I don't think so," she said. "But let's eat first."

Decan was hungry, but it wasn't for food. The fact that he could see all that she'd gone through what she called a "date", said it was important to her. That made it important to him. Besides, it would be a lot easier for him to talk to her about which direction her work for the Assembly should go in next.

"You were in the military which is a group of soldiers fighting to defend its country, but you do not particularly care for working with a team," she said after they'd both finished a whole sandwich.

She was sitting on one side of the huge bed and he was on the other.

"I'm not adverse to teams," he told her. "I've just found that it works out better when they're all working toward the same goal."

"Equality for all," she said. "Isn't that what we should be working toward?"

It sounded good, Decan thought. It also sounded a little naïve, all things considered. But a big part of him wished for what Nisa had just said, if for nothing more than to make her happy. When had that begun to make a difference for him? A long time ago, Decan admitted. The nights when he decided that it was better to follow her above ground so that she could have her run instead of telling her father that she was sneaking out.

"I'm glad you brought that up," he told her. "How soon do you think you'll have the new computer system up and running here in the Central Zone?"

Changing the subject seemed like the right thing to do. Until she blinked and looked over to him with eyes Decan had never seen before. There was disappointment in the brown orbs. Undeniable and packing more of a punch than if she'd physically assaulted him. He wanted to kick himself for not giving her the type of date she'd wanted, for just a little bit longer.

"I'll be working on it for the next couple of days. Since my dad gave the order for all zones to migrate to the new system, we were able to have the groundwork installed throughout the last few months. X did the traveling to oversee the initial process," she said without skipping a beat.

"The security shields are stronger on the holodeck?" he asked her.

She'd just finished wiping her hands with a napkin and tossed it inside the basket, before settling back against the pillows. Her legs were crossed at the ankles as she looked relaxed in his bed. This space was just as close to belonging to Decan personally as any other location in Oasis. Since he'd returned he'd never stayed in one place long enough to call himself settled. And when he had spent those months at the Assembly Headquarters, the room on the floor beneath Nisa's room, only served as a resting place for the time he wasn't following her around or in meetings with her father. This bed, after this time spent with her, would never be forgotten in his mind.

"Definitely much stronger," she told him. "But not only on the holodeck. We'll implement that new technology in everything from the comlinks the guards and enforcers carry to the vehicles we all use. That way nobody will ever be able to disable our tracking device without us knowing."

Decan's head jerked in her direction.

"Yes. I figured that out just before we left Keller's place. And I know that Keller Cross is still listed as being on some explorative sea voyage," she told him. "I figured you would tell me why when you were ready."

Dammit. Decan was so not ready to tell her any of that.

"Have you ever heard of a mercenary?" he asked her.

"I have," she said, "Just not in Oasis. There's no need for any such profession here."

"But in the world above there used to be. Now, after so much change has occurred, the job has taken a different turn, but Keller loves it. And he loves fighting for the Shadows in whatever capacity he can."

"I cannot ignore that bunker, or the fact that he has some type of technology designed to hack into the controls of our vehicles. I've already drafted an addendum to our maps and once the holodeck is installed everywhere his ability to get in and do what he wants will be severely hampered," she told him.

Decan did not have the heart to tell her that it didn't matter what she designed, Keller was not going to be deterred. He also couldn't help but feel as if he were stuck between two worlds.

"So what else do couples do?" He found himself asking, because flipping topics seemed to be his go-to method for surviving his time with her now.

D ECAN WAS NO DOUBT WISHING he'd kept that last question to himself right about now. Because Nisa had been quick to figure out another way she could learn about the shifter that had invaded her world for the past few days and that she was increasingly afraid was overrunning another part of her.

She'd immediately hopped off the bed and cleaned up the meal she'd had the kitchen staff prepare for them.

"I was also told that massages after a strenuous day at work are a good idea," she said when she was standing on the opposite side of the bed from him.

For the first time in her life Nisa felt nervous. She hadn't been at all sure of the things Shya had told her because she'd never done them before. And, unlike Shya, she hadn't spent her spare time reading stories of romance and love and finding one's perfect mate. That's where she and her best friend differed. Shya was a dreamer while Nisa had passed her time in Oasis by learning. Now, it appeared, Nisa had neglected one very important subject.

"I've got an even better idea after a strenuous day at work," he told her seconds after a low growl echoed throughout the room.

His eyes changed before she could respond. The blue took on that crystalline look she'd seen last night just before he ripped that guy's throat out and she gasped. But not in fear. No, she'd never been afraid of Decan and she wondered why. She'd also felt completely comfortable with him, right from the very start. That was strange as well. But if Nisa was standing there thinking about all the anomalies where this thing between her and Decan was concerned, there was one she could admit and accept without question—her cat was inexplicably drawn to his. From the very start, and even now.

She blinked and knew her eyes were different when she opened them. Her skin even felt different, more sensitive. And the room had definitely gotten warmer, just in the last few moments.

"What's your plan?" she asked.

The soldier and inventor in her questioned why it was so easy for her to submit to this shifter and his salacious looks. The jaguar inside easily pushed past those queries opening the door to the completely sensual side of her that craved his words, his stares, his touch.

"Take off your clothes," he said slowly so that there was no mistaking what he wanted her to do.

Nisa hesitated. Why, she had no idea.

He'd already seen her naked, more than once. His

mouth had found the most intimate part of her, twice. And she'd enjoyed every moment of it. So what was the deal?

Tonight had been a date and they were standing in the middle of a brightly lit bedroom. Not a dark creek or an almost darker room in an old cabin, even though shifters could see in the dark. She was being silly and that wasn't like her.

"Is sex how everyone relieves stress?" she asked even as her fingers went to the hem of her shirt in preparation to lift it up and over her head.

His hands went to the waistband of the black shorts he wore.

"I can't speak for what anybody else does," he told her. "But this is not going to be just sex."

No, it wasn't, Nisa thought.

Not for her at least.

She knew what sex was and how it played out between a man and a woman. But Decan wasn't just a man, and luckily for her, she wasn't just a woman. Nothing about this mission was turning out the way she'd expected. Not the things she'd been uncovering or the people who were now key players. Her father was worried about her. He'd expressed that throughout their lunch and then again when she'd gone to the main dining hall for dinner. He'd wanted her beside him and had repeatedly told her how much she meant to him and her mother. So much so that Nisa began to worry.

As for her mother, she'd watched Nisa quietly. Or what she thought was quietly but Nisa had felt Kalina's gaze lingering on her more than once. She hadn't been able to explain it, but then she hadn't really tried. Her mind had been someplace else.

On someone else.

She removed her shorts and the flat shoes she'd slipped on before coming to Decan's room. He pulled off his shirt, revealing ripped abs, sculpted pectorals and biceps so perfect she wanted to leap over the bed and grab hold of them at this second. The army of healed slashes over his chest horrified and held her still. They were a dark pink color in a violent pattern that wrapped around his sides. Her fingertips warmed as she recalled the feel of the raised and bumpy skin on his back.

She'd asked about that last night and he'd brushed her off. Nisa wasn't going to take that route again. This time she walked slowly around to the other side of the bed as he'd sat on its edge to remove his boots. She waited while he also removed his shorts and boxers. Then she was touching him.

Standing in front of him she rested her palms on his shoulders and gently pushed him so that he was once again sitting on the edge of the bed. His head came up and those intense blue eyes held her gaze. Strength, loyalty, power, were all the things she could see in his eyes and feel from being this close to him. There was no doubt that Decan Canter was a powerful Shadow Shifter. The muscled body and deadly quick maneuvers she'd witnessed last night cemented that fact in her mind. So how had he obtained these scars?

Shifters did not contract human ailments, and they had the ability to heal from most wounds. Additionally, there were now—thanks to Ary Delgado, the Lead Curandero—Shadows that had been previously trained as human doctors, with the added training to specifically treat shifters. So these scars should not be here.

Yet they were, and hurt suffused her when she touched them.

She gasped and Decan reached up to grab her wrists.

But Nisa was not to be deterred, not this time.

She continued to move her fingers over his chest. Some parts of the scar were still puffy, other parts had thinned. There were so many that when she went lower to just above his navel she could no longer remain silent.

"I don't understand," she said her voice so quiet she wondered if he'd even heard her.

He released her wrists and used his hands to cup her face, bringing her gaze back up to meet his.

"You don't have to," he said. "It's over."

But it wasn't. At least not for her.

Her chest heaved with the heaviness of the pain that pressed upon her as she looked down at his blemished skin once more. She placed her hands on his shoulders and leaned over to look at his back. Tears immediately sprang to her eyes and then the anger ripped free.

"Who did this?" she asked him. "And why?"

He moved his hands to her waist, lifting her from the floor and standing to turn them around. Decan lay her back on the bed and came over her.

"It doesn't matter," he said.

When she opened her mouth to tell him he was wrong, that it definitely did matter because whoever had done that to him needed to pay—possibly with their life, she hadn't quite decided between that and torture just yet— he lowered his face closer to hers.

"All that matters is this."

His words whispered over her lips just before his tongue touched them. Nisa parted her lips, but she did not close her eyes. He was staring down at her and she wanted to see him. All of him.

"I want you," he said and brushed his lips over hers.

"I want you," she replied.

"Do you?" he asked. "Do you know everything that goes with wanting me? Can you handle it, Nisa?"

She didn't know that, wouldn't know until she'd tried. What she did know without any doubt, was that this was happening. Again. And she had no intention of stopping it.

In answer to his question—or was it a challenge, she

didn't know—but she tilted her head and wrapped her arms around his neck to pull him down for a kiss. She adored the feel of his tongue against hers. He tasted wild and defiant and the more she arched into him, stroking her tongue over his, the more aroused she became.

His hands went beneath her then, grasping her ass and squeezing tightly. So tight for a moment she wanted to scream out. Then the pain lessened and his palms smoothed over the agitated skin. She sighed in response because the two sensations were so different, yet so tantalizing. She felt his fingers moving lower, down the back of her thighs as his mouth continued to work over hers. When he lifted her legs, pulling them up so she could wrap them around his waist, Nisa thrust her hips upward. Anxious did not quite describe the need clawing through her at this moment.

Nothing mattered. No sound. No event. No scent... wait a minute. He pulled his mouth from hers and she realized in that moment that the scent was thick and wafted through the air as if it were coming in through the vents. It was a sultry aroma that reminded her of the incense Baxter had brought back from The Gungi. A rich and woodsy smell settled over them and stroked against Nisa's cat until she could do nothing but let loose the growl that rumbled deep in her chest. Decan's head shot up, his eyes widened.

"Get ready," he mumbled, as if in reply, and lowered his head to her neck.

He kissed her there, softly at first, dragging his tongue over her skin while she arched her back to give him better access. This was exactly what she needed. She'd tried to take Shya's advice to have a date with him, to get to know him better to see if they were a good fit. But that question seemed as if it had already been answered. They fit just fine, which was why he knew exactly where to touch and what to kiss to keep her wanting more.

When his teeth scraped over her, Nisa sighed. The Lion, she thought as her eyes finally drifted shut. He'd been fierce in that room as he'd pulled that man away from her. So strong and ferocious. And she'd loved it. Every second of seeing him in action had drawn her closer to him. Sure, she would have handled the man if she'd had to, but she hadn't. He'd come in like a savior, and while Nisa knew she didn't need saving, she'd loved watching it unfold regardless. His eyes had pierced through her, just as they had only seconds ago. Her fingers dug into the skin of his back just before he pulled away from her all together.

"I want to taste you again," he growled. "I can't get your taste out of my mouth."

He was between her legs now, pushing them farther back. Nisa hadn't removed her panties or her bra but that hadn't mattered. With one tug the swatch of cotton had been removed and she was bared before him. Decan dipped his head down so fast, his tongue moving so wildly over the damp folds of her pussy she had to catch her breath. And when she did, Nisa planted her feet on the bed and pumped into him with every needy thread in her body. Her teeth clenched, head thrashed on the bed as he licked and sucked, thrust his tongue inside, toyed with her clit and started all over again just in case she'd forgotten what he'd done. She never would forget. As long as she lived, Nisa was certain she would never forget how good this felt.

When his fingers joined in, slipping through the rapidly flowing juices at her center to ease slowly into her rear, she gasped. This was a different sensation. A devilishly different one that had her pumping wilder.

"I want you here," he grumbled. "Right here. I want to be buried so deep in you I can't remember the time or the place."

As he spoke he pressed two fingers into her, spreading them slowly, stretching her. Nisa gripped the sheets, her jaguar's claws cutting through the material. He used his other hand to touch the tight bud of her clit. Rubbing there and thrusting in the rear drove her absolutely insane. Her teeth extended, pressing into her lips as she struggled to keep from screaming.

"If you want me, this is what you get," he said then. "This is everything you get."

The finger slid down from her clit to sink deep inside once again. Nisa didn't know which felt better. Either way she was completely full of him and she wasn't sure she could stand it.

"Tell me to stop," he said and the icy tone of his voice stilled her.

"Tell me to stop and leave this room. Don't come back. Don't look at me. Don't want me."

Despite his words Decan never stopped touching her. He never stopped either of his fingers from working her, stretching her, pleasing her.

So while her body hummed with pleasure, her mind tripped over his words. What was he saying? What did he mean?

The sharp prick against her inner thigh had her eyes jolting open. Raising up on her elbows she heard him growl just as she looked down to see the eyes of his lion staring back at her. His teeth were bared, his lips pulling back from them in a motion that would have been frightening to some. To Nisa, however, they only made her want more.

"I don't want you to stop," she told him as her legs trembled and juices dripped from her pussy.

He blinked and for a moment she thought he seemed confused. But he moved again, this time biting the inside of the opposite thigh. It stung and the pain shot through her so quickly and so intensely that her arms shook with the force of it. Just as fast as he'd bitten her, Decan's tongue came out to lick over the spot, soothing the pain and sending heat soaring through her instead. She let her head fall back and moaned. His fingers were still inside of her and they began to move again. Nisa trembled, her release coming in a powerful spasm that lifted her lower body off the bed.

His growl was low but rumbled through her reaching every corner until she felt like he was actually a part of her.

"You have to leave me," he told her. "I'm no good for you."

Her mind was still hazy after that fast and furious orgasm, but she heard him and she ached for him. It was the sadness in his voice that opened her eyes once more. Decan was a fierce lion and a soldier. He wasn't sad or weak, or needy in any way. Except that there was this overwhelming sensation in the pit of her chest that said differently.

He was pulling his fingers from her, moving as if he were going to leave her. Nisa sat up and wrapped her arms around his waist pulling him back onto the bed. When he was on top of her, looking at her with confusion she flipped him over, straddling him.

"Now, you can get ready," she told him.

She'd never done this before, but she'd thought about it. Ever since that night they were in the dining room at Keller's place. When he'd been standing just a few feet away and his crotch was eye level with her lips. The urge to reach out and find his length had been so strong it had almost pushed her right off that chair. But she hadn't been bold enough then, wondering what if he'd pushed her away. Now, she didn't have that fear. He was hot and long in her hands as she slid down his body and took his length. She'd wondered how they'd managed last night, as she recalled how full she'd felt when he was inside of her. Complete, might have been a better word.

"Put it in your mouth."

It was a command in a voice that brokered no arguments.

She stared down at the thick head of his cock and felt her mouth water, the folds of her pussy becoming soaked by her creamy essence.

"Now, Nisa," he spoke, this time his voice ragged, tortured.

That spurred her on and Nisa opened wide, covering him with her mouth, taking him deep as his hands flattened on her head to hold her down.

"Yeah, right there," he moaned. "Stay. Right. There."

She did for another moment, adjusting her lips, her throat, everything to him. Pulling back slightly she moved her hand up his rigid stalk and stroked while licking his tip.

"More."

Did he say that or was she thinking it?

Nisa didn't know, but she went down again, taking him in, sucking him hard. Again and again, until she felt as if her cat were clawing against every part of her body. That woodsy scent was everywhere now. On the bed, on his skin, in her mind, in the sound of his voice, on her fingers, the tip of his cock. She couldn't get away from it, nor could she get enough of it.

With a motion she hadn't planned and that took her and Decan completely by surprise, she released him with a popping sound from her lips. Then she was coming over him once more, lowering her hips until she could sink her coated walls down over his thick length. He jerked only once and then he was pumping rhythmically. She moved with him, thrusting her hips and arching her back. When his hands came up to grab her breasts she bared her teeth and growled. And when he came, this time, in contrast to last night, she felt something different.

Her body trembled, thighs tightening around him. She

could hear him roaring, a different sound than the man had made, this one all lion. The sound reached inside of her until she felt compelled to match it and when she did everything changed.

"WHAT IF WE ARE MATES? What if there is truth to this *companhiero connection* he was talking about?" Nisa asked her best friend as she dropped down into the chair the next day after lunch.

They were in her room after an eventful few hours and still, her mind circled back to early this morning and waking to find Decan gone. The sting of rejection had threatened to irritate her to the point of seeking him out and demanding a response. But she refrained. He wasn't far. Somehow she knew that for a fact and as long as she could feel him near it was okay. Right?

Shya sat on the bed and folded her legs beneath her. Nisa's best friend was a thin shifter with butter toned skin and a riot of black curls that framed her face. A thin silver hoop pierced the center of her nose and quiet brown eyes stared back at her.

"I think that's a good thing if you've found your mate," Shya said. "I mean, he's definitely hot, so you don't have to worry about being coupled with someone you're not attracted to."

"It doesn't work that way, right?" Nisa asked again. Then she snapped her lips shut tight because she was asking too many questions and she'd decided somewhere in the middle of the night as she'd lay in his arms that she didn't need all the answers, all the time. Of course that was in response to her growing curiosity of what had happened to his back and chest, not this mating thing.

"My mother says there's no reasoning to the shifter mating. Once the cat recognizes its mate, nothing else matters. And as for the *companhiero connection*, I've heard of it, but mostly from the elder shifters now staying with us. They say it used to happen a lot in the Gungi. Where the mated couple develop this sort of telepathy."

"Wait," she said trying to wrap her mind around what her friend had just said. "So now I'm a telepath *and* a shifter?"

Shya looked at her patiently before replying, "No. This power only exists between the mated couple. You said you thought you heard him say a name. He said he did not say the name aloud. Either he said it in his mind, or was reliving a memory or because of your connection to him, you were able to tap into that memory thereby experiencing it with him."

Nisa ran her hands through her hair.

"And this only happens to one part of the couple? Because Decan doesn't seem to be tapping into my thoughts," she said, but then stopped herself.

How did he always know when she was about to sneak out to go above ground?

"It happens in varying degrees to each person. My mother said the old shaman Yuri, before he went berserk, used to come to the village and speak about all the different powers the Shadows could possess. The younger Shadows in the forest believed it was a bunch of nonsense but it seems, as time goes on, some of the nonsense turns out to be true," Shya told her.

"Great," Nisa quipped. "So it doesn't matter that I've only known him for a week, even though he's watched me for months." She was now toying with the string that was used to tighten the sweatpants she wore.

"And it doesn't matter that my father wanted to kill him just twenty-four hours ago. Because of our weird genetic make-up and some shaman from the forest's legends, I'm now inside his head when I'm sure he doesn't want me there. And what about love?"

Shya shook her head. "All of those things probably matter a lot. Probably so much that they create the whole."

Of this duo Shya was definitely the more emotional one. She was the dreamer. The settled, calm, mature personality to Nisa's adventurous, inquisitive one.

"You know this isn't what was supposed to happen. It's not my goal in life," Nisa admitted.

"I don't think we get to dictate what happens," Shya said. "Besides, you are sort of doing what you wanted. You're helping Jace with his holodeck and you're showing your father that you can be valuable in other ways than just the computer."

Nisa thought about that and she recalled her meeting right after breakfast with her father, Jace and Amelia. She'd been able to install the new equipment that had been shipped ahead of her arrival. And with the codes and new security measures that she'd come up with had managed to get the Central Zone's upgraded holodeck running smoothly. She'd also gone over the specific documents that had been viewed by whoever had hacked into their system with them. Because Decan had assured her that Keller's hacking had only been into the vehicle controls. They weren't happy by the time she'd left them alone, but at least they all now knew exactly what they were dealing with.

"My father wants me to go back with you tomorrow," she said letting her head fall back against the chair.

"What is Decan going to do? Is his assignment over?"

Nisa shook her head. "I don't know. And that's a huge problem for me. I don't know what his plans are. Not for tonight or tomorrow or thirty years from now. I don't know why he came to be here, now or what will happen if whatever his plan is doesn't work. I don't know anything about him."

Shya slipped off the bed then. She moved to the dresser where she'd set the small pouch she always carried with her. Inside the pouch, Nisa knew, was the small disk that contained her daily medications. Shya had been very sick as a baby, as a result of a dangerous herb from the Gungi that her mother had ingested while pregnant with her. Nisa didn't need to look to see that Shya would remove the disk and place the small frosted orb over the inside of her wrist. In seconds medication would be released from the disk to seep through her skin and into her bloodstream. It kept Shya from feeling too weak, even when she'd done no more than walk from one end of a room to the next.

"You know that you are feeling something you've never felt before. Things are changing for you, Nisa. That is what you wanted, it just wasn't the way that you envisioned it," her friend spoke moments after the medication had been administered.

"Is that your way of telling me to stop whining?" Nisa asked as she sat up straighter in the chair just in time to see Shya closing the pouch and turning to face her.

Shya smiled. It was always a slow smile but one that could easily brighten any room she stood in.

"It's my way of telling you to for once in your life, go with it. Let the questions be answered when the time for the answer comes. To not push. To not try to control. To just be."

It sounded so simple coming from her. For Nisa, as she clenched her hands, then forcefully released them and placed them on her knees, not so much.

"What if I can't?" she asked, afraid of messing up, also for the first time in her life.

"You can do anything Nisa Reynolds. I've always known that and I believe your parents have too. It's time for you to believe it and to accept what happens as a result."

CHAPTER 14

———•———

S HE WASN'T IN CONTROL.
    She was accepting.

She was believing.

Nisa was driving herself insane. Decan had left her in bed for the second time. Only a few hours had passed since he'd been gone but she could still feel him as if he were lying right there. Actually, she could feel the waves of stress and anxiety that had covered him even though he'd insisted there was nothing wrong.

"There's something," she'd said when he'd sat in the chair across from the bed.

They'd had crazy hot sex...again. That may have been the only part about this that Nisa understood without too many questions. She was convinced that her body was made specifically for this shifter. Everything he did, every touch and kiss...all of it was exquisite and never failed to bring her to another soul-shattering orgasm. It was the before and after the sex that still perplexed her.

"There's nothing, Nisa," he'd said with impatience. "Everything is not a puzzle that you have to figure out."

She'd pulled her knees up to her chest as she sat on the bed, wrapping her arms around them as she continued to stare at him.

"Believe it or not, you're not the first person to tell me that," she'd admitted.

Decan continued to tie his boots.

"But there's still something," she continued regardless of whether or not he wanted her to. "It's like a weight sitting right between us."

He stood then, his face stern when he looked down at her. "It's nothing! Let it go!"

She thought about Shya's words and considered for another moment. Hell no, that was Shya's nature, not hers.

"I won't let go a feeling that's threatening my sanity, Decan Canter!" she yelled back at him.

Then she was getting off the bed and going to stand in front of him.

"You may be older and worldlier but you are not the only one in this room with a brain or an inclination to use it," she told him. "One of the first things I learned in training was to follow your gut. Well, that's what I'm doing and I'm telling you that something is going on."

There was a low rumble, his lion no doubt. Displeased with her too. Well, it could get in line. Her father was angry with her for not wanting to leave with him in the morning. Gold was still irritated with her she figured for what happened at the gala and Kyss who was normally all smiles and love for everyone hadn't shown her face in the last couple of days.

He inhaled deeply like the action would actually calm the lion inside of him. It hadn't, she could still feel the beast's restlessness. It was making her edgy, as if she were pacing the floor herself.

"There is nothing going on," he said, his voice calmer this time.

Unfortunately, his eyes and the lion that continued to give away everything the man did not want her to know, told a different story.

"You should be packing to leave with your father in the morning," he'd continued.

Whether or not it was intentional—which it probably had been to distract her—Nisa folded her arms over her bare breasts and stared up at him.

"Who said I was leaving with him?" She shrugged. "I didn't come here with him."

"You should leave with him," Decan told her and then he touched her chin.

His fingers had rubbed lightly over the line of her jaw, then back to her chin as he watched her. He continued to breathe steadily, in and out, focusing on each breath. Nisa had begun to focus too, mimicking her breaths to match his and wondering why the act wasn't calming her in the least.

"You've done what you came here to do. Now, you should go. You're safer at Assembly Headquarters with your father."

"I'm not in danger, Decan. Those innocent humans above ground who are being murdered because of a familial connection are. The shifter who hacked into our system is. But not me. I'm fine," she'd insisted.

"That's not true." His voice had been solemn. "You are a target to anyone who still hunts your father. That rogue scent we picked up that first night in Florida, they knew you were there."

"What?" Her arms had dropped to her side once more. "Nobody knows me above ground."

"Shifters and rogues knew that Kalina was pregnant at the time of the Unveiling. You may have been born in Oasis, but news spread quickly of the Assembly Leader's only child. You are his weakness and anyone wishing to harm him, will gladly go through you."

"Are you saying there've been threats against my father? Why? He's been hiding down here in the world he's created to keep us all safe. How could that still put him in danger?" she asked.

The right side of his mouth lifted into a grin. "You never run out of questions, do you?"

He did not give her a moment to answer.

"Pack your clothes, Nisa. Go home."

He'd turned and walked out of the room then and Nisa fell to her knees as a wave of sadness rushed over her with the force of a battering ram. She stayed there, hands flat on the floor, head down as she'd struggled to catch her breath. When she did, Nisa had quickly dressed. Then, she'd sat on the edge of the bed and waited.

That's where she was now, but she knew the waiting was over. It was just after midnight and as she stared at the door Decan had closed on her, she suddenly saw straight through it. On the other side was a war zone, or what looked like one with fire licking cement walls, the stench of burning flesh piercing her senses until she cringed. He was there, lying on the ground, his face pressed into the dirt. Blood poured from the deep slashes over his back and she knew instinctively his front. Around him people were running and screaming, things were falling from the sky—steel poles, flying debris, body parts. It was sickening and frightening and Decan was just lying there not moving. Not shifting. Where was his lion and why hadn't it appeared to help him move, to get away? Another question her subconscious thought, but one she answered quickly. He wouldn't let it.

Just as he wouldn't let her get any closer to him than sex, he was holding the beast inside at bay.

But this time, Nisa thought as she slowly stood from the bed, he wasn't going to be successful.

THE DOWNPOUR WAS TORRENTIAL ON the night of the full moon.

Rain falling so quickly in thick drops that flooded streets, while winds blasted through at rates that threatened to knock a mere human off his feet. Good thing Decan was only half human. He was a Shadow Shifter and he knew that from tonight on not only would the shifters in Oasis know that, but every human would know and they would remember that he was the one who killed Ewen Mackey.

Hurricanes of this magnitude, along with raging forest fires, catastrophic blizzards and other amazing weather anomalies had plagued the planet in the last twenty years. His father had spoken of those who had predicted climate change due to global warming in the years of Decan's youth. Now, he was sad to say that he'd witnessed the devastation and destruction of that very prediction.

Keller and Gold moved quietly beside them. The threesome making their way down the street where Mackey lived. This was where they'd learned he was having a private meeting with his top cabinet members. So they wouldn't get them all, as they'd planned, but Decan had agreed with Keller that this opportunity was too good to pass up.

While they remained in human form, the eyes of their cat and the extra-sensory sight came in handy as seeing through the cloud of rain and wind would not have been possible without it. They came closer to the house at the end of the cul-de-sac. Most of the large homes in this part of town had been vacated by people who either could no longer afford the exorbitant payments Ewen and his crew exacted from them or had been killed. Because they were shifters. Decan planned to avenge them all.

"There will be six of them present," Keller stated, the clicking sound of his claws breaking through his skin and the wind whistled around them. "After what happened the other night there will probably be armed guards at the door."

"Armed rogue guards," Gold added.

"Nobody lives," Decan said, the prick of his elongated incisors against his lips going unnoticed. "But Mackey is mine."

He was a killer. He'd been born with that natural instinct and the military, along with his shifter training, had perfected his skills. His father had never killed a man or a beast before. Decan had done both and was preparing to do so again. That wasn't the type of mate Nisa deserved.

"We don't have any back-up so let's get in and get out," Keller said.

His voice sounded off so Decan looked over at him to see that the cougar was straining to remain in human form. Water dripped from his hair down to the shoulders of his navy blue t-shirt and down his jeans. He was soaked and still, Decan could see the expanse of his shoulders increasing, the deep breathing that was steadily failing him. The claws and teeth were already visible and Keller's usually cloudy green eyes were now a vibrant hue as he stared straight ahead. He would shift soon. They all would.

"In and out. Leave them dead. Go home," Gold said as if he were struggling to read the words on a sign.

There was no fast fight for Gold. The rage this lion held within him came in bursts that ravaged for however long it took for the anger to subside. The Ruling Cabinet, the ones who had ordered the death of his parents all those years ago, was the proverbial thorn that would forever be in Gold's side. That is, until he killed every single one of them.

While the storm ravaged the other houses, ripping shingles from the roof tops and breaking through windows, the house at the end stayed intact. Mackey would have used the best materials for his house, everything new and innovative that the top scientists and engineers could come up with was at his disposal. While others, such as Marlee and the six children she sold her body to support, lived in squalor.

"We're going through the front door," Decan announced. "Just like we've been invited."

They were only about five feet away now and Keller had grown tired of waiting. The cougar took off charging through the wind and rain. Decan continued to hold his shift back, as did Gold. Keller's hatred for the Ruling Cabinet had always been a bit obscure to Decan, but the anger that simmered beneath the surface of that beast was real and so Decan had never pushed for details. Now, he ran toward the house, toward the destiny the three of them shared in common.

The plan had been to catch them off guard but to let it be known that they were being beat by shifters for Mackey's crimes against their kind, but the moment Keller crashed through that front window and sparks of electrical volts ripped through the air in glowing gold spikes, Decan knew the plan had been changed. Going for the door he used all the strength of his lion to kick the steel access off its hinges, watching as it indeed fell to the floor and bullets quickly flew in his direction. They seemed to have been prepared for the intrusion, but Decan didn't have time to think about that at the moment.

He removed the enhanced pistol he'd tucked in the back of his pants and returned fire until he was able to take out two of the shooters and enter the house. He had the advantage of being able to see clearly through the storm that had blown into the house with just as much force as the shifters had used. Gold brushed past him in a whoosh of growls and roars but Decan kept moving. Mackey was in here. Hiding, as was expected of such a coward. Decan was determined to find him.

The wind whipped around him as he moved through the house, a wall collapsing in front of him just seconds before he stepped into that spot. But he had the scent. It had stuck with him all these years, since he'd been set free of the SIC by that fire which had been set by someone intent on freeing their kind. He took the stairs, not caring that they creaked and moaned as if they too were about to collapse. And then he was there, as if materializing through the fog, the man stood with Lial who was showing his cougar eyes at his side.

"You," Mackey said the moment Decan stepped through the doorway into the dimly lit room.

There had to be a generator pumping power into this house because there were lamps lit all around this room while the rest of the house had been dark.

"Me," Decan answered as he looked into the eyes of the one who had put many of those scars on his back and torso.

"Kill him!" Mackey shouted at Lial.

The cougar still in his human form was dressed in all black with some form of body armor around his upper body and a long black leather jacket. He made a move, his teeth bared, a wicked ugly jagged edged blade in his hand as he leapt toward Decan. But he was quickly cut off as Gold roared into the room clamping his lion's teeth into Lial's side and taking the cougar down to the floor. They were rumbling and tussling on the floor when Decan moved quickly, leaping over their bodies and going for Mackey. He heard the shots more than he felt them and came down on top of the man, sending the gun rolling across the floor.

His clawed hands immediately went around the man's plump neck. Mackey immediately grabbed his wrists in a futile attempt to push Decan away.

"No you bastard, this is the time we've both known would come," Decan said, his lion pressing hard against the man's body.

It wanted out. It wanted this kill for itself.

Decan couldn't let it, not yet.

"I told you I'd kill you," he continued, the memory of the night he'd said those words flashing quickly through his mind.

"I'll kill you!" he'd yelled that last night as Mackey had stood behind him, wielding that steel rod that had been laced with some type of poison so that it stuck to Decan's skin with every contact, ripping his flesh in a way that could never be repaired. In the five years that he'd been held captive at SIC he'd never been able to completely heal from the beatings Mackey liked to personally give him.

"No, you dirty animal, I'm gonna kill you, just like I've been exterminating the rest of your kind!" Mackey had continued. "And when we find that cowardly leader of yours I'm gonna put his head on the end of my staff and hold it for all to see. We're in charge here, the humans! Not some twisted ass breed of feline monsters!"

He'd slapped that staff as he'd called it over Decan's skin once more.

"You won't," Decan had told him. "You will die instead. Mark my words."

The fear that instantly rose in Mackey's eyes was all the motivation Decan needed to remain in human form. He would take the beatings for now. He would not shift and give in to the lesser persona some of the humans had given them the moment they found out they were different. He had to be better. His father had told him that often. "Be better than any other shifter, or human for that matter. Show them that it can be done."

And Decan had. He'd gone to school and he'd served in their military. He'd walked like them, talked like them, lived and regretted in the same way that man had and still they hated him.

Now, was his chance for revenge. He leaned in closer to Mackey's face, roaring so loud and so long, tears poured from the man's eyes.

"Decan! Stop!"

Her voice was like spikes of ice piercing through the heat of his blood in painful intervals that snapped his head back as he struggled to distinguish between memory and the present.

"Stop!" she yelled again. "You don't have to do this. You're better than this. Better than him."

Decan roared again, this time feeling the crack of his bones as his body prepared to shift into the animal that wanted desperately to sink his teeth into Mackey's throat. The hand on his shoulder stopped everything. Her scent seeped inside him, filtering through his nostrils and moving quickly to fill each corner of his body, warming him until he wanted to lay docile on the floor. The animal bucked against the submission, but the sound of the jaguar's low murmur calmed the animal's soul.

"We'll take him with us. He's more valuable to our cause that way," Nisa said.

Mackey's grip on Decan's wrists slackened, the man's face turning an ashen color.

"Let him go," Nisa said, this time her lips close to his ear. "Take a deep breath and let him go."

Decan took that deep breath, his head throbbing with the effort. His fingers ached, claws sinking into the man's flesh. He could hear Nisa's heartbeat. It matched his own. He took another deep breath and even though he was still staring down at Mackey, he could see Nisa's face. She was everywhere and, Decan thought as the calm he'd always possessed covered him once more, she was everything.

He pulled his hands from Mackey's throat just in time for the man to choke out a breath just as an unfamiliar sound rocked them and everything in that house.

AFTER GAGGING AND TYING MACKEY as quickly as they could, Nisa and Decan ran down the steps toward the light that poured in through the front door. The rain had stopped and as they stepped through the door it was to see nothing but fog surrounding them. A thick fog that even their extra-sensory vision couldn't pierce through.

It had grown colder, the wind still blowing as an eerie sound filled the air.

"What is it?" she sked Decan, but before he could answer someone else did.

"It is Death."

Blaez Trekas with three other lycans stepped from around the side of the house. Decan hadn't even known the lycans were there.

Nisa didn't bother with introductions, but asked yet another question, "What or who is Death?"

"They don't live here," the lycan dressed in leather pants and jacket and who looked unmistakably like a sexy biker answered. "They are from far away but like all of us have been in a state of upheaval since the Unveiling and the supermoon that soon followed."

"The supermoon that reportedly ripped through the veil separating the Human Realm from the Otherworldly Realm," she said.

Blaez, whose eyes glowed that intense blue that Decan recalled seeing when the lycan was in his complete wolf form, nodded to Nisa.

"There are more here than shifters now and unfortunately, much more at stake than a lowly human who rules with hate in his heart," Blaez told them.

A screeching sound bellowed through the air then and they all stared ahead in silence. Waiting.

Decan stood near Nisa, pulling her close and reveling in the fact that she did not attempt to pull away.

Something cut through the fog. Something big and dark. The ground shook beneath them, almost to the point of sending them all tumbling. They managed to remain upright and continued to stare when the big and dark pierced the fog once more, this time in one quick motion that produced a heavy wave of warm air to fall upon them. In the next second more was visible, until it was no question they were staring at a wing. A more than one hundred foot wing so dark it appeared to be a deep purple color.

Nisa gasped as the second wing appeared and then a golden arch of fire was spewed into the air. The cold that had greeted them when they'd first stepped outside immediately vanished and heat filled the space. As suddenly as it appeared, the wings and the fire vanished. The fog rolled back in a motion that seemed as if the owner of those massive wings had sucked it in with its departure.

And lying on the ground just about ten feet away from where they stood was the body of a man.

Blaez moved first and Decan immediately followed him. They both came to a stop—Blaez's pack behind him and Nisa beside Decan.

"That's Cole Linden," Blaez said and looked up at Decan who stared at the man once more and then looked at Nisa.

CHAPTER 15

———◆———

"YOU THINK YOU KNOW EVERYTHING," Ewen Mackey said with a smirk hours later. "You have no idea."

Decan sat at the other end of the nine-foot table looking the evil bastard directly in the eye. They were back at Oasis, in a room with reinforced steel walls and automatic locked doors. The room had only this one table and four chairs. A smaller room connected by a narrow doorway held a mattress where Mackey would be sleeping for the foreseeable future. The man wore slacks and a button front white shirt, both of which were dirty and wet from the storm and the way Decan had been sure to drag him across the ground until tossing him into the trunk of the vehicle they'd traveled in. A few miles before entering into the forested area that would lead them back to an Oasis entrance, Mackey had been blindfolded and gagged and for good measure, Decan had knocked him unconscious with one punch. Nisa had frowned and called that overkill, but the fact that Gold was lying on the third row of the vehicle bleeding profusely from a wound Lial had inflicted with that fucking knife was motive enough for him.

"Then, please, fill us in," Amelia asked, her dark hair pushed behind her ears as she sat in the chair to Mackey's right.

She was closer to him as Jace had insisted she do the questioning instead of Decan. He probably thought that she would be more diplomatic than Decan who had made no effort to hide his rage toward the man when they arrived at the Central Zone Headquarters. Rome, Kalina and Nick, who had now delayed their trip back to Assembly Headquarters, were with Jace at the medical center where Ary was leading the curanderos in examining Cole Linden. Nisa was in the room with Decan, Amelia and the bastard. She stood by the door listening.

"Not a chance," Mackey said with a sick grin. "I don't answer to animals."

"You won't leave without providing some answers," Amelia said in that cool, professional tone she always used.

Mackey tossed his head back, strands of his frosty white hair were sticking up giving him a crazed and delirious look.

"You don't scare me. None of you!" he yelled.

Decan stood abruptly then, pushing the table until it pressed into Mackey's chest, sending his chair sliding back until the man was trapped between the wall and the table.

"Why are you paying Lial to kill for you? And how long has he been working for you?" Decan asked, his tone anything but professional.

Mackey sobered as he tilted his head and glared at Decan. His beady little blue/green eyes usually hid behind wire-rimmed glasses. Tonight, the glasses were long gone and his eyes were clear as they focused on Decan. His lips pulled back from his perfect—too perfect to be real—bright white teeth and he slammed his fists onto the table before coughing.

"I swear I should've killed your ass when I had the opportunity! The moment that hooker you were screwing reported you, I should have had them cut your fucking head off!"

Decan pushed the table again, until this time Mackey coughed, gasped, and his face reddened.

"We want him alive, Decan," Amelia said from where she now stood to the side of the table.

"Why?" Decan asked, whipping his head around to stare at her. "He's never gonna tell us anything useful and even if he does, it'll probably be all lies. You can't trust him. He's killing his own people as well as shifters!"

"You want me to tell you something?" Mackey asked in a wheezing voice.

Not giving a damn that he sounded like he might keel over at any moment, Decan only glared at Mackey in response.

"I'll tell you that this dirty bastard you've got here is a liar and a cheater!" Mackey spat.

"Why do you say that?" Nisa asked as she stepped closer. "Because he hates you?"

"Noooo," Mackey replied drawing the word out as he shook his head. "This isn't about me, is it Decan? It's never been about me?"

Decan's fists clenched at his words. Nisa's confusion was palpable. He did not turn so that he could look at her, but he did not need to. The questions were already running through her mind, ready to roll off her lips at any moment now. But Decan was more worried about the answers, the ones that might finally send her running.

"You know him personally?" Amelia asked before Nisa could speak.

Mackey laughed. "Oh yeah. Decan and I go way back. Don't we Decan?"

"If you mean back to the five years you held me and thousands of other shifters captive in one of your killing camps, yeah, I guess so. Why don't we talk about that?"

Decan knew it wasn't going to work, the moment he said it. Mackey had latched on to his leverage and was more than ready to play his hand. He also knew what Mackey was going to say and hated like hell that this was going to play out in front of other people, instead of when he and Nisa could be alone.

"No, I think this little lady here would rather hear about how that hooker's blood is on your hands and about how many had died since then because you and your friends wanted to play renegade."

He chuckled as he looked at Nisa. Decan was about to push the table again, this time hard enough to crush that sorry bastard's insides. But Nisa was faster. She moved around him, going to stand right next to where Mackey was pressed against the wall.

"Tell me everything," she said.

"Nisa, he's our prisoner," Amelia began after tossing an irritated look at Decan. "We need to find out where Lial is now and who else might die because of the work he's doing for the Ruling Cabinet."

"No!" Nisa shouted and looked back at Amelia first, and then Decan. "I need to hear this."

And she did, he thought as she slowly turned back to Mackey. She needed to know all the dark and ugly secrets so she would understand and stop looking at him with hope in her eyes. Or had that been his own reflection he'd seen each time he stared into her cat's eyes? Had he been hoping that the *companheiro calor* they shared would lead to a joining? Had he finally accepted that this woman, this stubborn and inquisitive warrior was the perfect mate for him?

"He ravaged her every night," Mackey said, his thin lips turning up as if in disgust. "Right in front of us he continuously took poor Marlee because he wanted to get her pregnant with his animal spawn. Then, when given a choice, he'd watched as her limbs were cut off while he decided whether or not to give up the name of the Desert Cat."

"Who? I've never heard of a Desert Cat," Nisa said.

"I have," Amelia added. "Years after the Unveiling, talk surfaced above ground of an elusive shifter that traveled through the desert land in the Pacific and Mountain Zones burning down the camps the humans built to contain us."

"This one here thought he was better than all the rest of the animals we had caged up," Mackey continued, his tirade against Decan.

This time it was Nisa who leaned in close, slapping her palms on the table in front of him.

"We're not animals!" she yelled into his face. "And you're going to start showing some respect or the next time, nobody will be around to keep him from ripping your throat out!"

A spurt of pride spread through Decan as he watched her. From the start of this mission she'd told him that she was in charge. He'd shot her down quickly enough and thought she'd shown exemplary training and respect for their security hierarchy by not continuing to argue over control with him. Instead, she'd continued to do her job, the one thing she knew that he could not do in place of her. She'd done it so well he hadn't even known about the things she'd uncovered until she'd told him, Jace and Amelia when they arrived at Central Headquarters.

"All he had to do was cooperate and he refused," Mackey continued as if Nisa hadn't spoken at all. "Then the Desert Cat struck again."

"Burning the New Mexico hell hole you unlawfully kept too many shifters in, to the ground, that's what happened next," Decan stated evenly.

"Yes, there was a fire," he said. "And then there was the break-in at my office and the taunting of the other members of the Ruling Cabinet. You and your friends have been busy these past months breaking into our computers, and stealing from us. You gave me no choice but to hire security."

"That's what Lial Johansen is to you?" Amelia asked. "He's security?"

"He's protecting us from the Desert Cat and this little band of mercenaries that unlawfully broke into my house tonight, assaulted and kidnapped me!" he yelled.

"I should have killed you!" Decan replied and flipped the table over.

As Amelia and Nisa avoided getting hit, Decan moved quickly to Mackey, yanking him up by the front of his shirt and slamming the man's back against the wall.

"When I watched you running from that fire in New Mexico I should have hunted you down and gutted you right then and there. And tonight—" he paused because he could feel her gaze on his back.

Mackey laughed.

"What? You can't control this you dirty forest scum! There are people in place to pick up where I leave off, so no matter what you do to me we're gonna get rid of all your kind. You don't belong here and we're gonna see to it that you get exactly what you deserve for trespassing."

Decan growled, his teeth bared. But he had control, now. He tossed Mackey across the room until he bounced off the other wall like a discarded toy before storming out of the room.

NISA'S MIND WAS WHIRLING.
    She came out of the room where they had been questioning Ewen Mackey, took two steps and had to lean against the wall to keep from falling to the floor. So many voices had been slamming into her head while she stood in that room listening. So many scenes had replayed

right before her eyes.

One in particular had her gasping for air now.

The walls were cinderblock, layered in four rows. The single door was made of thick iron bars, no latch or lock in sight. The cement floor was dirty and probably cold in the dark 9x9 space. Yet the smell there was sterile, clean, almost devoid of any identifying scent.

It was the same smell she'd picked up that first night at Keller's bunker when she was looking for a way out.

The tapping grew louder and louder, the source, a long stick with a metal edge and a black handle held by a man around five-feet eleven-inches tall. The man wore black leather gloves. His shoes were shiny tie-ups that clicked as he moved across the cement floor. He wore a business suit and tie, an outfit that did not seem to fit in this surrounding. He was tapping the end of the stick to the iron bars. Over and over. Tap. Tap. Tap.

Just like Nisa recalled hearing that night at Keller's place.

Her heart was beating wildly now, so fast and furious she lifted a hand to her neck as she tried desperately to take deeper breaths.

Finally, the iron bars lifted upward and the man stepped through the opening inside the small space. He chuckled as he looked toward one corner where a naked man's body lay crumpled on the floor. The man moved immediately, rolling over, leaving streaks of blood on the cement as he did. He stood quickly on strong legs, standing until his head was only a few feet from the ceiling. His chest was bloody, some old blood that had dried and was now peeling, other parts oozing fresh fluid. And his face... it wasn't distorted this time. It was the face of a man, the eyes of a lion.

Decan.

"Nisa."

Familiar hands touched her shoulders and Nisa leaned into them. Her eyes were closed, her hands shaking as the scene cleared from her mind, the remnants of it still sifting through her soul.

"Let's go in here and sit down," her mother said and guided her down the hall to another room.

This was a more homely place with tiled floors and deep cushioned hunter green couches. The walls were painted a warm orange color, a large screen TV was on one wall, a mahogany based bar in a corner. Nisa sat and Kalina did the same.

Just like when she was a child waking from a bad dream, Kalina kept one arm around Nisa's shoulders and grasped Nisa's hand with her free one.

"It's been an eventful night," Kalina began when Nisa was still trying to get the right words to form in her mind.

"It's been an eventful week," she said. "Or more like the last six months."

"What do you mean?"

Nisa looked to her mother. To the familiar hazel eyes and bronze hued short hair. She knew every part of her mother's beautiful face and the different tones of her voice. Her mother's scent was unique, the sound of her heartbeat still welcomed even though Nisa was now an adult.

"Did you know that Decan was at Headquarters all that time?" Nisa asked her. "Did you know he was in our home?"

Kalina replied immediately, "I knew when he first arrived. I knew of the meetings your father was having with him. And I knew of the plan to send him here with you."

"I knew too," she said and then sighed. "I didn't then, but now, thinking back, there were times that I felt different."

Her mother's lips lifted in a soft smile. "You were awakening."

"No," Nisa answered immediately. "I had my awakening long before that. You said I was early with my first shift, but it was still before I met Decan."

"I am speaking of another level of awakening," Kalina told her. "Think about it as a new awareness of yourself and everything around you."

Nisa waited a beat, recalling the times she'd felt tense in the last six months and that she'd attempted to do as she always did and please herself. It had grown increasingly harder to reach her own precipice. Her body wanted more. Even her mind had changed. When she would lay down to sleep at night her thoughts that normally circled around creating something new and innovative for the shifters, or fighting for the shifters, or trying to figure out how to change the world for the shifters. But with each night lately, her mind had grasped the fact that she was lying alone in a bed. That was why she hadn't minded when Decan first lay in the bed beside her and why she'd accepted these past nights that she spent in his arms.

"The awakening of a shifter female and a mate," Kalina continued rubbing her fingers over her daughter's. "It's different than simply accepting that you are a shape-shifter, Nisa. Because mine came so late in my life, my emotions and actions were different. But yours, I could see it blossoming in you in the weeks before your father announced this trip."

"You knew I had a mate out there and that I would soon find him?" Nisa asked because as much as she prided herself on knowing about the Shadow Shifters, she was now accepting that she hadn't paid nearly as much attention to the origin of the shifter mating as she should have.

"No," Kalina said with a slow shake of her head. "I didn't know who. Not at the time. I just knew that something was changing in you. I hoped that this mission would bring you closer to your place in this world. I think it did."

Nisa slipped her hand from her mother's and brought her fingers to rub her temples. She didn't know what to think at this moment, or how to come to terms with all that had happened in a seemingly short amount of time.

"He's not who I thought he was," she said after a few moments. "He's done things...unsanctioned things from what Mackey just said."

"You believe the human who has created camps to house the shifters that he captures, then tortures and kills them?"

Her mother's question was spoken in a level tone as if to soften the blow of shock she had in her daughter. Nisa rested her elbows on her knees and leaned forward.

"Decan did not deny the accusations. He's been keeping secrets this whole time," she said. "From me, from dad and the Assembly."

She was speaking specifically of Keller's bunker and all the things that Mackey had said Keller and Decan had done in the past year. None of it was mentioned in the databases. There was no record of any assignment that Decan and Keller were on that would have taken them above ground or anywhere near Mackey and his camps. None.

The comlink on Kalina's wrist buzzed and she looked down before dropping her arm from Nisa and standing.

"Ary has news about Cole," she told Nisa. "But before I go I want you to think about something."

Nisa stood as well because she planned to go to the medical center with her mother.

Kalina pushed back the hair that had fallen onto Nisa's forehead. She touched her daughter's cheek as she smiled gently at her.

"Finding a mate is unlike any other experience a shifter will ever have. There is no rule book as to when or how it occurs. It is just there one day and you are tasked with believing and accepting."

"What if I don't accept? What about love?" Nisa asked.

"Do you feel like you are in love with Decan? Think about it, Nisa. Think about your feelings from months back up to now. Consider how you felt in those first moments he was near you and in the moments tonight when things were happening and there was a chance that you could never see him again."

Nisa did think about those things. She thought about how tender and enticing his touch was and how heart wrenching it had been to see those horrible scars on him. She thought about how horrible five years in the SIC must have been for him and how she might feel if it had happened to her. Then she thought about how he hadn't told her father she was sneaking out to run above ground, but instead had followed her to protect her. Then, she thought about Marlee and the secret mission he and Keller seemed to be on.

She sighed heavily and replied honestly, "How can I know if I love him when I'm not even sure I can trust him?"

I T HAD TAKEN HIM LONGER than usual to calm down. Hell, Decan wasn't certain he was totally calm at this moment. Not this time.

She'd stopped him from killing Mackey. He wished she hadn't. Then again, he recalled the feeling of total contentment as he'd heard her voice through all the chaos that had broken out around him. It had been like a bright light through the darkness Decan swore he'd been in for the last ten years. Longer than that, if he were being totally honest. Growing up without his family had taken a bigger toll on him than he'd ever admitted. Until now. Until her.

He could leave now. Cole Linden was back and that's what the Assembly Leader had wanted him to do. Mackey was now a captive of the Shadow Shifters, the irony in that hadn't gone unnoticed. To an extent Decan figured that may have been better than the quick death he'd intended for the evil bastard. He would likely never see above ground again and even though he was pretty sure Rome would never order the man killed or tortured, living underground among the very species he detested wasn't going to be a walk in the park for the twisted leader.

There was no way that Decan was getting the job of Faction Leader now. Not with the *calor* surrounding him and the Assembly Leader's daughter. So there was nothing more here for him. He could move back to the eastern zone with Keller and they could continue to work to dismantle the Ruling Cabinet and all the havoc and destruction it had caused in the last years.

But he could do none of that without seeing her first. One last time, he told himself, and then he would walk out of her life. Decan had never heard of *companheiros* that did not stay together, so he had no idea how that scenario would actually work out. What he did know was that she deserved better. She deserved a mate she could be proud of, one that could stand beside her and fight for the same causes as she and her father before her. Decan wasn't that shifter.

He turned the corner into the medical center where he figured Nisa would be since the rest of her family was here waiting for information about Cole Linden. The first person he saw was the Assembly Leader.

"I'd like a moment, Decan," Rome said with a nod of his head toward one of the doors across from the waiting area where he was standing.

Decan thought about telling him it wasn't necessary and that he would simply leave right now, but he silently walked toward the door instead. Letting himself inside the tiny bright room, he waited while Rome followed and closed the door behind him.

"Tell me about what happened up there tonight," Rome said.

Roman Reynolds was a force. There was just no other way to put it. The man had been one of the top litigators in the country, running a billion dollar law firm and sitting comfortably on his family's fortune. He had been unanimously named Assembly Leader and was respected throughout the world for the strides the Shadows had taken in the years of his rule. Decan had nothing but respect for the man, even if he didn't agree with all of his methods.

"We received news of a private meeting Mackey was having with some of the Ruling Cabinet members. It was my decision not to take a full team above ground to carry out the mission. Once the attendees of this meeting were either contained or deceased, we left the premises. Blaez Trekas and his pack were there. Something left Cole Linden in the middle of the street. We brought the Faction Leader and Ewen Mackey back with us."

That was a succinct and fairly accurate version but Decan could tell by the way Rome was looking at him that it wasn't going to be enough.

"Is that all?" Rome asked.

Decan waited a beat before replying. "That is what happened while we were above ground."

And that was not a lie. It had happened that way. The fact that the mission above ground was unapproved and their goal was to kill and not kidnap which they ended up doing, was an omission. Not a lie.

"You took my daughter with you on this mission?" Rome asked him.

"Yes, sir," he answered immediately.

He was not going to tell Rome that his daughter had followed them into an unauthorized situation that involved guns, shifters fighting in cat form and something big and powerful enough to cause the ground to tremble. That was not an option.

Rome flexed his hands at his sides. He was standing with

his back facing the door, his legs partially spread, arms at his side. "Did you really think I had no idea what was going on?" he asked. "I'm the Assembly Leader. I'm the one the Shadow Shifters look to for guidance. My team and I took down Sabar, Crowe and Boden. We've been to the Gungi and back and forth across the US fighting for our cause, for our lives. So when some young renegades think they've got a better idea and decide to work outside my authority, I make it my business to watch every step they take carefully."

Decan did not reply.

"I knew who you were before your father introduced us and I knew who your friends were. Keller Cross believes he's been operating under the radar but I know about his bunker in Florida. I also know that he was the one who hacked into the vehicle security. X received an alert on the vehicles and I had Jace call you to see what was going on. And while I don't have proof just yet, I'm inclined to believe he's the one who broke into two classified files on the holodeck. Although, I have yet to figure out why."

Keep your enemies close. Isn't that what Nisa said her father had taught her? But he wasn't Rome's enemy, at least he didn't believe so.

"Our mission was personal," he said to the Assembly Leader.

"Because you knew I wouldn't approve," Rome replied. "We do not kill without being provoked."

"We were provoked. I was tortured and scarred for five years. Gold's parents were killed right in front of him. And Keller lost everything he'd worked to build when Mackey and his cohorts exposed him as a shifter and beat him until he had no choice but to shift in front of an office full of people and attack. A pregnant woman died in the stampede of humans hurrying to get away from the vicious cougar, scarring him mentally for the rest of his life. If that's not provocation, I don't know what is."

"We've all lost in this war, Decan."

"With all due respect, Assembly Leader, this is not a war," he said barely holding on to his anger at the moment. "You packed every shifter up and put them into a life of hiding with no escape plan. You've created this underground world with all the luxuries you could possibly think of. You're using your personal fortune to finance the bulk of this effort and you think that's fighting a war. I know what it means to fight a war! I've been on the frontlines of battle and this is not it. Not down here."

Rome gave a curt nod. "So you and your friends decided that the smart move was to take the battle to the doorstep of those responsible. Well, I can tell you that in the beginning, the other FLs and I contemplated doing the exact same thing. The problem with that was collateral damage. How many innocent lives would be lost because we stormed into what was once the White House, or the new Ruling Cabinet's house, shifted into our cat form and killed the ones responsible for causing the widespread panic about our kind? How many of the people who we want to convince we're not animals, would see that as an animalistic act?"

"We just think differently," Decan told him, refusing to back down.

"We've lived differently," Rome said. "We come from a different cat species. But our goal is the same, Decan. I not only wanted to keep you close so that I could be there to stop you the moment I felt like you were messing up for more than just yourself, but I also wanted to show our people that we could come together. That we could work on one accord."

"One accord meaning your way," Decan said.

"One accord meaning the right way," Rome stated and then turned to open the door.

When he had his hand on the knob, Rome paused and then turned back to look at Decan.

"In addition to leading the Shadows, you should remember that I'm her father."

His gaze was intent, the yellow of his cat's eyes, flickering between the dark brown of his human ones.

Well, damn.

"I have no intention of hurting her," Decan told him because he didn't. That had never been a possibility for him. Which also solidified the fact that leaving her was the best idea.

"You will have no mission, no revenge to appease, no life, if you hurt her," Rome said and then walked out of the room.

CHAPTER 16

———

ROME STOOD BEHIND THE PODIUM in the Grand Hall of the Central Zone Headquarters. It was the largest meeting space in the facility with three hundred cushioned seats, burgundy carpet and warm beige painted walls. Rome wore a dark gray suit with the silver Topétenia insignia pen on his left lapel. On the wall behind him were the shields of each tribe. They were positioned around the newly designed Shadow Shifter shield that signified their unity and loyalty to each other.

As Rome looked out to all the shifters in this zone and his family seated on the front row, he thought that what he was about to do was for all of them. It was his job to unify his people and to carry them into the next generation with the smartest and most innovative ideas possible. He believed he was about to do the right thing.

"Keller Cross of the Bosinia tribe is on his way back to Assembly Headquarters for debriefing and reassignment," he began.

"Golden Harris has been quarantined due to the poison that was on the blade Lial Johansen used on him. The medical staff as well as one of my Lead Enforcers, Ezra Preston, will be searching for the exact poison and how best to rid Gold's body of its toxins."

There were a few murmurs throughout the room and Rome made a point of looking all around as discreetly as possible. He inhaled deeply as he stood there quietly, searching for any scent, any sign of infiltration, but found none.

"Cole Linden, who served as the Central Zone Faction leader since its inception, has been found."

There were applause and cheers but none that wiped away the block of concern Rome still carried for his friend.

"He is currently in a comatose state," Rome continued. "Lead Curandero Ary Delgado is not sure how long he's been this way or how long he will stay in this condition. She will continue to work with the medical staff to find a way to bring him out of it."

He found Kalina's gaze and held it for endless moments. She was his rock. The one who had held him last night as he'd cried for the friend that he'd missed these last twenty years, and for the possibility that he may not ever open his eyes again. She was also the one who had soothed his irritation that Decan Canter was his daughter's mate.

When Kalina nodded Rome stood taller. He removed his hands that he hadn't realized he'd clenched against the side of the podium and prepared to speak again. To say the words that he knew would take many in this room by surprise. As for him, he'd known it would come to this. Baxter and Eli had told him the time for the Shadows was now. And he'd listened. Over the years Rome had gained a newfound respect for the Overseer who had raised him and who loved Nisa as his flesh and blood granddaughter. He'd also come to appreciate the Seer who Rome had watched being trained and recognized his leadership abilities and loyalty long before any other callings had come to the young jaguar. Together, their foreshadowing abilities had aided Rome on numerous decisions made on behalf of the shifters. He hadn't liked their last prediction, but none of this was about him. Regardless of what others might say.

"Decan Canter will be the Interim Central Zone Faction Leader from this day until I give further notice."

Nisa looked crestfallen and Rome instinctively wanted to go to her. To pull her up and hug her close the way he used to when she was a little girl. But his little girl had grown up. He wasn't sure when or what the hell he'd been doing while it happened, but she wasn't the spitfire that used to hide under his desk and read books while he was working just so she could be close to him. No, his baby girl had stopped following him around a long time ago. He'd just been too busy to realize that when she stopped following him, that meant she would inevitably find another man to look to. He only prayed—for the lion's overall safety—that Decan was up to the challenge.

The meeting ended shortly after his announcement and Jace's brief address to the shifters he'd been responsible for in the last twenty years.

"How could you?" Nisa asked the moment he walked through the stage door leading to a back room.

He'd had to tear his gaze away from the sorrowful look on her face when he'd been on stage and when the other shifters around had stood and began moving through the room, he'd presumed that Decan, correction, her *companheiro*, would go to her and take care of her. The fact that she'd made it through that crowd to catch up with him the second he walked through this door didn't bode well for how Decan was going to deal with her in the future.

"I've done everything right," she continued. "Everything!"

Rome watched her breeze past him and moved to close the door. He turned around to see her standing with her fists clenched tight at her sides. She had his complexion but otherwise looked so much like her mother it was eerie. She'd always kept her hair short like Kalina's, but in a curlier fashion that suited a minimalistic personality. Nisa wasn't interested in pretty things or primping and posing. She'd grown up with her nose in one book after another. Listening intently to everything Baxter had to teach her. She loved learning to fight with Eli and Ezra and hearing about the seriousness of security from Nick. And when X had let her climb up onto his lap while he'd been working on one of his many tablets at the time, she'd been in heaven. But no matter what, his little girl had always come back to him, cuddling into his embrace and looking up at him as if he could do no wrong. It was a powerful emotion for a man that had gone through the things Rome had to experience. She'd taken every part of him and made it brighter with just her smile.

Now she was glaring at him and he thought it might just make more sense to kill whoever had hurt her enough to put that look on her face. Unfortunately, that person was him.

"My job is to lead our people, Nisa. To do that I have to make the best decisions for us as a whole."

"And I'm not the best decision. That's what you're saying, right?" she asked and took a step closer. "I excelled in everything! You know it because everybody reported back to you when I finished a test or some tasks they threw my way. I even sucked up every complaint I had when you decided I needed a bodyguard to accompany me on this mission. I traveled with him and I didn't usurp his authority or report the things I knew he was doing wrong to you. But he gets the job! He gets to lead an entire zone and I get to what? Go back home and play in my room like a good little girl?"

Did she really not know? Rome thought.

She was correct in that she'd done everything right.

She'd passed all the tests, and he'd thought—after picking up the scent of their *calor* yesterday—that the logical next step of accepting her *companheiro* had been completed successfully as well.

"You don't go back, Nisa. Never go back, never look back. There's nothing there. Your future is in front of you," he told her. "That future is with your *companheiro*."

"Oh you mean the backstabber! He stole my job! I was supposed to be named Faction Leader. I came here and I updated the holodeck. You know the one that I created! I even found out that someone had broken into confidential files. I went on that mission above ground and brought back valuable information. And oh yeah, I snuck above ground last night and stopped your new Faction Leader from killing the best and most valuable witness we're ever going to have in this war. So how is it that he gets the job and I don't?"

"He's a Serfin."

She tilted her head, staring at him perplexed. "And? That's just DNA."

"It's evolution," he replied. "As this new world has evolved in the past twenty years—changing its climate, accommodating more types of shifters and other beings, and foregoing the leadership it had been built on—so have we had time to evolve down here. We're no longer in the positions we were in before, so it stands to reason that our beliefs need to change. So far there have only been Topétenia Faction Leaders. Now, there will be Serfin representation in the upper ranks. More changes are coming, Nisa and we need to be ready. My actions cannot only be about my family."

"But I'm just as qualified as he is, regardless of our DNA," she said, deflated.

Rome moved to her then, touching her shoulders. "You are qualified to take my job," he told her with a grin. "I've never known a more tenacious shifter in my life."

"I really wanted that position," she confessed, her voice softer now.

Rome leaned in and kissed her forehead. "I know you did, baby girl. But this is for the best and once you get over being pissed at me, I believe you'll see the strategic logic in my decision."

She sighed heavily, bringing her hands up to his arms. "We're stronger together. Uniting us means bringing us together on all fronts. I see your point. But I don't have to like it."

He smiled and hugged her. "I love you, baby girl. I love the woman you have become."

When she wrapped her arms around him, squeezing him almost as tightly as he was squeezing her, Rome could almost let every bad thing that had ever happened or that could possibly happen in the future vanish from his mind. Almost.

"I love you, Daddy."

He would never grow tired of hearing that and whatever it took, whoever he needed to put in leadership roles from this point forward, he would. Because growing old and continuing to hear her say it was what Rome wanted most. It was what he would give everything he had to accomplish.

LATER THAT NIGHT, NISA RAN long and hard along the indoor space that had been perfectly designed to mimic the Gungi rainforest. Her cat stretched its legs, moving until its flanks heaved from exhaustion. And then she pushed further.

She tried to let the cat take control, to move in the environment created to make it feel at home. She'd never been to the Gungi but even she had to admit that their engineers and scientists had been able to create a pretty realistic setting. The forest floor was heavy with moisture while the drone of cicadas and crickets echoed through the air. Absent the sun, during the day there were specially designed heated lights to assist in the livelihood of the plants and foliage. There were clearings with downed trees and shallow creeks. Buttress roots twisted into elaborate sinuous shapes crept along parts of the floor while verdant mosses and vines hung like beards throughout the area.

None of it silenced her recent memories.

"So what he's going to be the Faction Leader, that doesn't mean you can't finish the job you were meant to do," Kyss had said when she'd appeared outside of Nisa's room just as Nisa headed out for her run.

The cheetah had been leaning against the wall and pushed off once Nisa closed the door and fell into step beside her.

"I've learned that if you want something in this world, or the one up there, we've got to simply take it. So, you want to be a leader, take it. Show the new Faction Leader—and your mate, I might add—that you can do just as good a job as he can."

Nisa hadn't wanted to acknowledge her, but then again, she had been wondering where the shifter had been for the past two days.

"Where've you been?" she asked. "Why weren't you above ground with them when they attacked the Ruling Cabinet?"

"Your friend didn't tell you?" Kyss had asked.

When Nisa remained silent, the cheetah continued.

"I was coming out of my room, prepared to follow you because I knew that if Decan made a move, you would too. Tailing you was a lot easier than trying to keep up with Decan and those other two in his crew. Anyway, Shya was in the hallway and she didn't look so hot. So I ended up staying with her until whatever episode she had passed."

While Nisa normally took everything Kyss said as only half-truth, she knew this time was different. Shya had never been the same since her childhood poisoning. The remnants of which would last for the rest of her life. Nisa could only thank Kyss for being there when she should have been.

"Whatever, that's done now," Kyss told her. "What's more important is that you don't mess this up. You can make a difference here. Don't screw it up."

"What's in it for you?" Nisa had asked her, because she didn't believe for one moment that Kyss was simply looking out for her best interests, or for the interests of the Shadows as a whole.

Kyss had smiled. She'd worn skintight black pants and what looked like just a black bra. Her hair was down hanging past her shoulders.

"I get to watch how the new generation of shifter leaders will represent us in this war."

"And that entertains you doesn't it?"

"You're damn right it does. And you know I live for my entertainment," she'd said before smacking Nisa on the ass and walking off.

Nisa could only shake her head as she'd watched her walk away. There were still so many unanswered questions about Kyss and so many reasons not to trust her. Yet, Nisa kind of liked her. She liked her honesty and her courage.

As for what Kyss had said about taking advantage of this opportunity, well, Nisa hadn't decided how best to handle that situation.

Her cat padded through another shallow creek, then ran up an embankment and stretched out along a mossy hill. It heaved until its breathing evened and then its eyes slowly began to close.

Until it picked up the scent...of its mate.

She remained still as if waiting for her prey. Nisa

wanted to sigh or scream. She wanted to do something because she felt like she should. This wasn't how things were supposed to turn out and she wasn't supposed to be so confused by it all. Her cat, on the other hand, did not move and felt no trepidation.

As he approached she could sense the wariness. He didn't know how to approach her or what to say either. There was an all-consuming weight that pressed inside her now, filling her completely when she had no idea how empty she'd been all this time. She moved then, standing and turning to face the lion. The cats stood only ten feet apart, staring each other down. It was most likely a sight to behold, the majestic golden spotted jaguar and the illusive white lion, surrounded by an almost exact replica of the rainforest from which they had originated.

The lion made a sound, a low growl that was his signal to her cat that this was a friendly visit. They'd been in these forms together before, running, challenging one another and bonding, she thought now with a start. This had been happening since day one. She walked slowly toward him and completely around him. He did not make another sound, nor did he move, something he would most assuredly never have done with any other cat this close. When her tail was toward his head as she made her second circle around him, he growled once more. She paused and lifted her head to immediately pick up the new, more intense scent that surrounded them.

Even in cat form, their *calor* was recognized.

Nisa slowed, the cat's bones bending and adjusting until her human limbs extended, her body shifting slowly to her full human form. For a few seconds she remained on her hands and knees, her head held down as she took in the large animal still standing beside her. Lifting her head slowly, she looked up at the lion.

He was a marvelous creature. His mane was thick and fluffy, pure white as it stood out against the dark green of the backdrop. His body was massive, huge paws and flanks that only provided a glimpse into the power he could project. He was at least 6.5 feet long from head to rump, with a long curving tail. And then there were the eyes, the ones she'd looked into on so many occasions. The cat's eyes were different than the man's in that they were brighter, clearer, and deadlier. They were, right this moment piercing deep into her soul, touching not only her cat, but the woman, as well.

"Why are you here?" she asked, coming to her feet and continuing to stare directly into his eyes. "Why now?"

The lion did not make a sound, only waited for her to continue.

"I wasn't expecting you," Nisa continued. "I thought I was coming here to lead. To be a part of the solution for our kind. I wanted to make a difference. But you showed up."

She remained in front of him, in what would look to any human like a naked woman standing before a vicious killer. His eyes stayed trained on her.

"You lied to me. You touched me. You made me think about mates and all that entailed. I wasn't prepared for any of this," she continued and moved along his side.

"But," the word came out as barely a whisper as Nisa lifted a hand and touched his mane.

It was soft, just like the man's hair had been when she'd run her fingers through it. She continued, letting her fingers trail down his back. He did not move, but for his steady heartbeat. And she continued to run her hands along his fur knowing that on the man, this was where the scars were. But they were deeper, Nisa thought suddenly. Decan's real scars were much deeper than the ones she was able to see.

"I saw you in that cell at the SIC," she told him as she came around the other side of the cat's body. "I know what they did to you there."

Decan shifted into human form then, pausing on his hands and knees, his head bowed down.

"That no longer matters," he said slowly.

"But it does," she replied. "Because it's you. It's a part of you that I don't know because you didn't tell me."

"Nisa," he said and looked up at her.

She shook her head and backed away from him. "I don't know anything about you. I don't know you but I'm supposed to be mated to you for the rest of my life."

"You know that we are connected. You smell the *calor*," he told her.

"None of that was in my control!" she yelled. "None of this is. Before you showed up I knew what I wanted. I knew where I stood. Now, there's nothing. You're the Faction Leader now and I get to continue being the Assembly Leader's daughter."

He came to his feet then. The male body just as magnificent as the lion's had been.

"I won't be Faction Leader without my *companheiro* at my side," he told her.

"Why?" she asked. "Why us? Why now? What is it that you really want to happen now, Decan? Because I don't know. You came to me as my bodyguard. Never once did you say you wanted to rule this zone. I let you touch me because the arousal was too much to ignore. I gave you my virginity. Yet, you gave me nothing of you. I don't even know where your tribal tat is!"

She knew she sounded irrational. Knew that she should be reacting in a totally different manner, but Nisa hadn't lied. She didn't understand any of this. The why or the how and she didn't know what was supposed to happen now.

He turned his back to her then and Nisa wondered if she'd asked too many questions, or if the answers she required were simply too much for him.

"I want what both of us want," Decan finally replied.

"Neither of us agreed with how your father handled things with the shifters. We don't agree that we should be locked down here, hiding from the humans. Each time you went above ground without his knowledge you were screaming that very fact. At the same time you wondered why Keller's bunker wasn't recorded on the maps as all dwellings in Oasis should have been. You were torn between being loyal to your father and hating what he'd made you…and all of us become. I was the only one in a position to put things in motion."

"You were the only one cold enough to not only betray your tribe by openly going against our leader, but to do so while lying to my face," she spat. "I never lied to you, Decan. I never kept anything from you, not even when this *companheiro* stuff scared me to death."

"You never lied?" he asked as he whirled around to face her. "You sure about that Miss Perfect Daughter to the Perfect Assembly Leader? Because I don't recall you coming to me the night before last and saying you knew I was planning something and that you were going to follow me above ground to kill some humans!"

"Because you would have tried to stop me if I had," she spat.

"Exactly!" he yelled again. "That's what you do when you try to protect someone you love, Nisa. You keep them out of harm's way. I didn't know what to expect up there and I didn't know you would come waltzing into my life and changing all the fucked up parts until they suddenly seemed bearable. All the pain and rage I'd kept stored inside began to make way for all these new emotions. Ones that had me changing my priorities to the point where my own team questioned me. That's not how I work. It's not how I was trained."

She was blinking and staring at him as he stood no more than three feet away from her now.

"What did you just say?" she asked, having heard all of

his words, but still remaining stuck on just a few.

He ran a hand through his hair, his lips drawn in a tight line before finally replying, "I said I was fucked up until I met you."

She shook her head. "You know that's not what I meant."

"I don't know what I said, Nisa. I don't know what I mean. I just don't know. I can't remember or I don't want to contemplate what we just saw up there dropping Cole Linden off like he was some special delivery. He's in a coma now and none of us know why or how he got that way. Your father is going to ship Keller off to who knows where as punishment for hacking into your system. Lial attacked Gold, almost killing him with some poisoned knife and all I can think about is that if you walk away from me, how will I breathe?"

He hadn't answered her, or rather hadn't said what she'd so desperately wanted to hear once more, but Nisa had heard something different instead. She heard her mother telling her about her second awakening and becoming the female shifter she was meant to be. About Shya suggesting that maybe Nisa was doing exactly what she wanted here even though it wasn't the way she'd envisioned it. To go with it and let the answers come when it was time for them to do so. She also heard Decan's cry.

As he lay crumbled in the corner of that dank cell in the SIC his head bowed and eyes closed. He had cried, but not for himself, not for the situation he found himself in, but for them. For the Shadow Shifters.

"You could have escaped," she said softly.

Nisa was moving before she ever realized what she was going to do.

"Each time Mackey or one of his men came into that cell you could have easily killed them and got out of there. His baton, those guns, they wouldn't have stopped the white lion. You could have defeated them, but you didn't," she said.

He looked away from her momentarily and when their gazes met once more his eyes glistened in the darkness. The black and white mixture of his hair and beard more prominent, reminding her instantly of the lion's regal mane.

"After graduating from high school I came to Oasis to visit my family. I'd heard via the messages my mother had sent to her adoptive parents that were my human guardians about the changes that had been made in those first years after the Unveiling. The plan for Oasis was just beginning to be fulfilled, bunkers were being built, tribes were coming together. My parents were excited. I was disappointed because there was a freedom above ground that Oasis just couldn't capture. I felt claustrophobic down here, like I was going to die if I stayed."

Nisa nodded because she could remember feeling the same way most days of her life. She'd combatted that feeling by focusing on creating something better for them—the holodeck—always looking for an answer, a solution to how they could once again join in the world that had forced them out. That was why it was imperative that she run above ground, that she get at least those small opportunities to breathe the free air.

"I joined the Marines two weeks later," he continued. I came back to visit my family after finishing my tour. Nothing had changed. Sure, they'd built more bunkers and spread out further, but they were still trapped down here. And I hated it. I wanted them and every other shifter out and above ground living the way we were meant to live. But the Assembly Leader was adamant that the shifters stay in Oasis. That we not attempt to fight the humans. So I decided I would make my own plans. I went above ground and had just finished a meeting with Keller when I contacted a woman I'd seen before."

"Marlee," Nisa said the name and surprisingly did not

feel any twinges of jealousy the way she had before.

"She was a prostitute. She had children and lived in a small apartment. I paid her too much money every time I saw her because I knew she needed it. I didn't use any other woman, not because I had any serious feelings for Marlee, but because I wanted her children to also have some freedom and to live the life they were meant to live. I'd gotten my tribal tat on my last visit to Oasis. It was long past time but since I was living above ground and trying to fit in, my parents hadn't thought it was a good idea to have the identifying tattoo. Marlee saw it. Up until that moment she'd thought I was a human, just like everyone else above ground had and because of the fear that Mackey and his goons had helped spread throughout the world, she was afraid."

"She called the Task Force," Nisa finished or him. "And they took you to the SIC. They took Marlee too, leaving her children to fend for themselves. Mackey wanted information from you so he didn't kill you like he did so many others. But you didn't kill him then."

She'd been walking as she talked so that now she was standing in front of the man this time.

"The moment I woke up in the SIC I killed the first human that pulled a gun on me. It was instinct and training and my chest heaved as I watched his body fall to the floor, his throat torn out, blood pooling around him. I could hear the humans coming, screaming that they knew this would happen. That we were savages and all deserved to die. Mackey stopped them from killing me and that night they brought Marlee to me. He wanted to see if I could get her pregnant and what a half shifter, half human would be like. She would remain alive as long as I was there to serve a purpose."

"You took the beatings," she whispered and lifted a hand to move over the scars on his chest.

Pausing when she felt warmth under one particular set

of scars.

"Your tat was here," she said and looked down at the spot on his left pectoral where the strips of scarring were closer together forming a sort of patch of dead skin. "They burned it off."

He nodded.

"I wouldn't tell him who The Desert Cat was and when they heard that the infamous shifter might be close, Mackey decided that Marlee would be the deciding factor."

"He killed her in front of you to force you to tell him," she said. "But you don't know."

Decan shook his head. "I don't know who it is. But the shifter showed up that night and set fire to the SIC. I escaped."

"And began to plan to go against my father's rules."

The moment she said the words Decan grabbed her wrist, keeping her hand on his chest as he pulled her closer.

"I planned to free us, Nisa. We deserve to be free."

He was right. She'd believed that all her life, but she also loved her father.

"He has reasons," she said quietly.

Decan nodded. "I know some of them now. But Cole is back and even though we have Mackey, they won't stop. Not unless we stop them."

He was right again. She knew it as surely as she knew her name.

"I won't...I can't do this without you," he continued.

She looked up at him, wondering once more. "Because I'm your *companheiro*."

"No," he said, his voice lowering to a gruff whisper. "Because you're my heart. You're everything I was trying to hold onto each night in that camp. I knew that the moment I saw you at Assembly Headquarters. That's why I couldn't leave. I'm in love with you Nisa Reynolds."

There were no stars, no bursts of warmth in her chest the way Shya's books had always said there would be. Nisa didn't feel like flinging herself into his arms and having him lift her in the air and spin her around. There was no intense joy and thoughts of happy ever after. There was, however, peace. It settled over her like a fresh sheet in the morning breeze and wrapped her in security and comfort. She knew exactly what her mother had been speaking of in that moment. This was her second awakening. It was the moment she accepted the woman and the mate she was meant to be.

"I'll rule by your side?" she asked.

Decan wrapped an arm around her waist, his strong fingers splaying over her bare backside.

"You'll be my partner," he told her.

"No secrets?"

"No secrets?" he asked her in return.

She couldn't help the small smile that slowly spread.

"I'll plan the future of the Central Zone shifters with you," he said as he brought the wrist he'd continued to hold up to his mouth and kissed the back of her hand. "I'll listen to you and respect you."

His hands moved to her hips then, sliding down until he was lifting her up and wrapping her legs around his waist. "I'll cherish and protect you."

Nisa wrapped her arms around his neck and rotated her hips at the feel of the crest of his arousal against the already damp folds of her sex.

"I will help you plan the future of the Central Zone shifters," she said and gave a slow moan when he pressed his length slowly into her.

"I'll listen to you and respect you," she continued.

He kissed her forehead and then the tip of her nose.

"I'll cherish and protect you," she whispered when his cock went deeper.

His lips found hers and the words tumbled free as she

finally let go. "I'll cherish and protect. I'll love you, Decan."

He growled and pressed his full length into her. She clasped her feet and hugged him tight, never wanting to break this *companheiro connection*.

"I'll love you, Nisa," he whispered and began to move slowly and deliciously in and out of her.

"So I've claimed a lion's heart," Nisa said on another moan as Decan's hands spread her cheeks apart and thrust deeper into her.

He nuzzled her neck, licking along her shoulder before sinking his teeth into her skin and licking the spot when she growled in response. "Yes, baby, you've finally claimed this lion's heart."

A
COUGAR'S
KISS

A Shadow Shifters Rebellion Novel

A.C. ARTHUR

Coming 2018

H E'D RUN AS FAST AS he could, pushing his cat until its flanks heaved with each new breath.

He wasn't going to catch the beast. Not this time.

He hadn't caught it any of the last times that he'd been chasing it and that fact was eating away at him.

It was killing. Shifters and humans, anything in its path, ended up dead. The rage was deep and real, festering inside this beast until nothing but hate spewed out in return.

He couldn't run anymore, couldn't chase the beast and could not contain it either. He did not want to give up. But he had no other choice.

With his last breath the jaguar roared loud and long. It broke through the class that had contained it for years and roared once more before collapsing to the floor and letting the human take over.

K ELLER CROSS HATED HOSPITALS.

He hated the smell, the sounds, the stark white walls and the inevitability of death. That was the biggest reason he despised Rome's punishment for all the things he'd done against the Assembly Leader's command.

Standing guard outside the room where Cole Linden had been sleeping like a fifty year old baby for the last three months was boring and tiresome and futile. People died in hospitals. Most assuredly Shadow Shifters died in hospitals. He knew, because he'd watched it happen. The fact that this was a Shadow Shifter medical facility built in one of the adjoining bunkers to the Assembly Headquarters in the shifters underworld haven called Oasis, didn't really matter. It was supposed to. Ary Delgado took pride in the facility she'd designed and ran with efficiency. To her credit, the Brazilian born jaguar shifter was good at her job. She was the smartest and most talented curandero Keller had ever seen. But she wasn't a god and could not bring anyone or any shifter back from the dead. If there were such a person, Keller would have begged them a long time ago to save his family.

That was a miracle Keller had given up on a long time ago. There was no one to save them, they had to do it themselves. Which is exactly what he'd been trying to do before his plan of murder and revenge came crashing down in the form of the Assembly Leader's daughter and one of Keller's only friends getting caught up in that damned *companheiro calor*.

Another shifter anomaly that Keller refused to accept.

Rome had called Keller a renegade because he'd built a secret bunker and was able to hack into the holodeck vehicle control board. He'd also called Keller reckless because his plan for revenge had almost gotten him, Gold, Nisa and Decan killed. The Assembly Leader had raged at Keller once they'd returned to Assembly Headquarters and when Keller thought all the yelling and growling would be followed by a swift death, Rome had assigned him to babysitting duty.

It seemed that even though he'd screwed up when it was his turn to keep an eye on the Assembly Leader's daughter, he was now being given the chance to redeem himself by keeping watch over the most prized shifter of the decade.

Keller pushed away from the wall he'd been leaning against and moved to stand in front of the door leading into the room. He stared through the window to the shifter lying in the hospital bed, his arms still at his sides, eyes closed, white sheet tucked around him. It was late so the lights were out in the room and in most areas of the medical center. Keller pushed his hands into the front pockets of his jeans and continued to stare.

He wondered, as he had in the past weeks that he'd spent staring at this same scenario, where Cole Linden had been for the past twenty years. What had he been doing and how had he ended up on coma? The biggest and probably most ignored question was who…or what… had brought Cole back to them?

Keller had shifted early upon approaching Ewen Mackey's house that night and he'd taken down at least four humans before hearing Gold's roar of pain. He'd shifted back to human form in order to carry the wounded shifter out of the house, just in time to see what he and Decan now thought was a gigantic wing disappear into the fog and Cole on the ground.

Nobody had spoken of it since that night and they hadn't seen the lycans again. So Keller was left to wonder and stare at the comatose shifter leader as he was doing right now.

Nothing had happened in the past twelve weeks. Cole had not responded to any tests or stimulation that Ary and her team could think of. He simply lay there, sleeping, as if whatever he'd done in the last decade had completely tuckered him out. Or scared him into a place so deep and so dark, he dared not come back.

Keller dragged a hand down his face. He was irritable and tired of standing here and anxious from being stuck down here for so long. He was also horny, but that was a complaint for another day.

Tonight, he would do fine with a nap until his babysitting shift was over. He was just about to resume his position against the wall when something stopped him.

Through the darkness of the room yellow eyes glowed.

Cole Linden was awake.

FIND A.C. ARTHUR

LIKE AC Arthur's Book Lounge on Facebook
Follow Me On Twitter @AcArthur
or find
Award Winning Author, A.C. Arthur
www.acarthur.net

CPSIA information can be obtained
at www.ICGtesting.com
Printed in the USA
LVHW021551060421
683586LV00016B/1316